THE JOY
BRIGADE

Also by Martin Limón

Jade Lady Burning
Slicky Boys
Buddha's Money
The Door to Bitterness
The Wandering Ghost
G.I. Bones
Mr. Kill
Nightmare Range
The Iron Sickle
The Ville Rat
Ping-Pong Heart

THE JOY BRIGADE

MARTIN LIMÓN

SOHO CRIME

Published by
Soho Press, Inc.
853 Broadway
New York, NY 10003

Library of Congress Cataloging-in-Publication Data

Limón, Martin, 1948–
The joy brigade / Martin Limón.

ISBN 978-1-61695-397-3
eISBN 978-1-61695-149-8

1. Sueno, George (Fictitious character)—Fiction. 2. Korea(North)—
Politics and government—Fiction. 3. Korea (South)—Politics and
government—Fiction. 4. Intelligence service—Fiction.
5. Political fiction. I. Title.
PS3562.I465J6 2012
813'.54—dc23
2012010121

Printed in the United States of America

10 9 8 7 6 5 4 3 2

-1-

Yellow floodlights loomed out of thick fog. Atop the rickety wooden dock, soldiers paced.

"Red-star jokers," Mergim told me, squinting into the mist-laden night. "They inspect ship. After that everything okay. Maybe."

I leaned on a taut steel cable, gripping it tightly. The sea rumbled below: dark, listless, reeking of slimy death. We were five miles inside the Taedong River estuary in the Democratic People's Republic of Korea, or DPRK, better known as North Korea.

Mergim scratched his unshaven face, searching my eyes for signs of panic. Apparently, he found them. "Don't worry," he said, slapping me on the back. "I come here many times. Still alive." As if to demonstrate, he pinched the loose skin on the back of his hand. "You be okay." Then he turned back to the dock. "Maybe."

My name is George Sueño. I'm an agent for the Eighth United States Army Criminal Investigation Division in Seoul, South Korea. But now I was standing on the deck of an Albanian merchant freighter, a ship called the *Star of Tirana*. I was clad in unwashed woolen work pants, staring into the vast predawn darkness of communist North Korea, wondering if this entire operation had already been exposed and, more importantly, if I'd be tortured to death by those pacing red devils.

Mergim had briefed me on what would happen once we docked, and he was telling me again in an attempt to calm me. It wasn't working. My fear of North Koreans, "the enemy," ran too deep.

Concerned, Mergim reached into his dirty wool jacket and pulled out a green vial. He popped the cap. Grease-stained fingers held up a blue pill. "You want?"

I shook my head. If I were to survive, I would need my wits about me. I turned and stared at the dock, and the demons pacing upon it, willing myself to be calm. When a foghorn sounded, I nearly leapt off the edge of the boat.

"You okay?" Mergim asked, eyeing me.

"Okay," I said. The deck of the old merchant ship rolled slightly, or at least I thought it did.

"I go work," Mergim said. "You stay." He patted me on the shoulder. "Take deep breath. Don't think too much."

He turned and his soggy leather boots pounded down the iron-planked walkway.

When he was gone, I reached inside my crinkled canvas peacoat, making sure that my phony Peruvian passport was still folded into my inner pocket. I breathed deeply, willing myself toward calmness. The tart aroma of garlic wafted on the air. This country was definitely Korea, but a different Korea than I'd known.

My job here was clear. Once we were on dry land in this port city known as Nampo, I had to somehow make my way to the Nampo Southern Section People's Grain Warehouse. From weeks of studying aerial surveillance, I knew exactly where it was. The problem would be managing to evade our North Korean minders and slip away unseen from the area set aside for foreign merchant marines. Once I reached the grain warehouse—if I ever did—I'd be escorted elsewhere by a contact who would be waiting for me, a former soldier who went by the name of Hero Kang. That's all I knew about him. That and a password. If he betrayed me—or if Mergim betrayed me—I'd be lost in a world of pain. The North Koreans had tortured Americans before, most notably the crew of the USS *Pueblo*, a U.S. reconnaissance vessel captured on the high seas. The sailors had been beaten, hanged by their thumbs, left naked in their cells, and subjected to weeks of brutal interrogation. Those who survived the ordeal were released from captivity less than five years ago. The others were returned in coffins.

We docked with a thud. Sailors tossed thick ropes from the deck and dockhands scurried below to secure them. After a gangplank was lowered, uniformed men scrambled aboard—two squads, I figured—all of them armed with AK-47s.

The skipper of our little boat, Captain Skander, was already standing on deck. He had a long gray beard and a protruding belly, but in the glare of the overhead flood-lights he held himself like an admiral, shoulders thrust back. In my few days aboard, I'd developed loyalty for this ship and crew despite myself. The crew was mostly Alba-nians, and a smattering of other nationalities. I was proud that Captain Skander seemed so courageous amid this sea of swarming Korean Communists. Although I knew that Albanians were technically Communists themselves, these Albanians didn't seem like Communists. They seemed like workingmen on the sea—hustlers, all corrupt certainly, but okay guys.

North Koreans in brown uniforms and round helmets secured the deck, motioning for the crew to step back. We did. Finally, an officer climbed aboard. He was older than the other Koreans and had gold piping along the red epaulets lining his shoulder. He stepped toward Captain Skander and they conversed quietly. In English, I thought, because I caught a few words: ". . . inspection . . . contra-band . . . manifest . . ."

For most of the trip I'd been clueless about the chat-ter surrounding me because the main language spoken aboard was Albanian. In Kuala Lumpur, where I'd been sent by military intelligence to wait while they arranged my passage, three sailors from the *Star of Tirana* became unexpectedly sick only hours after they docked. Desper-ate for a strong back to help below with cargo, they'd hired me. I'd been aboard ship now for almost a month. We'd worked our way north along the Pacific coast of Asia, first to Hanoi, then Hong Kong, then Shanghai, and finally across the Yellow Sea to Nampo.

According to my passport, I was José Aracadio Medin,

an experienced cargo handler who'd been stranded in Kuala Lumpur after the owners of his previous ship had gone bankrupt. In fact, what I knew about working on the sea could fit into a tin teacup, but Mergim had been well paid to watch out for me and show me what to do—paid an additional stipend on the side, not by his ostensible employer but by someone who was in the employ of either the South Korean government or the United States government. Which one, I knew better than to ask.

All of this had been arranged. I never could have set it up myself.

The North Korean officer barked a command. The entire crew, along with Captain Skander, was herded into the forecastle. Then the armed North Koreans started a systematic search of the ship. The sailors grumbled, complaining because they'd been rousted out of their racks so quickly that they hadn't brought either cigarettes or matches. Despite their bellyaching, no one dared confront the armed boarding party. The captain sat down on an impromptu stool of wound hemp rope, looking resigned. It took the better part of two hours for the Koreans to complete their search. When they were done, Captain Skander was called across the deck to report to the North Korean officer.

As they talked, the Korean officer lit up a cigarette and held it with the tips of his fingers. He gazed into the still-dark sky. Apparently, accusations were made. Captain Skander waved his arms as he spoke. The North Korean officer didn't even bother to look at him.

Mergim, squatting beside me, tensed.

I wanted to ask what the problem was but resisted

the temptation because I didn't want to draw attention to myself. On this entire voyage I'd been as low-key as possible, making no friends among the crew except for Mergim. Mergim was in my work group, by design, and while on the job I mainly mimicked what he was doing. I wasn't sure if Captain Skander was privy to our charade. I hoped not. The fewer who knew that an American soldier was aboard this freighter, the better.

As the North Korean officer and Captain Skander argued, I regained my composure. This was beginning to look suspiciously like a shakedown. Maybe the North Korean customs officer and Captain Skander would haggle, a price would be settled upon and paid, and everyone would go about their business. That's what I thought back then. As I learned more about the DPRK, I would come to realize that nothing is ever simple.

Finally, the two men came to some sort of resolution. Captain Skander returned scowling.

Two armed Koreans emerged from below deck holding plastic packages wrapped in gauze tape. They set the packages on the deck. When their commander nodded, one of them pulled a knife from his belt and sliced open the first package. He held a pinch of the brownish powder up to the light. The commander asked where he'd found it, and the soldier replied. Other than the Koreans themselves, I was probably the only man on deck who understood them. They'd found it in one of the sailors' sea bags. The package was slashed with Chinese characters. When the beam from a flashlight passed across the thick ink, I was able to read them. *Antler horn.* A highly prized aphrodisiac used in Chinese medicine. But, like all personal business transactions, selling it was illegal in North Korea. The powdered horn of the Siberian caribou could be legitimately obtained only as a gift from the Great Leader.

One of the Albanians was called forward. I recognized him. A slender youth with a scraggly red beard named Zarkos.

The North Korean officer barked at him in English, "Is this yours?"

Zarkos stood dumbfounded, not understanding.

Captain Skander stepped forward to translate. Once he understood, Zarkos stroked his beard nervously and shook his head. Then he launched into a long tirade I didn't understand, the gist of which, according to Mergim, was that the powder wasn't his and he didn't know how it had landed in his sea bag. The North Korean officer was unimpressed. He said something softly to his men, and two of them stepped forward and rammed the butts of their rifles into the young man's back. He shrieked in pain. The men around me surged forward, but the business ends of half-a-dozen AK-47s immediately trained on them. The sailors backed off. Zarkos struggled briefly but was overcome by a Korean, who deftly knotted his arms behind his back. With the help of two more members of the boarding party, they shoved Zarkos toward the gangplank.

Captain Skander roared in protest, but the North Korean officer ignored him.

After Zarkos had been hauled ashore, the Korean officer, puffing serenely on his cigarette, stepped in front of the sailors. "My name is Commander Koh," he said in Korean. A young Korean soldier translated. "Welcome to paradise!"

The Albanian sailors shifted their weight, hunched their shoulders, and glanced surreptitiously at one another. None of them laughed, a tribute to their long experience of living under Communist regime.

"Our country is paradise," Commander Koh continued, "because our Great Leader, the shining light of our people, hero of the Korean War, and fearless general of our invincible forces, provides us with all our wants and needs. You are fortunate to be here, in this land of plenty, even if it is for only these few short days." Commander Koh paused, took a last drag on his cigarette, and flicked it overboard. "Your ship has passed inspection. All except the man who's been taken ashore. He will be competently dealt with. The rest of you will be guests of our Great Leader tonight in the People's Hall of International Friendship. Due to the open heart and generous spirit of our Great Leader, entertainment will be provided."

Below us, Zarkos had somehow broken free from his captors. He struggled toward the gangplank, but his dash for freedom was cut short by an alert soldier's swift kick to the groin. Zarkos curled into a ball, rolling on the deck and moaning in pain. His body convulsed and he vomited onto the splintered planks.

"The entertainment begins at eighteen hundred hours," Commander Koh continued, ignoring the performance below. "You will not be late." Then he turned away, adding, *"Kutna."* Finished. The entire armed boarding party retreated down the gangplank.

Captain Skander stared helplessly as Zarkos was dragged away. When the groaning sailor disappeared from view, the captain turned and spoke to the men in a somber tone.

Later, Mergim explained that Captain Skander believed that the bastard North Koreans only wanted money. It was routine with them. The North Koreans would negotiate a deal with the Albanian shipping cooperative and the contract would be signed, but all along the North Koreans would consider the price too low and make plans to extort more money to bring the contract up to a level they thought appropriate. Captain Skander assured the crew that the shipping cooperative would come up with the money and Zarkos would be freed and back aboard before the *Star of Tirana* left Nampo.

Grumbling, the sailors returned to their duties.

Mergim agreed with Captain Skander's analysis. For one thing, the powder that the North Koreans called antler horn was too finely ground to be a natural product from Siberian caribou. "Customers want chunks," Mergim explained, "to see what they're buying. Then they grind it down themselves. That stuff in those packages is some other kind of powder, not real antler horn." Then Mergim added, "The red-star jokers want to show us who's boss. Every time I come here, they push sailors. Push too hard sometimes."

After he left, I stood at the railing alone, holding my hands in front of me to make sure the quivering had stopped. Then I went below to help with the cargo.

"She's a hot number," Mergim said, leering.

There was only one woman in the People's Hall of International Friendship who was less than geriatric, and most of the sailors were watching her each and every movement. She was a slightly portly young woman, probably in her mid- to late-twenties, with thick legs and sturdy hips. Ample breasts were pressed tightly beneath a high-necked red cotton dress and a full-length white apron, her straight black hair held in place by a matching bandanna.

I'd already noticed that the other Korean workers called her Pei. Food Worker Pei. I hadn't let on that I understood, of course. To have done so would have brought attention to myself that could have proven more than just embarrassing. It could have proven fatal.

The other workers in the People's Hall were either frail older men who scurried about in the back galley or grandmotherly types who wore the same uniform as Food Worker Pei but didn't fill them out nearly as voluptuously. We'd all been at sea a long time and none of us could take our eyes off her.

"She wears rubber gloves," Mergim told me.

"Huh?" I sipped on my hot barley tea and set it down. "Rubber gloves? What do you mean?"

"She's not wearing them now," he said.

We watched as Food Worker Pei slid a platter of stainless-steel soup bowls onto the center of a round table of Albanian sailors. Showing complete egalitarianism, the sailors were required to pick up their own bowls, along with the spoons and the wooden chopsticks and the plates piled high with brown rice. Once the platter was empty, Pei hoisted it back up, swiveled, and sashayed back to the kitchen.

"Later," Mergim continued, "when the old women are cleaning up, then she wait in front hallway."

"Waits for what?"

Mergim grinned. "For rubber glove treatment." In short strokes, he pumped his fist up and down.

My eyes widened. "You're serious."

"Of course, I'm serious." Mergim puffed on his cigarette, looking slightly offended.

I glanced at the armed men guarding the three exits. "What about the guards?"

"They smoke outside. Don't look. Probably they get money too."

The People's Hall of International Friendship was not like the fleshpots of the Orient one reads about. It was fenced in, about a hundred square yards, with an outside patio that could be used in good weather and a large dining hall where most of the sailors ate their evening meals while in port. There was no menu. Whatever was served was served, take it or leave it. The menu du jour was a dish I recognized from my years in the South, *komtang*. Sliced beef with onion and egg in a hot broth. No pork—the Koreans had assured us that no pig product would be used since they knew that most of the Albanian sailors were Muslims. Not that the Communist governments of either country approved of religion, but the sailors were paying for their meals, cash on the barrelhead. The strapped North Korean government, meanwhile, was greedy for money they could exchange on international markets, so they complied with the Albanian sailors' bourgeois requirements.

During my briefings in Seoul, I'd been told about the corruption among the staff of the People's Hall of International Friendship. I'd even been told that some of the bolder foreign sailors had smuggled in contraband and then paid staff members to lead them to illicit dealers who operated near the port. The North Korean authorities almost certainly knew about these things but turned a blind eye, probably because much of the profit ended up in their pockets. It was a safe bet that Commander Koh, the customs officer in charge of the Port of Nampo, kept the lion's share of the money earned not only from smuggling but also from Food Worker Pei, with her voluptuous figure and her rubber glove.

After the dinner plates had been removed, the half-dozen older women brought out glass bottles, about the size of American pop bottles, filled with a clear fluid. They plopped three bottles in the center of each table. The label said *Red Star Soju*, in both Korean and English. Immediately, the sailors started squabbling over the bottles. The Korean women shook their heads in disgust. The custom is to pour for your comrades first and then one of your comrades pours for you. Mergim, who'd been here before, offered to pour some of the clear rice liquor into my tin cup. I refused. I'd stick with barley tea.

"You don't want to get drunk?" he asked.

I nodded toward Food Worker Pei. She stood in the foyer, flirting with one of the guards.

"Ah, that first." Mergim tapped the side of his head. "Smart."

The Albanian sailors were tossing back huge shots of the fierce rice liquor, and some of them had already called for more. Once they laid Hong Kong dollars on the table, the old women delivered.

A shrill voice erupted from ancient speakers. Static screeched but the voice kept on, unperturbed, extolling the glories of the Great Leader and the paradise that was the Democratic People's Republic of Korea. The strident message was delivered first in Korean, then in English. None of the Albanian sailors paid any attention; they were more interested in guzzling soju. But then the voice stopped and strains of martial music erupted out of the old speakers like an ancient brass band. A side door opened and a troupe of men and women wearing the brown-wool, high-necked uniforms of the Korean People's Army marched in. The men wore round caps lidded like ancient jars, the women soft caps with short brims, both emblazoned with huge red stars. They goose-stepped toward the front of the hall, swinging their fists as they marched. Soon they were posing before us, raising the red-star flag of North Korea, singing, striking new poses, and finally engaging in something that could loosely be called a dance. It was more like a series of poses that they switched to on cue, creating a tableaux that illustrated events narrated by the lyrics. When one song stopped, another started without pause. As best I could gather, they were telling the tale of the Korean people's epic struggle against colonial forces—the Japanese, who had occupied Korea from 1910 to 1945; and then, to hear the North Koreans tell it, the United States from 1945 onward, in the southern portion of the country. The twentieth century had been a constant struggle for them, a series of tribulations they saw as ongoing.

The sailors glanced occasionally at the entertainment but mostly ignored it. The men in the troupe were all baby-faced and slender, their movements nothing less than effeminate. The women were strong, determined, and assertive, and their cheeks glowed crimson when they belted out tunes praising the Great Leader. Since they were fully clothed in heavy wool uniforms, including thick tunics, long skirts, and black combat boots, the sailors didn't have much to look at.

It was an hour before the performers took a break, promising to be back for more. Finally, the scratchy speakers subsided into silence.

"I want to go back to Hong Kong," Mergim said, slugging down another shot of soju.

I'd noticed some movement in the front hallway. "I'll be back," I told him, then stood up and strode past drunken and arguing Albanian sailors.

The truth was that I didn't plan to return at all, not if I could help it. I hoped Mergim would be all right. He'd been a good friend to me, and even though he'd been well paid for his efforts, I'd grown fond of him and respected the tough life he'd led. My handlers in Seoul had assured me that the Communist Albanian government would look after him. I prayed they had been telling the truth.

The guard talking to Food Worker Pei noticed my approach and turned and sauntered away. Without looking at me, she stepped into a hallway that led toward the back of the building.

I followed.

It was dark back there, but I saw her a few yards ahead, moonlight filtering though a smoke-smudged window. She was slipping something on over her right hand, something that creaked and flapped like thick rubber. Not supple like the synthetic materials made in the West. More like a flipper.

▪ ▪ ▪

My mission was to avoid another war between North and South Korea. Or at least that's what Major Bulward, the executive officer of the 501st Military Intelligence Battalion, told me. I didn't really believe him. The military of both the North and the South had been longing for war ever since the ceasefire had been signed in June of 1953, more than twenty years ago. The Korean War had settled nothing, despite the death of two or three million people—depending on whom you asked. Korea, a four-thousand-year-old society, was still divided. Families were unable to communicate, either by phone or by letter, and people who were separated by the Demilitarized Zone that slashed through the center of the country couldn't even be sure if their loved ones were dead or alive. And the U.S. military, despite all its talk of peace, was aching to become involved in another conventional conflict. Now that the Vietnam War was all but wound down, the American brass was sick of guerilla warfare. They wanted a good old-fashioned head butt: major armies, tank battalions, naval armadas, squadrons of jet fighters—the fun stuff—all slugging it out in a defined field of conflict. So when Major Bulward told me that my mission would help us avoid war, I knew it was bull. I also knew that if I were successful, the information I sought might actually ignite a war, by encouraging the South Koreans to go north. I hoped not, but I knew it was possible.

My mission—my real mission—was to find an ancient manuscript that contained a description of a vast network of caverns and underground waterways that led from an area in North Korea near Mount Osong to an area in South Korea near Mount Daesong. In other words, a secret passageway beneath the DMZ. The existence of such a manuscript had been rumored amongst scholars for centuries, but I'd come into possession of physical proof that it actually existed, a fragment that had been confirmed to be genuine by experts.

Despite its name, the Korean Demilitarized Zone—or DMZ—is the most heavily militarized border in the world. An estimated 700,000 heavily armed Communist soldiers guard the northern side and an estimated 450,000 ROK soldiers guard the southern side, assisted by 30,000 American GIs of the United States Army's Second Infantry Division.

For years, the North Koreans had been diligently tunneling beneath the DMZ. Two of the tunnels had been discovered by Southern forces. They were impressive constructions, high enough for a grown man to walk through. Down the center of one of the tunnels, railroad track had been laid. Military intelligence estimated that with the help of rolling transport, a battalion of armed North Korean infantry could be smuggled beneath the DMZ to the southern side within two hours, an entire division in one night. According to aerial reconnaissance, the scope of the North Korean drilling effort on their side of the DMZ indicated that there were at least a dozen more tunnels that had yet to be intercepted. In addition to the threat of the tunnels, Major Bulward told me, the entire logistical effort of the North Korean military in the last few months had been moving steadily south.

"Kim Il-sung, the Great Leader, has reached *huangap*," Major Bulward told me, "the age of sixty, when a Korean man traditionally retires. He's appointed his son as a full-fledged member of the Workers' Party's Central

Committee, and he's vowed to unite the country before he turns over power. We believe they plan to do that now, while the American public is still wallowing in self-pity over the failure of political will in Vietnam."

The failure of political will. That's the U.S. Army's way of blaming somebody other than itself. Saigon hadn't fallen yet but we were mostly out of it already. Nobody expected the ARVN, the Army of the Republic of Vietnam, to hold on much longer.

Major Bulward went on to imply that if South Korea didn't find a way to tunnel north and insert our own infantry behind enemy lines, the North Korean armored assault across the DMZ might prove so overwhelming that we'd be forced to use nuclear weapons.

"We don't want to do that," Bulward assured me, "but we might have to."

Inwardly, I hated him. Not only for even contemplating using nuclear weapons on the Korean peninsula, but also for choosing me for this job. But I knew that was unfair. The reason I'd been chosen had nothing to do with Major Bulward. It actually had nothing to do with me or my less-than-stellar qualifications. The reason I'd been chosen was because I'd received a note from an old girlfriend. A woman of substance. A woman I'd once loved and maybe still did. A woman known as Doctor Yong In-ja.

Food Worker Pei's pretty, round face was sullen. Pouty. She pointed toward my crotch. "I touch," she said in Korean. "You no touch." She gestured toward her breasts.

Dumbly, I nodded.

She held out her left hand, the one without the glove. "Money," she said in English. A word I figured even Albanian sailors understood.

I reached beneath my leather belt into a cloth pouch. I pulled out one large silver coin and held it up to the light. Food Worker Pei smiled. As she stepped forward, I shoved her rubber-gloved hand out of the way.

"I want to trade this," I said in English, "for ginseng. Red ginseng."

The most prized type of wild ginseng is the red ginseng, sometimes called royal ginseng, that is found only in the remotest areas of Hamgyong Province, in the mountains of North Korea. In Hong Kong, wild red ginseng could be sold to wealthy old men for a small fortune. Ten to twenty thousand dollars was not unheard of as a purchase price for one of the gnarled crimson roots.

Pei frowned. She didn't understand a word I'd said. She thought I was bargaining for something other than ginseng. She slipped off her rubber glove and let it fall to the ground. Stepping closer, she upped the stakes and unbuttoned the collar of her dress. I didn't have time to continue trying to communicate with hand signals and her rudimentary English, so I said the words in Korean, the words that had been relayed to me in the middle of the night in a secluded spot on the edge of the Port of Pusan.

"The Nampo Southern Section People's Grain Warehouse," I said. "I must go there."

Her mouthed gaped open. She'd probably never heard a merchant marine speak Korean before.

"*Bali*," I said. Hurry. "*Na insam sago sippo.*" I want to buy ginseng. Still speaking Korean, I asked her how I could get outside of the fence surrounding us so I could make my way to the grain warehouse.

Pei's mouth closed. She stared at the silver coin, rebuttoning the collar of her dress. She seemed frightened, confused. I needed to reassure her, so I slipped the coin into her open palm. The flesh was rough and calloused. She gazed up at me, thinking it over. Her brow wrinkled.

"No one will know," I said in Korean. "A friend told me you've done deals before. I'll be careful."

Finally she nodded. Her fingers closed around the coin.

Quietly, we stepped farther down the dark hall. She opened a door that led outside, turned, and motioned for me to wait. A few yards away, a guard stood at a side gate. He seemed bored as he stared into the mist-soaked darkness. As Food Worker Pei approached, he turned, clutching his rifle. She bowed and stepped closer to him. When she was almost touching him, she spoke.

If she wanted to betray me, now was the time.

The guard whispered a few questions. Pei answered. Finally, the guard glanced around, ensuring that no one was watching, and took a couple of steps away from the gate. Pei motioned for me to come forward. I did. The gate guard couldn't have been much more than a teenager. He stared up at me, insolent.

"*Tambei*," he said, silently snapping his fingers.

I pretended I didn't understand. Food Worker Pei mimicked the act of smoking.

I didn't smoke, but I knew that one of the best ways to inspire cooperation was to always have cigarettes on hand. The ones I pulled out of my pocket were British-made, purchased in Hong Kong. The guard stared at them greedily. I slipped one out of the pack and handed it to him.

Like a magic trick, the cigarette disappeared into the pocket of his jacket. Then he snapped his fingers and said, "*Doh.*" Again.

I hesitated. Food Worker Pei nodded. I took two more cigarettes out of the pack, handed them to him and, with an air of finality, stuck the remainder of the pack deep into the recesses of my peacoat.

The guard seemed pleased. He glanced around, pulled something from another pocket and handed it to Food Worker Pei. He sauntered off, not looking back. As his footsteps faded, Food Worker Pei bent toward the gate and fiddled with a lock. Metal clinked on metal. She stepped toward me and asked me in Korean, *"Odi inji allayo?"* Do you know where it is?

I nodded.

This shocked her, the full realization finally hitting her that I was not only a foreigner who spoke Korean but one who knew where the People's Grain Warehouse was located. The fingers of her left hand rose to her lips, as if the full import of what she was doing was finally coming clear to her. I grabbed her shoulders and spoke to her urgently.

"Kokchong hajima," I said. Don't worry. "There's another silver coin for you when I return. Tell that guard to expect me after one hour. I have more cigarettes. Don't betray me. If I'm caught, both you and he will be punished."

She gazed at me in terror. "One hour?" she asked.

I nodded. "One hour. Maybe a little more."

Then I turned and pushed through the gate, closing it behind me.

I watched as Food Worker Pei scurried forward and snapped shut the lock, feeling guilty about getting her into so much trouble. I had no intention of returning to the People's Hall of International Friendship. At least not voluntarily.

I had long since memorized the path to the grain warehouse. Eighth Army's aerial reconnaissance of North Korea is state-of-the-art and covers every square foot of this poor, targeted country. The North Koreans have a small air force but no capacity to stop the U.S. overflights of supersonic aircraft, and certainly no capacity to stop our satellite surveillance. The zoomies tell me that they purposely make sonic booms over the North Korean capital of Pyongyang to remind the Great Leader that we can take him out whenever the spirit moves us.

Back in Seoul, I'd spent hours studying black-and-white blowups of photographs of the Port of Nampo and the surrounding area. I trotted now through cold, narrow alleys, mud sloshing beneath my feet, with few lights to guide me. Only at major intersections did the occasional yellow street lamp stand guard. I avoided these, sticking to the shadows.

The sailor who'd brought me the message back in the safety of the Port of Pusan had specifically said that I must contact a man called Hero Kang at the People's Grain Warehouse in the southern section of Nampo. It was only a few hundred yards from the People's Hall of International Friendship and other sailors had gone there to transact black-market deals. Who Hero Kang was or what he looked like, I had no idea. The only thing I was told was to use the code word "orphan." In Korean, *ko-ah*. Child of bitterness.

The People's Grain Warehouse was right where the recon boys told me it would be. Luckily, North Koreans retire early, and on the way I'd seen only a few people from a distance: laborers trudging their way home, an occasional man pushing a wooden cart. I'd managed to avoid them.

The rotted wood door at the back of the warehouse was open. I stepped inside carefully, prepared for anything. Inside, a candle flickered on a low wooden table. The odor of fermenting grain was overpowering. Dust floated in the air. Not dust, I realized, probably minute particles from the husks of rice.

The candle still burning indicated that someone was working late. Hero Kang, I hoped. He couldn't have known which ship I'd be arriving on—we'd had no communication since the initial message—but certainly he'd be here any night a foreign ship pulled into port, which was only, according to the intelligence boys in Seoul, two or three dozen times a year. A desk sat in a corner and in front of it were square wooden slots, an old-fashioned filing system with yellowed paper rolled and stuffed into various pigeonholes.

I didn't want to say hello—what if Hero Kang wasn't alone? What if he'd been joined by a surprise visitor and had led the visitor away, hoping I wouldn't barge in at the wrong time? I decided to find a hiding place and wait. Before I did, I couldn't resist peeking through a double wooden door. Stepping gingerly on the creaking wood, I pushed the door open slightly and peered into the vast darkness of a high-ceilinged storage area. Something flitted amongst rafters. Bats. I was about to retreat and find a hiding place in the outside alleyway when the soles of my shoes slid on something rough, like tiny pebbles. Grain—millet, I thought—had been strewn purposefully along the floor. As my eyes adjusted to the dim light, I realized that the grain had been dropped to form the shape of a crooked arrow, an arrow that pointed deeper into the warehouse. Quietly, I scattered the grain with my shoe and followed.

Moonbeams streamed through a skylight. I passed ancient wooden pallets piled high with sacks of rice. North Korea was a fecund country, rich soil in the lowlands, profitable minerals in the mountains. Begrudgingly, some of my briefers in Seoul had admitted that the standard of living in communist North Korea—as judged by the per capita annual caloric intake—was higher than that in democratic South Korea. But they were quick to add that the Soviet bloc was spending millions subsidizing the North Korean lifestyle, and South Korea was gaining on them rapidly.

At the far end of the warehouse, another tiny candle wavered. It sat on the floor in the center of a short hallway. The door at the end of the hallway had been propped open by a stone. Near the flame, more grain had been scattered. I knelt to examine it, this time expecting a message. It formed two words. The first was a Chinese character. Three lines, the outer two angling in on the straight line in the middle. It took me a second and then it came to me. *Su.* Water. The second word was in shadow. I lifted the flaming plate of oil. It was in English. Then I realized what it said.

Run.

-2-

A narrow pathway ran along the edge of the Taedong River. I slipped on the muddy precipice and almost plunged into the roiling water below, at the last minute grabbing shrubbery, steadying myself, and moving forward. Besides the three-quarter moon, the only visibility was provided by the glare of the floodlights of the port behind me. I was heading north, not sure if this was the right way but knowing that I didn't want to return south toward the port. If anyone were following me, they'd be coming from that direction. The message written on the floor of the grain warehouse had been clear. Head for water and run.

Doc Yong knew that I'd studied the Korean language and memorized a few dozen of the Chinese characters that educated Koreans sprinkle amongst their phonetic hangul script. Had she told Hero Kang about me? Was she here? The thought excited me but also frightened me. Frightened me because I wasn't sure what to say to her after being separated for so many months, and frightened me even more because I didn't want her to be in danger. I shoved such thoughts out of my mind and concentrated on keeping my footing on the slippery precipice.

A breeze flowed from the land above, caressing my cheek, wafting down toward the Taedong River and joining the swirling current below. The wind carried guttural male voices and shoe leather slapping on stone, from how far away I couldn't be sure.

I didn't think Food Worker Pei and the gate guard had blown the whistle. They had too much to lose. Also, if it had been them, Hero Kang or whoever was waiting for me at the warehouse wouldn't have known I was being followed. Not that quickly. Somehow Hero Kang had been tipped off already, which means that he had contacts feeding him information from inside the Port of Nampo.

Occasional flashes of light glinted from between the wood-and-brick walls that lined the top of the cliff. I increased my speed, plowing ahead for what must've been at least a mile. Abruptly the pathway ended, or at least it appeared to end. It curved sharply up the muddy incline. There was nowhere else to go, so I clambered uphill, following as the path squeezed between the walls and fed into a stinking pedestrian alleyway, barely wide enough for my shoulders. The ground was layered with mud except for a narrow center channel lined in flagstone. Waste flowed freely through the channel, gurgling beneath my feet.

Eight-foot-high walls loomed above the alleyway. Behind them, all was quiet. It was probably close to midnight by now, but this was more than just the silence of exhaustion in a working neighborhood. It was as still as death. So far, that's what this country seemed like to me. Like death.

I ran my hands along either side of the narrow walkway, stepping widely to avoid the central gutter. I passed alleys between buildings that were even narrower than the one I was on, veering off at odd angles to the right and the left. The only light left now was the glimmer of the overhead three-quarter moon.

Finally, the alley ended, merging into an open area paved in a circular array of old-fashioned cobblestones, which surrounded a naked elm tree bracketed by flat wooden benches. I knelt in the mouth of the alleyway, catching my breath, studying the darkness. Across the little plaza, candlelight shone through a crack in the walls, golden beams bobbing like mischievous imps. The electricity in this area had probably been switched off by the local authorities—a routine practice to conserve energy, according to my briefers in Seoul. I stared up at the stars, bright among drifting clouds. No one followed me anymore. Where were the running footsteps I'd heard before? I listened for what must have been two minutes. Nothing.

I thought about the message on the warehouse floor. There had only been one pathway along the river's edge and only one way to climb back up to ground level. It led here, to this spot. Whoever had left the message for me was the same person who'd lit that candle across the plaza. I was certain of it. I stared at the flickering light, appreciating the fact that someone in this vast wilderness of death had lit a candle for me, and enjoying the sensation of sweat pooling beneath my coat. But the night was growing colder. Soon I would begin to shiver. The light on the far side of the cobblestones portended warmth and safety.

Just as I was about to stand up and step out into the open, I heard footsteps. Rapid. Too rapid for me to react. Shadows appeared at the far end of the clearing. I crouched back into darkness. Demons of the night, maybe a dozen, filtered across the cobblestones.

I suddenly became aware of something behind me. Back some thirty yards, where this pathway opened onto the muddy cliff, I heard heavy breathing, and cursing.

Only seconds ago, I'd been counting on being saved. Now I was trapped.

No time to think. I retreated back down the alley, away from the central clearing. Ahead of me, along the main path, I heard sloshing. The cursing had stopped but the breathing was still audible. Whoever they were, they were only a few yards off in the darkness, moving toward me. I had no choice. I slipped sideways into one of the cracks between the buildings and sidled my way north, moving as quickly as I could without making noise.

Spiderwebs and moth cadavers hung from rafters. I shuffled along the narrow opening, which became even narrower, the moss-smeared walls in front and behind pushing in on me. Just as I was about to be hopelessly wedged in, the building in front of me ended and another, slightly wider lane emerged. I ducked into it, holding still for a moment, listening, not breathing. I couldn't be sure because the sound reverberated off oddly juxtaposed walls, but I believed the footsteps passed the narrow crack and continued toward the central square. Still, I dared not go back there. I edged my way along these brick-and-stone walls, occasionally passing a window boarded up with ancient wood. The alleyway turned and turned again and finally widened. A slippery brick pathway opened in front of me, lined with a sturdy metal railing. Below me, water surged through a cement channel, narrow enough for me to hop across, moving downhill toward the Tae-dong River.

Behind me, someone shouted.

They'd realized I'd slipped away. In a matter of seconds, they'd be searching between the buildings. Toward the river, the pathway along the edge of the narrow channel hit another building. A dead end. In the other direction, the pathway wound out of sight but led, I believed, back toward the central square. Someone would be waiting for me there. Once again, I was trapped. For a brief moment, I considered leaping into the water and taking my chances plunging downstream. But who knew what tunnels or grates or underground reservoirs loomed between me and the open river? Frantically, I searched my surroundings. Then I saw it. An indentation in the wall on the far side of the channel, large enough for a man. If I managed to make it over there, I'd be spotted easily. Was there a similar opening on this side?

The footsteps and heavy breathing were louder now. Someone was making his way down the same narrow crack I'd just traversed. I climbed over the metal railing, lowered myself, and searched the cement on my side of the channel. About ten yards downstream, I saw it. A recessed opening, directly across from the one on the far side, probably designed to anchor a footbridge or a sluiceway yet to be constructed. I pulled myself toward it, hand over hand. When my feet reached the recessed ledge, I fought for purchase, but only my toes balanced on the slippery lip. If I didn't lower myself flush up against the cement wall of the channel, I'd plunge backward into the river. Luckily, the wall angled forward slightly.

Loud cursing above gave me courage. I let go of the railing, and hugging the smooth cement in front of me, lowered myself straight down until I could reach inside the opening. I was tilting backward and grabbed frantically for a handhold. Just as I was about to fall, my fingertips found jutting stone. Holding all my weight by straining digits, I managed to pull myself slowly into the narrow opening.

The sound of footsteps exploded onto the brick walkway above. I curled myself into a ball and prayed they hadn't seen me. More shouts. Men cursing, trotting up and down the pathway. Then, after the sounds of a thorough search, more shouted orders and a pack of them headed off, away from the river, back toward the open central square.

All was quiet. Still, I waited. I knew better than to expose myself too quickly, before I was sure no one was up there. I lay curled in a fetal position for what seemed a long time, listening. Finally, a comet streaked through the air and hit the rushing water, sizzling. A flaming cigarette butt. Someone coughed directly above me. More coughing, more spitting, and then a silvery stream of glowing water rushed down directly in front of me, steaming and splashing into the canal.

Not water, I decided.

The sentry above me was taking a leak.

After an hour, the sentry left. When I was sure there hadn't been any coughing or soaring cigarette butts in a long time, I peeked out of my cubbyhole. Moving slowly, I managed to twist myself out of the opening and sidle up the slippery cement. I pulled myself up the metal railing onto dry land.

I felt a sense of triumph. They'd searched for me but they hadn't found me. I retraced my steps, listening at every intersection.

Back at the edge of the plaza, all was quiet. I waited ten minutes until I was certain there was no movement before stepping out of the alley. When I was halfway across the plaza, beneath the branches of the withered elm, someone off to my left shouted. Before I could react, armed men poured out of dark apertures. An electric torch sliced the night, shining brutally into my face. I raised my hands to cover my eyes. Heavy boots tromped toward me and soon I was surrounded. One of the men shoved me back toward the elm tree and others grabbed my arms. Within seconds they'd cinched my wrists behind my back with a wire cord. I cursed myself for being so careless. Before anyone could say anything, a man wearing a full-brimmed cap with a gold-backed red star in the center pushed his way toward me.

The beam of the flashlight was lowered. In front of me

stood Commander Koh, the man who had led the boarding party on the *Star of Tirana* this morning and the man in charge of the Port of Nampo. How had he become aware of me so quickly? Had Zarkos talked? Once they'd taken the young sailor into custody, he'd have been so frightened he would have told them anything, traded any tidbit of information, no matter how inconsequential, to regain his freedom. I was the odd duck aboard the *Star of Tirana*. He'd have told them about me. It was only natural. Still, I had my cover story and I was determined to stick to it.

Commander Koh raised a cigarette to his lips, his eyes narrowing. He didn't ask me anything, he just stared.

Finally, he stepped back. As he did so, another man armed with a rifle sprang forward. Before I could prepare myself, the butt of his AK-47 slammed into my stomach. My knees gave way and, finding nothing to break my fall, I tumbled headfirst to the ground. My tied arms prevented me from clutching my stomach, but I brought my knees up as far as I could in a vain effort to ease the pain. In seconds, I was vomiting my dinner onto the cobbled ground: *komtang*, coarse brown rice, and three glasses of barley tea. I must've passed out briefly because when I came to I heard a roar, as if the Minotaur of Greek legend had entered our stone ring.

Doctor Yong In-ja was the most exciting woman I'd ever met.

"A bookworm," was my CID partner Ernie Bascom's opinion. But Ernie didn't have much time for the intellectual side of life. He was too busy living, which for him included fighting, drinking, and chasing women, not necessarily in that order. To him, a book was a waste of precious time, time when he could be carousing.

We'd met Doc Yong because she was the chief of the Itaewon branch of the Yongsan District Public Health Service. As such she was in constant contact with the "business girls" who serviced the American GIs—young, impoverished women from the countryside of South Korea who gathered in Itaewon, the red-light district of Seoul. The business girls were constantly appearing on the Eighth Army blotter report—victims of rape, robbery, assault. These reports were routine, and Doctor Yong In-ja at the medical clinic often received the complaints first and passed them on to us.

Doc Yong was the most intelligent person I'd ever met. Through thick-lensed glasses, her serious dark eyes sized you up as soon as you were fortunate enough to step into her realm. I fell for her probably the first time I met her, and I felt awkward around her, but I wasn't able to get to know her until we worked on a murder case together. It was a cold case dating back twenty years, to just after the end of the Korean War. We'd become close, very close. When it was over, she had to flee to the homeland of her ancestors, to North Korea. I wasn't sure, but I had indications that she was pregnant at the time. So when I received the message, months later, I realized that it was her calling me to join her.

She was smart enough to know that in order for the Eighth Army brass to release me, and to risk having an American soldier enter communist North Korea, they had to have an incentive. That's what the ancient manuscript was all about. It had supposedly been written in the fifteenth century under the reign of Sejong Daewang, the Great King Sejong. It told the story of a chase for a man who had been considered dangerous by the authorities at the time. This "wild man" was extremely resourceful and managed to elude his pursuers on horseback by entering a network of caves in the Kwangju Mountains. Upon entering the caves, the officials discovered a network of tunnels that took them much farther than they imagined, beneath what in modern times is known as the Korean DMZ. Some scholars thought the manuscript was a myth. Now, by hiring a merchant sailor to contact me in the port city of Pusan and place a wrinkled fragment of the ancient parchment in my hands, Doc Yong had offered physical proof, confirmed by experts, that the narrative actually did exist. All this was lovely from a historian's perspective, but to the military, the manuscript had a much greater importance. Specifically, it offered a ready-made pathway beneath the Demilitarized Zone. The honchos at Eighth Army had swallowed the bait whole. And since Doc Yong had further insisted, through the merchant marine who relayed her instructions, that I was the only messenger she would trust, I was selected for the mission. In order to provide the remainder of the manuscript and the information it provided, Doc Yong wanted something in return. What that was, we weren't quite sure yet, but Eighth Army seemed ready to pay a very high price.

"There's not much time," Major Bulward told me. "When the rice paddies freeze, the terrain near the DMZ will become solid and therefore passable for the North Korean armored battalions. Tanks, personnel carriers, self-propelled guns—they'll find traction on the ice and won't have to worry about getting bogged down in mud. This winter, after the snows come, that's when the North Koreans will attack."

Kim Il-sung had publicly and repeatedly vowed to reunify Korea before he retired. Eighth Army believed him. The time for that to happen was now. This winter.

Here in Nampo, the leaves were off the trees. Cold winds were already blowing out of Manchuria. Soon, Old Man Winter would rouse himself from his snowy home in Siberia, lumber across the Asian landmass, and find his way into the long-suffering peninsula known as Frozen Chosun. He'd bring with him ice and snow and, it was believed, war.

I was still doubled over from the butt of the AK-47 that had been rammed into my gut. Commander Koh still puffed on his cigarette, studying me as if I were some sort of vermin that had to be stomped into submission. But even he seemed startled by the roar that emanated from the man in a brown felt army uniform who stood at the edge of the plaza. What he said was incomprehensible, but he left no doubt that he was enraged. The man was enormous for a Korean. He stormed across the plaza, shoving armed soldiers out of the way, and within seconds he stood toe-to-toe with Commander Koh.

"*Weikurei!*" he bellowed. What the hell are you doing?

The voice was as deep and as full-throated as any voice I'd ever heard. His bulging cheeks turned red and shook as he spoke, spittle erupting from moist lips. He leaned so close to Commander Koh that their noses touched.

Like Commander Koh, the enraged man wore a cap with a gold-backed red star in the center, but his was a soft cap, the cap of a workingman. He also wore the ubiquitous broach with a picture of the smiling face of the Great Leader pinned to his chest. Something dangled from a lanyard around the big man's neck, flickering in the light of nervous torches: a photograph, apparently of this man, standing next to and shaking the hand of the Great Leader, Kim Il-sung himself. It was the type of photo that in the West we'd have tacked to the wall of our office.

Commander Koh held his own. He squinted up at the taller man, pointing at me, hollering back that I had escaped from the Port of Nampo and therefore I was his prisoner.

The bigger man's eyes bulged, and, like a great torrent unleashed, words rushed out of his mouth, washing away any argument Commander Koh was trying to make. The big man pointed at me, waggling his forefinger. He was shouting that it was ludicrous beyond belief that Command Koh should think that he in any way had any jurisdiction here, outside of the port, or any reason in the great wide world to be arresting a man who was clearly the responsibility of the People's Police of the City of Nampo.

Or at least that's what I thought he said. The words came out so fast and furious, tumbling over one another; they were like a crowd in a burning theater rushing for the exits.

Commander Koh protested.

The big man leaned into him until their foreheads

touched, shoving the rattled Commander backward even further, screaming at the top of his lungs. He would brook no argument. I don't believe I'd ever seen a person so outraged. In America, we would've long since been exchanging blows, or gunshots.

Koreans believe that throwing a punch reflects poorly on the person who throws it. The person who does such an uncouth thing reveals himself to be an uneducated oaf and his victim wins the argument, at least in the public mind, by default. The greatest fear, much greater than the fear of physical harm, was the fear of losing face.

Gradually, the big man's argument concerning jurisdiction seemed to be gaining traction. Between shouts, Commander Koh looked pensive, probably calculating the cost of defying this man—whoever he was—and comparing it to the cost of backing down and returning to his little fiefdom at the Port of Nampo.

The bigger man sensed Koh's wavering and pressed his advantage, shouting louder than ever, waving his arms, his face turning so beet red that I expected him at any moment to keel over. But the big man maintained his footing and Commander Koh turned his face, now staring at me kneeling on the ground, then staring at his men, who, still clutching their automatic weapons, shuffled their feet nervously across the cobbled stones.

Finally, Commander Koh threw up his arms.

"*Kurom*," he said. So be it. "If that's the way you want it, take him. Take him! He's your problem now. Just, whatever you do, don't return him to us." Commander Koh waved his hand in front of the big man's face. "We don't want him."

For once, the big man remained passive.

Commander Koh swiveled and bellowed at his men. "What are you doing? Have you no military discipline? Form your ranks! Stand straight like soldiers. Let's go! Get moving!"

Commander Koh, his back to the bigger man, maintained an air of scholarly dignity. Without looking back, he followed his troops into one of the larger alleys. In seconds, their footsteps faded in muddy lanes.

The big man, still breathing heavily, stood with his arms akimbo, the redness in his face ebbing. I dared not move. Finally, he turned and looked at me.

"*Iro-nah!*" he said. Get up!

I did.

"Follow me." He turned and strode away, but after a few steps he turned back, noticing that my hands were still tied behind my back. He stopped and reached into a coat pocket, pulling out a knife. The blade flashed open. As he approached, I held my breath, standing stock-still. Roughly, he grabbed me by the shoulder and twisted me around. He was only a few inches shorter than I, huge for a Korean, since I stand six foot four. He must've weighed two hundred pounds easy. From the wisps of gray in his hair and the slightly loose texture of his jowls, I estimated that he was older than I by a couple of decades, in his early- to mid-forties, but he was still strong and quick. With a deft slash, he cut the wire cord and the loose ends fell away. I rubbed my wrists. He stared up at me, subdued now after such an unseemly public display of emotion.

However, there was no public to be seen. During all this commotion, not a peep had come from the surrounding homes; not so much as a window being lifted, nor a door sliding open, nor a candle being lit.

The man who had saved me from Commander Koh seemed to be thinking something over. Finally he said, "*ko-ah.*" Orphan. The password.

I replied with the response: "*Manju-ei ko-ah.*" An orphan from Manchuria.

The big man looked at me impassively, then he said, "*Bali ka-ja.*" Quickly, let's go.

I followed him toward the flickering light.

His name was Hero Kang. He showed me the photograph hanging from his neck. It was framed in varnished wood and showed a much younger version of himself standing in full military uniform next to the Great Leader of North Korea, Kim Il-sung, shaking hands. Both men were smiling. Hero Kang told me that the photograph was taken in Pyongyang in the Great Hall of the People almost twenty years ago, after the end of the Korean War.

"You must've been very brave," I said, "to receive such an honor."

His round face grimaced. He changed the subject.

After we'd escaped from the plaza of the barren elm, Kang led me down a narrow alleyway and opened the door to a dirt-floored storage building that held the flickering candle I'd seen from the opposite side of the plaza. After bolting the front door from the inside, he lifted the tin tray that held the candle and I followed him out a back door. He secured the door with a padlock. Then he doused the candle and we proceeded to wind our way through the narrow alleys of Nampo, lit only by moonlight. We must've traveled at least a mile, and during all that time we encountered no major intersections, no roads wide enough for a truck or even a small automobile. Hero Kang seemed to know this warren of byways as if he'd been born into it.

Finally, we reached another wooden warehouse. Hero Kang shuffled through a ring of keys in his pocket, popped the padlock, and we pushed through the splintered door. After relighting the candle, Kang motioned for me to sit on a raised platform partially loaded with sacks of grain. In front were a series of handcarts, and I realized this small warehouse and the one we'd been in before were part of a distribution network that started at the large warehouse closer to the port. Food is not sold in North Korea, at least not officially; it is issued based on rations. The rations themselves are based on a complicated set of rules. For example, a laborer receives more rice than a child or an elderly woman who no longer has a job outside of the home. On paper, it sounds fair, but in practice, at least according to my Eighth Army briefings, those in positions of power—the military, the police, and especially the Communist cadres—receive the lion's share. I figured Hero Kang must be an important man in Nampo if he was in charge of grain distribution.

After I sat down, I took off my peacoat and used the back of my hand to wipe perspiration off my forehead. I was about to thank Hero Kang for rescuing me when he said, "You must help me with a chore."

I sat very still, and waited.

Hero Kang studied me. "I've been told that you are bright and resourceful."

"Who told you that?"

His cheeks started to redden. "You ask too many questions. Listen! That will serve you better."

I chided myself for speaking too soon. Wait. See what he was proposing.

Hero Kang slipped off his left shoe. Brown low quarters, not boots, well worn but apparently well made. I wondered if they had shoe factories in North Korea or if there were still cobblers who made shoes by hand, as they did in South Korea. A pebble dropped out of the shoe and Hero Kang slipped it back on, retying the laces carefully. Then he looked back at me.

"I have a chore to complete," he said. "A vital chore." He spoke slowly, enunciating every word, wanting to make sure that I understood his Korean. "Do you understand?"

I nodded. He continued.

"It is a chore I don't really want to do but one that, for the sake of the people, I must do. It is a difficult chore and I will need help, but amongst the people of this country, this frightened country, there are few I can trust. You are a foreigner. You have nothing to lose. No parents, no children, no wife."

He was right. More than he knew. I had no one back in the States. I was an orphan—my mother had died years ago, and I'd been brought up in foster homes, thanks to the largesse of the superintendents of the County of Los Angeles. The one person I did have, I hoped, was Doctor Yong In-ja.

"The only thing you have to lose," Hero Kang continued, "is your life."

He waited for me to react. I didn't. At least I don't

think I did. I'd known how dangerous this mission would be when I took it. I'd even written out a will of sorts, in longhand. It was taped to the inside of my wall locker back at the Eighth Army compound. I knew Ernie would find it if I didn't come back. I didn't have much in the way of material possessions to leave—clothes, a portable typewriter, a few dollars in a bank account—but what little I did have I left to a Catholic orphanage on the edge of Itaewon. That and my Servicemen's Group Life Insurance, which I'd designated to go to my heir, if it turned out I had one.

Satisfied with my silence, Hero Kang continued.

"My country is filled with evil men," he said. "They betray our revolution daily, but to hear them tell it, they are protectors of the people." Hero Kang laughed sardonically. "Protectors of the people." He shook his head in disgust. "They are parasites on the backs of the people. They are rapists. They are cannibals."

As if suddenly realizing that he'd said too much, Hero Kang glanced around the warehouse.

"I would never talk like this to a Korean," he said. "The chance of betrayal is too great. It's not that my people are evil. But if by betraying you they can obtain a better job, a larger food ration, a chance for their children to go to university, they will do it. Because they are desperate. Because they know no better. Because they are constantly told that to betray someone's trust is patriotic." Hero Kang shook his head. "With foreigners, people from outside our world, one lets one's defenses down. And it's been so long since I spoke frankly to anyone. And besides, it's too late now." He sat up straighter, throwing back his shoulders.

"Tomorrow," he said, "we leave on the train. We will be traveling to Pyongyang."

I thought about this for a second, remembering my main reason for being here. "There's someone I must meet," I said. "It is my duty. Is she there? In Pyongyang?"

Kang shook his head. "Not there, but it is a necessary stop. After this chore is completed, she will be safer. Then, I assure you, I will take you to her."

"No," I said, surprising him. "Before I do anything, I must see her, make sure that she's safe."

Hero Kang studied me, amazed apparently, at my temerity. So far, he was my only point of contact in the entire country. All I knew about Doc Yong's whereabouts was that she was somewhere in North Korea. I either trusted Hero Kang or I was worth less than a handful of *nurungji*, the burnt crust on the bottom of a rice pot. But maybe I was burnt crust anyway. Before I did anything, before I was either killed or captured or tortured by the North Korean authorities, I wanted to see Doctor Yong In-ja. My cooperation was my only bargaining chip and I'd withhold it until I saw her.

"There is a tournament," he said slowly, as if speaking to an idiot, "for foreigners. Every year the winner is allowed as an honored guest into a place that is reserved only for the highest echelons of the Korean Workers' Party. We have managed to slip one agent in there, but no others. How that agent is faring, we do not know. We've received only one message, a message of the highest priority. A plea for immediate assistance."

"What," I asked, "does all this have to do with me?"

"You are a *foreigner*," Hero Kang roared. He glanced

around, surprised by the rage in his voice. When he spoke again, his voice was more controlled. "It is a Taekwondo tournament, for foreigners only, in Pyongyang. You are a black belt, are you not?"

I nodded. I'd been studying Taekwondo for almost three years now, if not as diligently as I should. My instructor in Seoul, Mr. Chong, criticized me often for not attending every class. I told him it was my job. That didn't mollify him.

"If you win this tournament," Hero Kang continued, "you will be able to enter the confines of their compound and make contact with our agent. You will be able to tell us what their plans are."

"Their plans?"

"You're not a fool," he said. "You know that at this moment, when our so-called 'Great Leader' is about to step down . . ." He flicked the photograph hanging at his neck with his forefinger, ". . . every mind in the country is on his succession."

"You want to stop his son from taking over the government."

"Don't worry about such things," he replied. "Let others worry about that. Only worry about the mission."

"I haven't accepted the mission. I came here to meet Doctor Yong In-ja."

Hero Kang leaned forward, as if he were about to spring at me, and let out a sigh of exasperation. He cocked his head to the right for what seemed a long time. I tensed, prepared to defend myself. Finally, he turned his head and gazed up at me. "All right," he said finally. "We'll see what we can do."

"No," I replied. "Not 'what we can do.' I must see her."

His face flamed red. He held up a thick forefinger, as if to waggle it at me, then thought better of it and let it drop to his lap.

"It will be dangerous for her," he said. "But if that's what you want, that's what we will do. Wait here."

He left through the back door, slipping off into the dark alleys of Nampo. I'm not sure where he went, but I spent the time sweating, wondering if he'd decided I wasn't worth the trouble. I wondered why I had been so obstinate. After all, I was alone in North Korea and this man held all the aces. I'd never escape from here alive if he didn't help me. Still, the more I thought about it, the more I believed I was right. I had to see Doc Yong. That's all that mattered.

After more than half an hour, Hero Kang returned.

"I sent a message," he said, shutting the door behind him. "Tomorrow, early, we go to Pyongyang."

"I'll see Doc Yong?"

"Yes." He was angry now. "I already told you."

He hadn't already told me, but I didn't argue the point. "On the way to Pyongyang won't we be stopped?" I asked. "Won't I be arrested?"

He raised his eyebrows. "You don't trust me very much, do you?"

When I didn't answer, he shook his head.

"No, you won't be arrested. In this country, no one is arrested as long as they act boldly. What you must do is spread fear; with every step, with every glance, with every word, you must spread fear. Then others will wonder what powerful people are behind you and they will respect you. Then they will do your bidding."

From what I'd seen so far, Hero Kang was good at spreading fear. He rummaged through a duffel bag and pulled out a brown uniform. He tossed it to me.

"Here," he said. "Fold this neatly, lay it on the hot floor, and sleep on it tonight. Tomorrow, at dawn, the wrinkles will be gone."

I held the uniform up to the light. Pants. Tunic. He also tossed me a pair of boots. Apparently, Hero Kang had been briefed on my size. Everything looked as if it would fit. I set the uniform down.

"You want me to wear this?"

"Yes. It is the only way."

I had recognized the uniform immediately. I'd seen it in innumerable intelligence briefings. It was the uniform of an officer of the Warsaw Pact.

-3-

We didn't bother to buy tickets. In fact, I'm not even sure there was a booth. Hero Kang already had what he called *yoheing zhang*, travel permits, two of them. All through the station people gawked at me. But when I looked back, they quickly averted their eyes. Afraid, I suppose, that I might stop and talk to them. In a country that prizes loyalty to the Great Leader above all things, being spoken to by a foreigner could prove fatal.

The uniform fit well, except for the sleeves, which were about two inches too short. This morning, behind the warehouse, Hero Kang and I had washed up at the single faucet and he let me borrow his old-fashioned straight razor to shave. After scrubbing my armpits and rinsing my teeth, I felt human enough to face the world. Hero

Kang told me to leave behind the old peacoat and wool trousers and leather boots I'd worn on the *Star of Tirana*. They weren't the type of clothing an officer of the Warsaw Pact would be carrying around.

"Someone will burn them," he told me.

I didn't ask who. It was enough to know that Hero Kang wasn't acting alone.

The two of us, both wearing our military uniforms, were about to board the train when a commotion broke out behind us. Nervously, I swiveled and looked back. An old woman, bearing a huge bundle in her arms and balancing another on her back, was arguing with a uniformed official. Apparently, she wanted to travel to Pyongyang, carrying dried mushrooms and garlic cloves to present to her family there as a gift. But the rail cop accused her of planning to sell the goods in the big city. She kept moving forward, arguing, trying to make her way onto the train. Finally, the uniformed officer shoved the old woman. She stumbled backward, tripping over her own bundle, and crashed to the ground. Her skull hit the blacktop with a crack.

I stopped on the metal steps of the train, staring at the scene, my fists clenched. In South Korea, no cop would ever do that to an elderly woman. The spirit of Confucius wouldn't allow it. Hero Kang grabbed me roughly by the arm, and when I didn't budge, he shoved. "Move," he hissed, almost spitting in my ear. "Not here. Not now."

The old woman's bundles had busted open. She lay on her back on the ground, moaning. Passersby, instead of helping her to her feet, surreptitiously knelt and stuffed a few cloves of garlic or a few handfuls of mushrooms into their pockets. One of them mumbled *"bobok juija."*

Revanchist. In Seoul, I'd studied the Marxist terms that people learned during their two-hour daily indoctrinations sessions. Now I knew they actually used them. The guard who had shoved her stood with his hands clasped behind his back, staring off above the heads of the crowd, a posture of triumph stiffening his shoulders.

"I ought to punch him," I said in Korean.

"No!" Hero Kang replied, shoving me again. "Move."

We boarded the train, but I kept glancing out the window at the old woman lying supine on the ground. Hero Kang bulled me forward and reluctantly I marched toward the front car.

Hero Kang's *yoheing zhang* were the best kind issued. It wasn't called first class, that would be too bourgeois, but there was a sign saying that the front passenger car was a restricted area. Unlike the hard wooden benches in the other passenger cars, the seats here had plenty of legroom and were padded and covered with something that resembled leather. The windows were clean and the aisle swept clear of the debris found throughout the rest of the train. This car was for the *dongji*, Hero Kang told me. The comrades. The Communist cadre.

I would've thought these were exactly the people we'd want to avoid, but Hero Kang's style was to confront them head-on and dare them to question us. It was Hero Kang's size, his bulk, his aura of confidence that made people move out of his way. That and the photograph of the Great Leader hanging from his neck. I wanted to know more about how he'd attained his exalted position as Hero of the Nation, but last night he'd seemed reluctant to talk about it, so I dropped the subject.

Other cadres took their seats around us, a few of them nodding in recognition to Hero Kang. Bored, he nodded back. Some of them were military officers and I noticed their ranks, almost all colonels or above. A lot of brass in this car. The ones who took on the greatest air of superiority, though, even greater than the military men, were the ones wearing military-type clothing but no symbols of rank. Both men and women, they had bright red badges pinned to their chests. I figured these for the Communist Party cadres. They crossed their legs, lit up cigarettes, and chatted calmly. People of power and ease. In the West, they would've been wearing suits tailored in London and talking to one another about stockbrokers and offshore tax shelters. Here, they spoke of the Great Leader.

I felt like a rabbit on a live-fire range. Everyone in this restricted passenger car, with the single exception of Hero Kang, was my enemy. I sat staring grimly ahead, trying to control my breathing. As long as I held tightly to the wooden armrest, I figured my hands wouldn't shake too much. So far, no one had approached us and I was praying that no one would.

My uniform was that of an officer of the Warsaw Pact in Eastern Europe with the rank insignia of a lieutenant colonel. Last night, Hero Kang informed me I would pose as a Romanian officer by the name of Enescu. The identity, including the papers, had already been established, but when I asked if we had backup at the Romanian Embassy, he interrupted me and warned me not to ask too many questions.

"We are a professional organization," was all he'd say.

Apparently, they were very professional. If he could

buffalo the boss of the Port of Nampo, establish safe houses amidst the city's grain distribution network, send messages to Doc Yong, and set up contacts within a foreign embassy, the organization of resisters he belonged to was very professional indeed. But the more people participating, the sooner they'd be compromised.

When I pointed out to Hero Kang that I neither spoke nor understood Romanian, he said not to worry, no one we were likely to run into on the train did either. Military officers from other Communist countries are occasionally seen in Pyongyang, usually Russian or Chinese, but a Romanian shouldn't raise too many eyebrows. As long as we kept moving. Like that rabbit on the firing range.

A whistle sounded and the train started its engines. Slowly, we chugged forward. Outside the window, ratty old wooden buildings rolled by, some made of brick but nothing that looked too permanent. I hadn't expected there to be. During the war, Korean cities had been bombed mercilessly by the American Air Force, so much so that the pilots complained that all they were doing was making "rubble bounce on rubble." Since then, the North Korean government had been in constant preparation for the resumption of war. The only structures that were designed to last were military fortifications.

I expected someone to walk down the aisle, as in South Korea, with trays full of drinks and cigarettes and snacks. But not here. The only people who marched through the train were a couple of rail-line policemen. When I turned to look back, I saw that they were checking the other passengers carefully, not only for their travel permits but also for their fare tokens. In our passenger car, the men did nothing more than nod at the various dignitaries and, without checking anyone's permits or fare, scurried out of the car. No wonder Hero Kang had chosen to sit here.

Five minutes out of the station, we were in rolling countryside, heading north past fallow rice paddies toward the capital city of Pyongyang, the heart of the Democratic People's Republic of Korea. I fought panic, taking deep breaths, reminding myself that Hero Kang would take care of me.

On some inaudible cue, people all around started to rise from their seats and make their way into the next car. Hero Kang rose and motioned for me to follow. I didn't want to move. Impatiently, he gestured for me to get up, so I did, fighting a brief moment of vertigo. Then I pulled down my tunic, thrust back my shoulders, and followed Hero Kang.

It was a dining car.

All the cadres were taking seats at round tables, each of which could accommodate eight to ten. Hero Kang guided me to a stool in the corner. Just as we sat down, we were joined by a group of people wearing the same bland Communist uniforms everyone else was. Immediately, I went on alert. They weren't speaking Korean. They wore high-collared jackets and the men's hair was combed across their heads and cut in a severe straight line; the women had soft caps pulled over short hair. They were chattering to one another in the singsong dialect of Mandarin, the language of Beijing.

Hero Kang ignored them. Already, men in military uniforms were shoving trays filled with noodle soup in front of us. Each person grabbed for a bowl, offering it to the person next to him or her, until we all had steaming bowls in front of us. Then the same servers ladled white rice into smaller bowls and passed those around. Spoons and wooden chopsticks were distributed. Without further ado, all the comrades started shoveling soup and rice into their mouths. Two large bowls, each of turnip and cabbage kimchi, were placed on the table, the pieces cut in rough chunks. Hero Kang dipped his chopsticks into them with gusto. A couple of the Chinese women tried some morsels. I decided that, as a Romanian, I would steer clear of the kimchi. I even pretended to fumble with the chopsticks and then set them down and ate strictly with my spoon, which made shoveling clumps of noodles into my mouth awkward.

I'd been in Korean restaurants before, plenty of them, and usually in addition to the standard cabbage and turnip kimchi, various types of pickled vegetables, up to a dozen, are served on elegant plates. Also, rice is never served with noodles. But this was plain peasant fare, filling, in no way trying to be elegant. Nothing to drink was served, not even barley tea, and the staff had disappeared into another section of the dining car. If you were expecting a dessert menu, you could forget it.

None of the Chinese looked up while they ate. Neither did Hero Kang. I was grateful for the lack of attention. In South Korea, as the only Westerner, I would've been the center of attention. People would've been showing me how to use chopsticks and explaining the various dishes on the table—and, more importantly, practicing their English.

When he finished eating, one of the Chinese apparatchiks pulled out a pack of cigarettes with a drawing of Chairman Mao on the front. He offered it first to Hero Kang, who took two, and then to me. Without saying anything, I shook my head, pointing to my lungs. The Chinese nodded sympathetically and continued to pass out cigarettes to the men at the table, ignoring the women. All the other tables were lighting up now and soon the bare-walled dining car was filled with acrid smoke. The serving staff reappeared and cleared the tables, not bothering to ask whether we were finished or not.

Now was the time to leave. I was afraid someone would speak to me, but Hero Kang continued smoking, apparently unconcerned. One of the Chinese spoke to him in broken Korean.

"You are famous, comrade. How fortunate you are to have met personally with the Great Leader."

Kang nodded dreamily, his eyelids half closed, allowing smoke to drift out of his nostrils.

There was no nameplate on the Chinese man's tunic, only his pin of Chairman Mao. Nor did he wear a rank insignia. Therefore, he was political and possibly of very high rank indeed. He grinned and continued to speak to Hero Kang.

"And your friend, a comrade from Eastern Europe, I see."

Kang nodded again. The Chinese man turned to me and said something in Russian.

Hero Kang sat up as if electrocuted. "He's a Romanian, not a Russki."

"Ah," the Chinese man said. "But he's an officer. Certainly he's been educated in Russian."

"The hell he has." Hero Kang was raising his voice now. "He's like me, promoted because of his ability to fight. In the Czech uprising he killed ten counterrevolutionaries, with his bare hands."

Hero Kang reached out his big, bear-like paws as if to demonstrate. The Chinese man leaned back. I stared ahead sternly, showing as little reaction to what was going on around me as possible.

"Don't provoke him," Kang said, waggling his finger, "or he'll think he's back on the field of combat and then you'll have to watch out."

Kang barked a laugh, stubbed his cigarette out directly onto the wooden table, stood up and strode out of the dining car. I glanced at the wide-eyed Chinese without nodding, stood up, and followed Kang. Behind me, I heard them chattering. I wished I could understand.

We were the first to return to the passenger car. Hero Kang flopped down in his seat. He looked worried. I was too. I doubted that Kang's little charade about me being a combat veteran who didn't speak Russian fooled anyone. I felt certain we'd been exposed. In a low voice, I asked Hero Kang what we should do. He waved me off.

"When the time comes to fight," he said, "we will fight."

I glanced back at the dining car. No one had emerged yet, but they would soon. If I was going to do anything, now was the time.

Hurriedly, I stepped past Hero Kang until I reached the spot where the Chinese had been sitting. In the overhead rack, they had sequestered a few traveling bags. I reached in my pocket and pulled out one of the packs of British cigarettes I had purchased in Hong Kong, the half-empty one, and slid it into a side pocket of one of the bags, quickly rebuckling the clasp.

When I returned to my seat, I quietly told Hero Kang what I had done. He said nothing but nodded, pleased. He kept his eyes open for a few moments as other passengers filtered back into the car. Then he let his eyes droop and, after a few minutes, softly began to snore.

Most everyone slept throughout the rest of the slow trip to Pyongyang. Often we traveled at speeds of twenty miles per hour or less. I believed this was to preserve coal, but it might have been because of the poor condition of the tracks. The iron wheels screeched and occasionally lurched from side to side, making for some interesting moments along the banks of the Taedong River. Even at our reduced speed, the trip to Pyongyang should've taken only an hour, but we stopped at every country village, stretching the trip out to almost three hours.

Behind us in the regular passenger cars, during the loading and unloading, there was much argument and discussion centering around travel permits and fare tokens. If I hadn't known that I was traveling in the "people's paradise," I would've guessed that the conductors and the rail guards lengthened the stops in order to eke out the maximum number of bribes from harried peasants, many of whom were traveling with bags of grain balanced atop their heads or clutching wicker baskets filled with dead fish or live fowl—presumably to barter with, which was strictly illegal. The old woman who had been knocked out back at the Nampo Station had been either unable or unwilling to pay a bribe.

At least the North Koreans were eating well, I thought. And so far, I hadn't seen any beggars. No filthy men, or even children, sleeping on sidewalks and sitting listlessly near commuter stations, holding out hats or tin cups for loose change. Life was grim here in North Korea. But from the point of view of a people who had suffered through colonization, occupation, war, starvation, and disease in the last fifty years alone, maybe things weren't so bad.

The train whistle shrilled and, with iron brakes grinding, we screeched into the Pyongyang Train Station. A large clock tower sat atop a sturdy stone building lined with plate-glass windows. Behind each one of them stood a uniformed guard, some of them peering at us through binoculars. When we came to a halt, the other passengers, particularly the small cadre of Chinese, were up and heading for the door. Hero Kang took his time, staying in character as a tough hombre who didn't much care what anyone thought of him. I don't think he was acting.

We followed the crowd to the departure gate. The uniformed woman checking documents there merely bowed to Hero Kang and waved the two of us through. It was in the foyer of the huge domed building that I spotted them. I pulled on Hero Kang's sleeve.

The Chinese man we'd spoken to in the dining car was conversing urgently with two men with red security armbands. They were having trouble communicating; the Chinese man had an exasperated expression on his face and kept gesticulating wildly, receiving blank looks from the security guards.

Hero Kang sized up the situation quickly.

"Come on," he said.

We headed for a side exit. About halfway down the hallway, a sign said: PEOPLE'S SECURITY, PYONGYANG TRAIN STATION. Hero Kang stepped inside. A smartly dressed young man stood up from behind a counter, tugged on his tunic, and half bowed to Hero Kang.

"I have a case of smuggling to report," Kang said. A supervisor was brought out and Hero Kang quickly explained the situation. Within seconds, a detail of security guards was dispatched to detain the Chinese apparatchiks who were so brazenly smuggling counterrevolutionary tobacco into the Democratic People's Republic.

In the main lobby of the train station, the Chinese man must have finally made his point, because a policeman's whistle blew. But the whistle sputtered out as a larger contingent of security guards surrounded the Chinese and placed them under arrest.

Hero Kang and I exited the train station from a side door.

There are no taxi stands in front of the Pyongyang Train Station, mainly because there are no taxis in North Korea. Automobiles, all automobiles, are gifts from the Great Leader, given selectively to those who contribute most to the revolution. Which means mainly Communist Party bosses and the military. Even the police are usually left on foot. And the fire department can forget about it; there are just not enough internal combustion engines to go around.

Hero Kang and I caught a ride on the back of a garlic truck. The driver was a farmer from a cooperative outside of town, and the young man with him was his nephew. They were in awe of Hero Kang and repeatedly thanked him for saving their country from the American imperialist aggressors in the Great Patriotic War. They seemed afraid of me and mostly tried to pretend I wasn't there. The old truck was Russian-made and coughed and wheezed through the wide Pyongyang streets. There weren't the teeming masses I was used to in Seoul, only small groups of uniformed students or organized workers marching to and fro, sometimes belting out songs in praise of the Great Leader.

My briefers in Seoul had told me that only the most loyal Communist subjects were allowed to live in Pyongyang, handpicked for their socialist credentials. The buildings were mostly huge apartment-like complexes made of cement. What was odd was the lack of signs or advertisements of any kind, and there were no stores where one could purchase food or cigarettes or soju. If you couldn't buy what you wanted when you wanted it, that meant you were dependent on the generosity of the Great Leader. Which, I suppose, was the plan. After meandering through the city for a couple of miles, we hopped off in an area of town that sat beyond the central monuments and parade grounds, beyond the rows of shoebox-like cement apartment buildings. It was an area of town that looked almost as if it were fit for human habitation.

"The bosses don't let foreigners come down here," Kang told me. We stepped down muddy alleys surrounded by wood- and brick-walled buildings, nothing much more than two stories and all of it jumbled in a maze that led up the side of the hill. From there, the neighborhood spread off to the left toward the Taedong River. A few women with bundles of laundry balanced atop their heads passed us. One of them stared at me goggle-eyed. The others averted their gaze, cringing as they did so, as if I were some predator escaped from a zoo.

"The children are at school," Kang said, "their mothers and fathers at work. Only the grandmothers remain."

"Won't those women report me to the police?"

"No. You're wearing a uniform, for one thing, and even if you weren't, they dare not talk to the police. They or their family might be accused of sedition."

"Sedition? For what?"

Kang shrugged. "Just talking to a foreigner is a form of disloyalty."

"How about you?"

Kang laughed and flicked the photograph of himself shaking hands with the Great Leader. "I'm a hero of the people."

Like the rest of the city, this jumble of buildings lacked storefronts. Even the poorest neighborhood in South Korea would have a few shops selling dried cuttlefish or puffed rice or ginseng gum, but there was nothing like that here. Not even any noodle stands or chop houses.

Another thing I didn't see were cops. Hero Kang seemed to read my mind.

"The police mainly patrol the government offices and the homes of the cadres."

"But if we see one?"

Kang's face set grimly. "I'll take care of it. Come on."

We slid into a narrow alley lined with brick-and-stone walls. The pathway ran straight for a while and then began to wind sinuously in various directions until I was completely disoriented. I would've navigated by the sun, but it was hidden behind banks of gray clouds. Finally, the walkway started to rise uphill. I felt hidden back here, and safe.

"Commander Koh," I said, "in the Port of Nampo, he will alert the authorities about me. And the Chinese aboard the train, eventually the train station security office will corroborate their story and confirm that a Romanian officer who couldn't speak Russian is wandering around Pyongyang."

Kang shook his head. "No. Neither one of them will report it. Neither Commander Koh nor the security people at the train station."

The road became steeper and finally, leaning forward, Hero Kang explained.

"Things are different here. No one dares to report failure." I thought of the headquarters of the Eighth United States Army in Seoul. There wasn't much failure reported there either. Kang continued, "The price of failure is too high. Commander Koh would never report that he allowed a foreign sailor to escape from the Port of Nampo, nor would the security office at the Pyongyang Train Station report that a man posing as a Romanian officer slipped through their grasp. They will remain silent and hope that your escape is not traced back to them."

"And if it is traced back to them?"

"They will cut a deal with someone to keep it quiet."

"They will be blackmailed," I said.

Hero Kang nodded. "Precisely. But that is unlikely."

"Why?"

"Because they will take other action."

"Other action? You just said they won't report me."

"No, they won't. Not officially. But they have other options."

"Other options? Like what?"

"Like reporting you to one of the fixers."

"Fixers" wasn't the exact word Hero Kang used. In fact, it wasn't a single word at all but a North Korean term he took pains to explain to me. It has to do with people who find ways to solve problems so they are never brought to the attention of the official governmental authorities. They also act as intermediaries between the various factions within the government. According to Kang, the fixers are exceedingly efficient—unlike the government—and are highly paid for the work they do.

"So Commander Koh and the railroad security people will go to someone they call a fixer?"

"Yes. A foreigner wandering around North Korea is like a bomb rolling across the deck of a ship. They have to do something."

"Do you think they have already hired a fixer?"

"Almost certainly."

Hero Kang made a left turn into a short alley draped with tattered canvas. At the end of a short walkway was a wooden storage bin heaped with stinking refuse. The stench was so awful I squeezed my nose.

"Back here," he said, pointing into the darkness.

"There's nothing back there. Just a wall."

"Come."

Hero Kang crouched on the far edge of the refuse bin,

fiddled with some of the splintered wood, and a small portal opened. The aperture was pitch black, darker than its surroundings. He entered and waved for me to follow.

I gazed behind me down the alley, at the gray light, at a sparrow that flitted across my vision through the cold, fresh air. Then I looked back at the foul opening. I had no choice but to follow this man. I was lost in a country that despised Americans, like a fat carp swimming among sharks. I went through the opening into the muddy pit.

After a few yards, I was able to stand almost upright. An electric torch appeared in Hero Kang's hand and he used it to guide his way over the jagged floor of the tunnel. Stones jutted down from the roof above me. I dodged most of them but clunked my head a couple of times, cursing as I did so.

The tunnels were used, Hero Kang told me, during the Korean War to hide from American bombs.

"We were most afraid of the napalm," Hero Kang said. "You Americans splashed it everywhere, turning us into cowering moles. The Great Leader had his headquarters in a cave not far from here. That's why the network is so huge. In addition to the army, the average citizens, with their bare hands, tunneled into the mountains too. For safety. After the war, the army used explosives and closed most of the tunnels, but the people have reclaimed them, pulling out dirt and lumber and boulders to develop a little world back here where we can live free of constant surveillance."

Ahead of us, men grunted in cadence. And then I heard some familiar words: *"Kyongnei. Chunbi. Shijak."* Bow. Prepare. Begin.

A door opened into a vast chamber lit by glass lanterns. In the center of the chamber, a raised wooden platform, a *dochang*, had been constructed. At least two-dozen men stood facing an instructor, some wearing white karate robes, most not.

"A Taekwondo class," I said to Hero Kang.

"Yes."

Taekwondo is taught to everyone in school and in the military, for the defense of the country. In its advanced forms, however, it is taught only to those favored by the Great Leader.

"So these men practice here in secret," I said.

"Yes."

We watched the men go through their choreographed moves. I'd studied Taekwondo in Seoul, on the base. A lot of GIs did. So far, I'd advanced to the first level of black belt, but I was a rank amateur compared to these men. Their kicks, hops, punches, and parries were carried out with a blinding precision and speed.

"So why have you brought me here?" I asked.

Hero Kang grinned. "You need to practice. Take off your clothes." He pointed to a bench covered with jackets and hats and shoes. Then he walked over to a line of pegs in the stone wall and selected a white uniform. He tossed it to me. "Put this on."

"Why?" I asked. "Is this about that 'tournament' you mentioned?"

Hero Kang grinned even more broadly. "We're going to find out what kind of fighter you are."

▪   ▪   ▪

I lay collapsed on a cold wooden floor. The pummeling I'd taken from the Taekwondo experts had been brutal. I was bigger than any of them, my legs and arms longer, my body heavier. Still, they'd kicked me around as if I were an overstuffed beanbag. When I was a kid, I'd studied boxing in a sheriff's program at the Main Street Gym in Los Angeles and I considered myself to be pretty good. More than once, my left jab had pulled me out of a jam. But Taekwondo emphasizes the use of the feet and the legs and more contact is allowed with kicks. Punches, by contrast, have to be pulled. So much for my advantage. I rolled over and groaned, longing to take a shower. Hero Kang assured me that in this worker's paradise there was no hot water available.

"Tonight," he said, "food will be brought to you. Until then, you are to wait and make no sound whatsoever."

After the workout, he'd had me change back into the Romanian officer's uniform. I'd been perspiring so much from the workout that the once-clean Warsaw Pact uniform was soon soaked through with sweat and the coarse wool rubbed mercilessly against my skin. We'd slipped out of a different exit from the underground tunnels and made our way about a half-mile, with me hobbling as fast as I could behind Hero Kang. Finally, we stepped into a deserted building constructed like a *yoguan*, a traditional Korean inn. There was a double door out front, a small wood-floored foyer, and a central stairway that led upstairs to long halls with cubicle-like rooms behind small doors. The only problem was that there was no proprietor. As usual, Hero Kang strode in like he owned the place and bade me follow him upstairs to the last room in a long hallway, where, once inside, I collapsed on the floor. In the next five minutes or so, I heard a few distant footsteps in the building and the occasional bump of wood on wood.

Hero Kang turned to leave. "I will lock the door from the outside."

I sat up, feeling the bruises along my thighs and forearms. "Lock it from the outside? When will you be back?"

Hero Kang shushed me. "Tomorrow. Early. But like I said, someone will bring you food."

"What if I have to go to the bathroom?"

He pointed at an iron pee pot in the corner.

I nodded, realizing angrily that my options for self-controlled action were rapidly diminishing.

"Don't worry," he said, reading my thoughts. "There are many out there looking for you, but right here in the middle of the city, you are well hidden. And there are many of us too, to protect you."

"Why is it so important to bring me here? I told you before, I must see Doctor Yong In-ja first. Before I do anything."

Hero Kang backed out of the door. A metal hasp squeaked closed and a padlock clicked. I groaned and lay back down on the floor. It was cold in there. Almost freezing. The perspiration turned clammy on my skin. I rolled over and groaned again, hungry, miserable, frightened. There was a world of hostility out there, and I hadn't a friend in the world except for Hero Kang. And who knew when he'd come back?

These thoughts caused my stomach to churn, and so, with an effort of will, I thrust them out of my mind.

Eventually I dozed, for how long I'm not sure. Finally, after what must've been two or three hours, a metallic clang brought me fully awake. I sat up. The room was dark now, illuminated only by moonlight seeping through a transom-like window.

I listened carefully. At first nothing, and then the sound of someone rummaging around near the front of the room. I crouched and searched for something to use as a weapon. Nothing available but my fists.

Another metallic clang as a small hinge creaked open and then what sounded like something being dropped into a chute. I recognized the sounds. I'd heard them often in South Korea: someone replenishing the cylindrical charcoal briquettes in the underground heating system. I placed my hand flat on the floor. No heat yet. Then more clanging as tongs and a metal pan were being put away. Footsteps approached the front door.

Someone fiddled with the lock, the rusty hasp was pulled back, and the door swung open. Whoever it was held a candle low in front of his or her body, head bowed and hooded. I couldn't see a face. Then I saw a long woolen skirt rustle forward, and the candle being placed on the floor. The woman, whoever she was, had a huge wooden disc strapped to her back like a shield, and tied to that were three layers of tightly folded material. In her left hand she held a large brass pot stuffed with a brown paper bag, and in her right a canvas bag smeared with soot. She let both drop to the floor.

"Who are you?" I asked.

The woman ignored me as she closed the door and slid shut the inner bolt. Then she placed the candle atop the wooden box meant to hold shoes. She shrugged off the shield and the material strapped to it, and a canvas bag, hidden between the layers, plopped out on the floor. Finally, she turned and knelt in front of me. I waited, afraid of what I thought I was seeing, terrified to allow myself to believe what my mind was telling me—not until I was sure. She slid back her hood.

There are moments in our lives that, because of pain or joy or terror, are unforgettable. This, to me, was one of those moments. I felt as if a surge passed through my body. Until that moment, I had suppressed my feelings of longing, of loss, and of loneliness. As I beheld the face I thought I'd never see again, I realized how much I'd missed her.

Doctor Yong In-ja stared at me somberly, not smiling. Hers was a smooth face, even-featured, with short bobbed hair and thick-rimmed glasses. No one, at least in the West, would accuse her of being beautiful. But I thought she was. In fact, at that moment, I wanted to embrace her, but I knew better. Being Korean—and a most reserved Korean at that—she kept her distance for this formal moment. Then she did an odd thing—she lowered her forehead to the ground, held it there, and said, "*Choesong hamnida.*" I am terribly sorry.

As far as I was concerned, Doctor Yong In-ja had nothing to be sorry about. I told her that.

"You are wrong," she replied. "I have much to be sorry about. Due to my own selfishness, I have brought you into terrible danger."

She was speaking English now. One of the things that always fascinated me about her was that even though

English was her second language, she spoke it better than most GIs did. Including me.

"No. You have nothing to be sorry about," I told her. "I wanted to come here. I would've had it no other way."

She stared at me quizzically. "Why?"

"Because of you," I said.

She turned away. "You will change your mind when I tell you all that I came here to say."

"No," I replied. "I won't change my mind."

Then she turned back and stared deeply into my eyes, evaluating what she saw, turning it over in that finely tuned mind of hers. Finally, she did what I hoped she'd do. She made a decision. The right decision. She held my eyes steadily and then smiled. The most beautiful and the most radiant smile I'd seen in my life.

"You're filthy," she said.

"Yes."

She gestured toward the charcoal briquettes in the dirty bag and the brass pot. "I'll heat water for your bath."

"And then?" I asked.

"You'll eat. Rice. Bean curd soup."

She unfolded four short legs on the wooden shield and set it on the floor.

"And after that?" I asked.

"You'll sleep." She allowed the folded sleeping mat and comforter to flop loosely onto the floor.

"Alone?"

"We'll see," she replied.

Doc Yong shook me awake. In the pale moonlight, she placed a forefinger against her pursed lips, warning me to be quiet. I sat up. Outside, boots pounded on pavement. I rose to my feet and crossed to the transom, trying vainly to reach the top latch. Doc Yong knelt on all fours and motioned to her back. I understood. She wanted me to use her as a stepladder to reach the latch. I was too heavy, I knew, but she pointed again to her back, insisting furiously. Gingerly, I stepped on her back with one foot, pulling myself up on the transom's ledge, supporting most of my own weight, and reached the latch. I slipped it back, pulled open the transom and, for just a second, peeked out.

There, standing on the sidewalk, in the glow of the headlights of a military vehicle, stood a female military officer. She was tall and wore high leather boots and a dark-blue overcoat tied tightly around a slender waist. Black hair hung long and loose, glimmering from beneath a leather-brimmed cap. She barked orders. Armed men trotted down the sidewalk at her command. They were moving fast, apparently searching the area.

I lowered myself quickly, breathless now, not at the exertion but at the shock of seeing so many armed men across the street. But I was also stunned by something else. I was ashamed of myself for thinking of it, at this moment of emergency, but I was thinking of it nevertheless. I found myself focusing on the face of the female military officer: a long oval with smooth, white skin and puffed lips and angry eyes. She was very possibly the most beautiful woman I'd ever seen.

Doc Yong stared at me, knowing something had changed. She hopped to her feet and, still motioning furiously, indicated that I was to lift her up to the level of the transom. I flexed my knees, grabbed her securely around the waist, and hoisted her easily into the air, holding her there while she clutched the edge of the transom. More boots pounded on pavement. An engine purred and began to fade. Finally, just as the muscles in my arms started to burn, she motioned for me to lower her to the floor. Then she pointed for me to close the transom. I did. Quietly.

She knelt in the center of the floor and relit the single candle.

We squatted opposite one another.

"She's very beautiful," she said.

"Who?"

"Don't play dumb with me. You saw her."

"The officer, you mean?"

"Yes. A *daewui*."

"A senior captain," I said. Before leaving Seoul, I'd memorized the ranks of all the branches of the North Korean military.

"Yes. They are searching the area, moving fast. This is a densely populated neighborhood and they don't have enough men to knock on every door and search every room. That means she's working alone, not in an official capacity."

"She's a fixer," I said.

"Who told you about them?"

"Hero Kang."

She nodded at that.

"What do you suppose they're looking for?" I asked.

"A Romanian officer," she replied, "who can't speak Russian."

"Or an Albanian sailor who escaped from the Port of Nampo."

"By now," she said, "they know you were traveling on a Peruvian passport."

"And you know too."

"Yes. I know too."

"We can't just sit here," I said. "They'll find us."

Doc Yong shook her head vigorously. "A full door-to-door search will attract too much attention. I don't believe they'll do that. Attention is what they're trying to avoid, to make sure that the superiors of the authorities at both the Port of Nampo and the Pyongyang Train Station are not alerted to their miserable failure."

"You mean their miserable failure in allowing me to enter the country."

"Yes. What they'll do is sit tight and hope that you'll become frightened and poke your head out. Instead, we must wait for Hero Kang. He'll know how to get us out of here."

"You could leave," I said. "They're not looking for you."

Doc Yong shook her head again. "Not yet."

She grabbed the canvas pack that had been strapped to her back, untied it, and pulled out a large bag. It was rectangular, wrapped in water-resistant oil paper. Beneath the paper were the tattered remnants of a leather binding, reinforced with varnished bamboo slats. A book, not bound at the spine but rather shot through with half a dozen brass rivets that held the thick sheaf of yellowed paper intact. What scholars call a codex. The paper I recognized—it was the same thick vellum as the scrap that had been given to me by an

Eastern European sailor in the Port of Pusan. Doc Yong thumbed through the pages.

"Here," she said. "Here is the section I cut out. We must replace it."

"We will," I said. "It's in Seoul, in a safe place."

Actually, the fragment had been stolen from me by a homicide investigator of the Korean National Police known as Mr. Kill. As part of the deal for me to come up here, I demanded that he return the fragment. He did. Now it was locked in the CID safe at Eighth Army headquarters.

Gently, I touched the rough leather of the codex. "Tell me about it," I said.

Outside, we heard the abrupt shouts of soldiers. We froze for a second, listening as their footsteps passed.

Doc Yong turned back to the manuscript. For years, she explained, scholars thought that the codex was nothing but a myth.

"Supposedly," Doc Yong said, "in the early fifteenth century, during the rule of our Great King Sejong, a strange man was spotted in the mountainous precincts of Hamgyong Province. A 'wild man,' he was called, and some said he was not a man at all but a beast. A court official was appointed to track him, an inspector of the king's, a man who held the rank of Five White Horses."

"A cop," I said.

"More like what the Europeans call an ombudsman."

"A what?"

"Somebody appointed by the government to investigate anything unusual. Or anything that seems to have gone awry."

"Okay," I replied. "So this inspector of the Five White Horses starts chasing this wild man through the mountains. What happened?"

"He was accompanied by a scribe who wrote it all down. His name was Clerk Yi." Doc Yong placed her hand on the codex. "That's why we have this manuscript. It's difficult for me to read not only because the writing is archaic but also because Clerk Yi had a very fluid style of penmanship, a style the Chinese call 'grass writing.'"

In ancient times Koreans had no written language of their own. Educated people learned to read and write Chinese. If they were well off enough, they traveled to China to continue their studies. Indeed, some of the most revered poets in Chinese literature were Koreans.

"I've managed to translate about half of Clerk Yi's manuscript so far," Doc Yong said.

"Into English?"

"Both modern Korean and English," she replied.

I shook my head, never failing to marvel at her brilliance. "So did they catch the beast?"

"I haven't gotten there yet."

"What was it? A man or an animal?"

"I'm not sure," Doc Yong replied. "But I did get to the part about the tunnels, where the beast was being chased by the inspector and his minions and eluded them by entering ancient caverns."

"The ones that tunnel beneath the DMZ."

"Yes."

"You got their attention at Eighth Army," I said.

"I thought I would. And that's why you're here."

"No. That's not why I'm here."

She waited, holding her breath.

"I'm here for you," I said.

It was at that moment, while she gazed into my eyes, that someone kicked the door in.

-4-

Shards of wood erupted into the room, and a brown boot
followed. A pair of hands grappled with the small door,
ripping it off its already twisted hinges.

I grabbed the short table, dumping rice bowls and
porcelain and pickled vegetables. Doc Yong clutched my
bicep instinctively but was forced to let go when I rose
to my feet and charged. Speed is everything in a fight—
speed and unbridled aggressiveness. The small table was
my shield; I rammed it full force into the face of the startled man who'd kicked our door in. He reeled backward
under my onslaught. As he fell, I kneed him in the gut and
he went down with me and the table on top of him. He let
out a grunt and a whoosh of air, then lay very still.

I scrambled to my feet, searching for more enemies,

but the hallway was empty. Doc Yong reacted quickly. She tossed my shoes to me and as I slipped them on and my uniform tunic, she put on her hooded cloak and grabbed the canvas bag that she'd packed in preparation for just such an emergency.

"Let's go," she said in English and ran past me toward the stairwell. As she did so, I knew that something was not right. The man lying at my feet wore a military-type uniform, even though these "fixers" were not a regular military unit. They wouldn't have sent him alone; they might be shorthanded, but surely there had to be someone backing him up. Before Doc Yong reached the stairwell, I lunged forward, grabbed her elbow, and jerked her to a stop, just in time. A club whistled from around the corner in a vicious arc, missing her head by inches and slamming with a thud against the wall.

I leapt past her and grabbed the club, turning my back against the hand holding it. I pinned the arm against the wall and twisted, elbowing the backup man in the face. He released his grip on the club, but I kept twisting his arm until he bent forward at the waist. I grabbed the back of his head with both my hands, braced him there, and slammed his nose and teeth against my knee. As he collapsed, I lost my grip and he tumbled, arms flailing, down the steps.

Doc Yong shrieked.

I clasped my hand over her mouth. Wide-eyed, she nodded that she was okay. I straightened my tunic and cap and, hand in hand, we trotted down the steps. The second fixer lay in a heap at the bottom. I checked his carotid artery.

"Strong pulse," I told her.

She nodded, looking relieved. We crossed the short entranceway and peeked out the double doors. All clear. The fixers, apparently, traveled in pairs, not squads. As we stepped outside, Doc Yong glanced around, getting her bearings. I followed her down a dark alleyway, watching as she adjusted her backpack. The terror of what had just happened to us was gradually draining from my body, making me want to throw up. I fought the feeling and instead glanced at Doc Yong. We were both frightened but overjoyed to be free.

At least for the moment.

Boot heels surrounded us. Giant cement boot heels. We'd hidden in the middle of a massive megalithic monument. A group of revolutionaries—a soldier, a factory worker, a farmer, and a woman holding a rifle—rose thirty feet above us. A circle of light illuminated the outside of the heroic structure, but here, in the center of the monument, it was dark.

"What's it called in English?" Doc Yong asked.

"A fallback position."

"Right. A fallback position. Hero Kang told me to come here if something went wrong."

And it had gone wrong. The fixers had somehow gotten wind that a foreigner was staying in that particular room. They hadn't searched any of the other rooms in the building. If they had, I would've heard boots pounding and doors slamming throughout the thin wooden structure. Probably the two men had sniffed out a lead and rather than informing their superiors they'd tried to take us on their own. If they'd been more patient, and merely put us under surveillance, a larger group of fixers could've been summoned and then we would've been caught. As it was, we were lucky to be free. And now I knew something more about the fixers than I had before. They were undisciplined. Undisciplined can be good, sometimes, but it can also be dangerous.

I rose from my squatting position and peeked at the empty streets radiating from this monument like spokes from a hub. No sign of the fixers. But nor any sign of Hero Kang.

"Be patient," she said. "He will be along."

"When?"

"At dawn."

The fixers had probably found their injured comrades by now. Although we were over a mile away, it wouldn't take them long to include this area in their search.

And then it started to snow. Doc Yong and I huddled together, she doing her best to cover me with her hood, I wishing I had some good old-fashioned GI-issue winter gear to keep us warm. Doc Yong used the time to complete my briefing—partially, I'm sure, to keep our minds off our misery. I listened patiently, enjoying the nearness of her, and at the same time keeping a weather eye out for approaching fixers.

She told me of a group of people called the Manchurian Battalion, of which she was a member. They were one of the original units of the Korean People's Army, she whispered, snuggled next to my neck. The Manchurian Battalion had started in the thirties, long before the founding of the Democratic People's Republic of Korea, as a ragtag group of bandits and malcontents who fled to the mountains to avoid the heavy boot of the Japanese Imperial Army's occupation of their country. They'd fought back sporadically, but it hadn't been easy. The Japanese formed special antiguerilla task forces that hounded them through the northern provinces of Korea and into the vast wilderness of Manchuria. The peasants whom they relied on were harassed mercilessly, rounded up, not allowed to grow crops. Starvation was rampant. Despite heavy losses, the Manchurian Battalion survived and kept fighting. Finally, at the end of World War II, the Japanese were defeated and forced to withdraw from all of their conquests in the Far East, including Korea.

Kim Il-sung, the Great Leader, had been comrades with the leaders of the Manchurian Battalion, and in later years, even through the chaos of the Korean War, the Manchurian Battalion maintained a certain level of autonomy. Now, they guarded the passes that led to Mount O-song in the Kwangju range, flush against the northern edge of the DMZ's Military Demarcation Line.

"There is much pressure on the Manchurian Battalion," Doc Yong told me. "Kim Il-sung is consolidating power, preparing for the transition to his son's leadership. His advisors tell him that his old comrades in the Manchurian Battalion are untrustworthy, that they will not accept his son's leadership, and will attempt to take power themselves. This is a lie. Still, we believe the Manchurian Battalion is marked for destruction. The forces arrayed against us are overwhelming, but Hero Kang has devised a plan that can save us."

"And you trust him?" I asked.

"Completely."

That was good enough for me. She took my hand in hers. The skin was no longer soft, as it had been in Seoul; now there was an extra layer of roughness.

"We need information," she told me. "Information that Hero Kang will guide you to. But only a foreigner can gain final access."

"Only a foreigner?" I asked.

"Yes. There is a man, a well-connected apparatchik, his name is Commissar Oh. Our information is that he and the commander of the Army's First Corps have been tasked with dealing with the Manchurian Battalion."

"Dealing with them?"

"Eliminating them," she said. "That is what we believe. But action must be taken soon, before the winter freeze, before the planned invasion of the South."

"You're sure of this?"

"We're not sure of anything," Doc Yong told me. "Our information is spotty, from multiple sources. We need to know more. We need to know when and where the First Corps is planning to strike. That's why we need you."

I brushed snow off her shoulders.

"Commissar Oh is a secretive man," she continued. "That's one of the reasons he was chosen for this mission. But he also has his vanities. Every year, he and the First Corps commander sponsor a foreigners-only Taekwondo tournament. The winner is invited into the inner sanctum of something called the Joy Brigade. That's where our agent is waiting. She needs help to obtain the information. Once you gain the trust of Commissar Oh, she will contact you."

"She?"

"Yes. The Joy Brigade is composed strictly of women. Once you have the information, she will lead you to Hero Kang and he will, in turn, help you escape and lead you to the Manchurian Battalion."

I thought of what she was saying, of how dangerous it would be, all the while staring down the spokes of the wheel that surrounded us. All was dark, quiet, unmoving, except for the silently falling shroud of snow.

"Where will you be?" I asked.

"In the Kwangju Mountains with the Manchurian Battalion. They are my protectors and they are the ones who guard the caves that lead to the passageway beneath the DMZ."

I gripped her small shoulders and stared into her eyes. "But why don't we escape now? Go to the Manchurian Battalion, find the passageway beneath the Kwangju Mountains? Then we will be free and we can convince Eighth Army to help with weapons and ammunition, maybe with ground troops."

"That's what we hoped before, but there is so little time. The attack on the Manchurian Battalion could happen at any moment. And who knows if the Americans will act quickly enough, or act at all?"

She was right about that. The motives of the American Army were often obscure, even to me.

"So we are fighting for time," she continued. "If you can obtain this information and pass it to Hero Kang, we can sabotage their plans, delay the First Corps attack long enough to seek American help. But if we escape now, if you and I run off to the Kwangju Mountains and manage to reach South Korea, the Manchurian Battalion will be destroyed."

She allowed me time to let this sink in. I could see her point. If this planned attack by the First Corps was delayed, or nullified, that would allow us time to make our way south and convince Eighth Army to reinforce the Manchurian Battalion. Still, I wasn't exactly sure who these Manchurian Battalion people were and why I should be worried about them. After all, they were Communists, supposedly, my avowed enemy.

"They are my people," Doc Yong told me, as if she were reading my mind. "I must help them."

"Your people?" In the ambient glow of the electric bulbs surrounding the monument, I studied her eyes.

"They are the ones who helped me in South Korea," she said. "The ones who, through their agents, paid for my education. They are the ones who helped me avenge the murder of my parents."

It was that series of killings against a group of thugs who ran the red-light district of Itaewon in Seoul that had forced Doctor Yong In-ja to seek asylum in the DPRK.

"Your parents were members of the Manchurian Battalion."

She nodded.

This time I looked away. "And if I decide not to help?"

"Then I will do my best to get you out of North Korea. I will show you the directions in the ancient manuscript and take you as far as I can into the tunnels. After that, you will be on your own."

"You won't come?"

"No. I will stay and fight with the Manchurian Battalion."

"You won't win," I said.

"No. Probably not."

Then she took my hand and placed it on her belly. After having spent the last few hours with her, I was certain she'd borne a child—the child I suspected she'd been pregnant with when she'd fled South Korea a year ago. Still, she hadn't spoken of it and I hadn't pressed her.

"We have a child," I said.

"Yes," she replied. "A son. His name is Il-yong. The First Dragon. He is full of life, and full of fire. So much like you."

It took me a moment to adjust to this new reality, although I had suspected it. Finally, I said, "We should leave, escape from North Korea, the three of us. You, me, Il-yong."

"I can't," she said. "Not until the Manchurian Battalion has at least a fighting chance." She clutched my hand more tightly. "Will you help us?"

Before I could answer, she pulled a photograph out of her backpack.

What is it about children, about our own flesh and blood, that moves us so? As I studied the photograph, she clutched my hand tightly. He was an aware-looking child, bright, his little fists clenched, his eyes staring straight into the camera.

I handed the photograph back to Doc Yong.

The chances of us surviving, any of us, were slim. The North Korean regime, when it felt threatened, had proven itself to be ruthlessly efficient. Still, now that I'd seen my son, now that I knew I had a family, I knew I'd never abandon them, not like my father had abandoned me. If it came to that, I'd rather die first.

"I'll help," I said finally.

▦ ▦ ▦

An automobile engine rumbled, growing ever louder. I peeked over the cement toe of the heroic factory worker. A beat-up old Russian sedan, probably left over from the Stalin era, cruised slowly around the monument. Doc Yong sat up.

"It's him," she said. "Come on."

We clambered over the massive foot of the monument and ran toward the vehicle. It stopped. Now I could see clearly the man sitting behind the wheel. Hero Kang.

"*Bali,*" he said, opening the door and climbing out. Hurry. "Let's go before those fixer bastards and their lead bitch get a bead on us."

Their lead bitch?

"Here," Hero Kang said. "Put this on." He tossed a black overcoat and a black chauffeur's cap to Doc Yong.

She handed her cape and her backpack to me and I shoved them into the backseat of the car. After she'd slipped the overcoat and the chauffeur's cap on, Hero Kang handed her a pair of white gloves. She slipped those on also.

As if she were born to it, Doc Yong climbed behind the wheel, adjusted the seat, and started up the engine. Hero Kang, positioning himself proudly in his usual military uniform, sat up front next to her. I crouched in the backseat. Doc Yong shifted the tank-like engine into gear and we lurched forward.

As we pulled away from the monument, I glanced back at one of the dark alleys. In one, a lonely figure stood. A woman with long, straight hair, wearing a leather cap and a leather jacket, hands shoved deep into her pockets. She seemed to be staring straight into my eyes.

"Who's that?" I asked.

The car swerved and Hero Kang and Doc Yong glanced to where I pointed. But now the alley was empty.

"What?" Hero Kang asked.

"There was a woman standing there," I replied. "A woman in military uniform."

"You're imagining things," Hero Kang said.

But I knew I hadn't imagined anything. The woman standing in the alley had been the same beautiful officer I'd seen outside the room where Doc Yong and I had been holed up.

The big Russian engine growled angrily as Doc Yong shifted gears and we left the monument behind. Slowly, we wound through broad lanes. The plan was that after Doc Yong dropped us off, she'd ditch the car, resume the role of a peasant woman traveling to visit relatives, and return to a place of safety in the Kwangju Mountains.

Hero Kang told me to sit up straight.

"Remember," he told me. "You're an officer. A hero in your own country. Everyone else is nothing. Less than nothing."

I sat up straighter in the seat and thrust my shoulders back, smoothing out the wrinkles in my Warsaw Pact uniform as best I could, staring about imperiously. Not that anyone noticed. In the distance, work groups carrying hoes and rakes marched through the gloom like military units.

We turned onto a massive road lined with monuments to the Great Leader and to the struggles of the North Korean people against the Japanese colonists and the American imperialists. Freezing fog and the slowly rising sun cast the quiet city in a somber red glow. Eerily, there were no other cars out yet, except for one military vehicle that whizzed past us. At the larger intersections, even at this early hour, attractive young women in police uniforms with skirts just barely covering their knees pirouetted and pointed and waved, blowing their whistles and coordinating an elaborate flow of imaginary traffic.

"She must be freezing," I said, as we passed one.

"Yes," Doc Yong replied. "Poor thing."

"You're an officer!" Hero Kang barked, aiming his rebuke at me. "You have no time for sympathy." Then he turned to Doc Yong. "Have you briefed him?"

"Thoroughly."

What he meant was had she convinced me to go through with all this. She had. Still, I longed to turn this vehicle toward the Kwangju Mountains, find my son, and escape with him and Doc Yong beneath the DMZ to freedom. But that would have to wait.

We turned down a side street, narrower than the rest, and wound slowly up into wooded hills. Finally, we reached a huge building, as broad as an aircraft carrier, but elaborately carved and splashed with the bright colors of an ancient royal palace. A red wooden arch was painted with golden hangul letters that said *Inmin jayu undong gong.* The Palace of the People's Freedom Movement. Yellow-eyed dragons with green-scaled bodies slid red tongues past ivory fangs.

At the main entranceway, four armed soldiers saluted. Two of them stepped forward smartly and opened the side doors. Hero Kang and I climbed out. Before we marched up the granite steps, I turned and caught Doc Yong's eyes.

She stared back, worried. I smiled and winked and she nodded slightly. Then I turned and walked past the North Korean soldiers, not looking back.

Steam billowed upward in moist, warm clouds. Hero Kang lay naked on a massage table covered in white linen. I sat on wet stone being scrubbed with a stiff sponge by a faithful female follower of the Great Leader of the people. She went about the job with all the joy of a butcher preparing a hog for slaughter.

Hero Kang's masseuse wore only a coarse white towel pinned around her shapely body and a smaller towel piled atop her head like an ancient Egyptian headdress. My attendant wore a stiff cotton medical smock buttoned meticulously to the top of her neck.

I wanted to ask Hero Kang why we were being treated differently, but I didn't want these women, or anyone in this massive gymnasium, to know I spoke Korean. Besides, I thought I knew the answer. Hero Kang was a revered hero of the people. I, on the other hand, was something putrid, to be cleansed and purified. In short, I was a foreigner. In North Korea, even those foreigners who were political allies, such as an officer of the Warsaw Pact, were considered objectionable, not of the "pure race" and, in most people's eyes, less than human.

We'd been fed earlier with expensive white rice, not the coarse brown rice or thick-fibered corn most North Koreans ate, and with savory side dishes: cabbage kimchi, diced turnip, pickled cucumber, and *bulkogi*, grilled slices of marinated beef. Now I was being washed. All of this pampering, I thought, was simply preparing me for the kill.

Hero Kang moaned in pleasure as his masseuse dug her pudgy fingers into the muscles at the base of his neck. My attendant dropped her sponge in a bucket and slipped on a glove of coarse, wiry cloth. Pointing, she ordered me to lie down on the stone. I did. She slapped soapy water on my back and then, with a vengeance, began to scrub. I winced in pain and started to rise, but she shoved me back down with her free hand. She was surprisingly strong. I could've thrown her off, but I decided that I was man enough to take it. I lay back down, clenched my teeth, and vowed not to show weakness.

I'd seen gloves like this one in South Korea. They were designed to clean the skin so thoroughly that they scraped off the first layer of flesh and sometimes the second and third. Dirt and oil built up in the pores appears like magic atop the reddened skin in black, rubbery pellets, which the Koreans call *ddei*. The woman scrubbed and scrubbed and whole handfuls of *ddei* appeared. "*Toryowoyo,*" she said. Dirty.

"*Yangnom da kurei,*" the masseuse replied. All foreign louts are the same.

Hero Kang laughed, his massive back shaking. "How do you know?" he asked them. "How many foreign louts have you scrubbed?"

The masseuse didn't answer. Instead, she slapped him playfully on the butt, her face reddening at her own boldness.

Grimly, my female torturer ordered me to roll over. I obeyed. When she finally ordered me to stand up, my entire body was as red and as raw as a lobster without its shell. Holding my arms away from my body so as not to irritate the inflamed flesh, I hobbled over to the huge tub filled with steaming water that she was pointing to. When I'd lowered myself to my shoulders, she grabbed the top of my head and shoved me under. I came up sputtering.

After soaking for less than a minute, she ordered me out of the tub and handed me towels. As I dried off, I thought of what Hero Kang had told me. My life and Doc Yong's depended on me finding the information that would protect the Manchurian Battalion. As did the life of the new person I'd only just learned about. He was already trying to walk and talk. Maybe maternal pride made Doc Yong exaggerate a little, but I didn't think so.

I was right about being prepared for slaughter.

I stood in my *dobok*, my pure white uniform, in the center of the massive gymnasium. Bleachers filled with North Korean Army soldiers lined both walls, males on one side, females on the other. Behind a low row of skirted tables sat stern middle-aged men. The judges.

The other participants were foreigners, like me. Sixteen of us, from countries in Asia, Eastern Europe, and Africa. Countries that were all, in one way or another, affiliated with the Communist Bloc. We were ordered in English to line up and then to bow to the judges. They nodded back.

Then we turned and faced a huge bronze statue of Kim Il-sung at the far end of the gymnasium. His face beamed, and with his left hand he was pointing to some sort of Marxist paradise. Little girls dressed in traditional *chima-chogori*

Korean dresses scurried forward and handed each of us a bouquet of roses. Where they found roses this time of year, I didn't know. We were ordered to march forward in unison. Cameras were pointed at us and it became apparent that this was a propaganda exercise. When we stood about twenty feet in front of the statue, we were ordered to kneel and lower our heads to the floor. One by one, we were made to rise and lay our roses at the feet of the huge statue. In the background, a voice droned on through rusty speakers about how people from all over the world prostrated themselves in front of the Great Leader in gratitude for spreading his shining light for all to see.

None of the participants complained. Hero Kang had told me that most of them were the family members or employees of various foreign embassies and consulates here in Pyongyang. However, the government's official line was that we were all Taekwondo enthusiasts who had traveled at great expense to bask in the glow of Korean martial arts and, most importantly, in the shining sun of the people, Kim Il-sung.

Personally, I wanted to throw up.

Hero Kang had registered me as one Captain Enescu from the Warsaw Pact country of Romania. Although they'd devised a phony passport for me, Hero Kang hadn't had to show it; instead, he'd been able to utilize the power of his personality to overwhelm tournament officials.

After the ceremony, we were allowed to return to our trainers, who stood on the sidelines of the central wood-slat floor. Hero Kang, my trainer, slapped me on the back.

A whistle was blown. The first two combatants trotted out onto the floor, faced the judges and bowed, and then faced each other and bowed again. The order *"Junbi"* was given. Prepare. And finally, *"Sijak."* Begin. The two men started bouncing around each other, fists raised. One of them shot out a side kick. It missed. The other countered with a roundhouse, which also missed.

I glanced at Hero Kang and raised my eyebrows.

"Kisul-ee potong an imnida," he said. Their skills are remarkable.

It was a joke. He'd told me earlier that many of the contestants were chosen just to fill slots in this supposed final round of the tournament and make it look as if there were a huge international throng here in Pyongyang to study Taekwondo. Some of the combatants, however, would be tough. They were security people who kept themselves in good shape, and, according to Hero Kang, some of them had taken up Taekwondo with true dedication.

In Seoul, I had earned a black belt studying part-time when my work schedule allowed. In the secret *dochang* Hero Kang had taken me to yesterday, the martial artists had coached me on tournament technique, the best way to score points and impress the judges who would be deciding the winners here today.

I glanced around. The men throwing practice kicks on the sidelines showed various levels of skill, but one of them, a tall black man, sliced the air with some serious punches and kicks.

"Maputo," Hero Kang told me, "from the Mozambique freedom fighters. He won last year."

"Only among the foreigners?"

"Of course. Against Koreans, he wouldn't stand a chance."

And I knew this was true. Every child in North Korea studies Taekwondo from the time they start school. Those with potential are pulled out and sent to study at special schools for athletes. Once they're in the military, highly skilled young men face enormous competition to land on the top military teams. If they make it, their only duty is to train and participate in martial arts competitions throughout the Communist world.

On the far side of the gymnasium, the People's Army First Corps Taekwondo team was limbering up. They would be giving a demonstration after the foreign competition was completed.

The two men fighting now completed their third round, bowed to each other, and—breathing heavily, fists hanging to their sides—awaited the decision of the judges. The judges conferred, the combatants bowed once again, and the winner was announced. Another whistle was blown and two more men took the floor.

Here was the catch about this plan. I had to win the tournament. Not merely do well and come in second or third place, but win. Take the brass ring. If I didn't, Hero Kang told me, I'd never be invited into the inner sanctum presided over by the political advisor to the commander of the First Corps, the army unit that guarded all access routes to the capital city of Pyongyang. And if I didn't reach that inner sanctum, I'd never make contact with the person the Manchurian Battalion had embedded in the upper echelons of the North Korean Communist elite, the person who had the information Hero Kang needed. This is why Hero Kang needed a foreigner. If I didn't win this Taekwondo tournament, our best chance of escape would fall apart.

In North Korea, as I was learning, nothing was ever easy.

My first fight was with a Cuban security guard. He was quite good, but he made a few fundamental mistakes, such as overextending his roundhouse kick, thereby leaving himself off balance if it failed to connect. Which it did, repeatedly, as I moved in and then hopped back just in time and countered with a short front kick that caught him one, two, three times in the midsection. The judges were fair. Although the Cuban's fighting style had been flamboyant, with long legs and long arms flashing everywhere, he never landed anything more than glancing blows, whereas I made direct contact with his solar plexus three times. In a real fight, the Cuban would've been dead. The judges ruled me the winner.

When I returned to the sidelines, Hero Kang beamed. "Only two more," he told me. "Then you can face Maputo."

I noticed the tall black man eyeing me. Maputo, like the judges, had been impressed with my performance.

Hero Kang elbowed me. Entering on either side of the gymnasium, at the base of the bleachers, were armed security men. After about a half dozen of them stationed themselves near the exits, a woman entered. Tall, dressed in black leather boots and coat with a matching red-star cap. A military officer, a senior captain. The same beautiful woman I'd seen last night. Her long black hair framed an oval face that was white and unblemished. Her lips were soft, petulant, and her luminous black eyes stared straight at mine.

"Don't look at her," Hero Kang said, turning his back toward the security people. I turned and pretended to be stretching my hamstrings. "Her name is Rhee Mi-sook," he told me. "A notorious fixer. Probably sent by the railroad security people."

"To arrest me?"

"Secretly. So they can interrogate you first and find out who you really are."

"Great," I said, still bending over so no one could see we were talking. "How do we shake her?"

"Only one way," Hero Kang told me. "Win the tournament."

Maputo mowed down everyone he faced. As did I, although not nearly as impressively. I counted on movement and scoring points, knowing by now that the judges were experts at realizing which moves were truly effective and which were just for show. Maputo, on the other hand, humiliated his opponents. He pelted them with side kicks and roundhouse kicks and, once they were backing away in fear, launched a showy reverse swivel kick that, despite being telegraphed by a mile, landed more often than not. A couple of his opponents had been bloody by the time the three rounds were over. Each time, Maputo easily won the decision. Even the members of the First Corps Taekwondo team were watching him, if with smirks on their faces.

Hero Kang whispered in my ear about strategy, using pidgin English when someone was close enough to hear, Korean when they weren't. His plan boiled down to one thing: move in close, inside his big roundhouse kick, and stay there. Maybe easier said than done.

Finally, after everyone else had been eliminated, it was down to just me and him. That's when an officer at the side of the hall shouted at the top of his lungs, *"Charyo!"* Attention! Everyone rose to their feet. An old man tottered in. He looked like he might be ninety. But he wore the uniform of a general of the People's Army and his chest was weighed down by what must've been twenty pounds of medals.

"General Yi," Hero Kang whispered, "the First Corps commander. Here for your match."

Two aides hovered near the old man's elbows, but he shrugged them off, straightened his shoulders, and marched into the gymnasium like the proud soldier he must once have been. He wore a leather-brimmed military cap with a flat, comically large crown, like the lid of some enormous jar.

Behind him was a much younger man, wearing the same uniform but without the epaulets and the medals. And without the cap. His long brown hair was slicked back, unusual here in North Korea, where most men wore their hair short. Also unusual was the thin mustache, the first I'd seen north of the DMZ.

"That's our target," Hero Kang whispered. "Commissar Oh, the political advisor to the First Corps commander. He's a personal friend of Kim, the younger, and the leader of the Joy Brigade."

Commissar Oh moved with all the grace of an eel through water, staying only a step or two behind the general. When they took their places of honor in the bleachers, he sat at the old warrior's right elbow, pulled out a pack of cigarettes, and offered one to the general, who declined. The younger man lit up, blowing smoke straight up into the rafters.

"He's a scoundrel," Hero Kang said.

In Korea, it's considered impolite to smoke in the presence of an elder. The old general seemed oblivious of the insult.

"And he's dangerous," Hero Kang continued. "Don't ever trust him. But he's the one who must invite you back into his headquarters after the tournament. That's where you'll be contacted by our operative."

"But first I have to win."

"You *must* win," Hero Kang hissed. "Commissar Oh doesn't tolerate losers."

Maputo was still warming up, smashing the air with wicked punches and kicks. Not very respectful to the elderly commander, but the Koreans ignored him. After all, foreigners don't know any better.

As I stretched, I watched Maputo's moves. He glanced in my direction and our eyes locked. Ritual scars stretched across his cheekbones. He smiled briefly and then his lips curled into a sneer. Hero Kang told me the freedom fighters he worked for received arms, clandestinely, from North Korea. Like Doc Yong, Maputo was fighting for his people. Only the desperate enter North Korea. Only the most desperate manage to leave.

Involuntarily, my eyes turned to the armed men at the exits. There were more of them now, but the beautiful senior captain had disappeared.

"Where'd she go?" I asked Hero Kang.

"I don't know. Forget about her. Concentrate on winning. It's our only chance to get out of here."

"You know her," I said.

"Yes. She's famous."

"For what?"

"Never mind now."

A whistle shrilled. Maputo approached the center languidly, with all the grace of a leopard on a hot summer day. A hushed wave of tittering flowed through the crowd, especially from the female side. Once we were facing the judges, we both bowed, then we turned and bowed to each other. The referee shouted, *"Junbi!"* Then, waving outstretched arms toward the center of his chest, *"Sijak!"*

Maputo hopped forward with a vicious side kick.

Unfortunately, I had been lost in thought about Captain Rhee Mi-sook. I'd been wondering if our cover had already been blown and if she'd really let me leave this gymnasium even if, somehow, I managed to win this match. I was doing exactly what Hero Kang had warned against. I wasn't paying attention.

The side kick landed hard against my left shoulder and I reeled backward, tripping myself. I fell with a thud.

The gymnasium erupted in laughter.

I bounced to my feet. Everyone was laughing, even the old general. But not Commissar Oh, who puffed on his cigarette and studied me with more than curiosity. With fascination.

Maputo didn't take advantage of my fall. To reach me, he had overextended and lost his own balance. His footing regained, we faced one another, fists raised, eyes locked.

I felt the burning in my face and behind my ears. I'd been humiliated by the fall and the laughter, but the side kick hadn't been a decisive blow. Not, at least, since

Maputo had been unable to follow it with anything more lethal. I did my best to calm down. I'd lost points, but not many, and I knew that the judges hadn't written me off yet. More than one man had been dropped in a fight and come back to win.

I stepped in, exposing myself to one of Maputo's round-house kicks. He couldn't resist the temptation. And while the kick was in the air, I dropped, swiveled with one leg extended, and slapped Maputo's remaining foot out from under him. He went down. Again, the laughter exploded like thunder.

I could've kicked him when he was down, but that would've violated the tournament rules. I held out my hand, and he took it, grinning, and started to rise. Half-way up, he jerked me to the floor and hopped away. For the third time in less than a minute, laughter filled the gymnasium. I doubted this much mirth had been witnessed in North Korea since the founding of the Democratic People's Republic. Minders waved the audience back to sobriety, reminding them that they must maintain order. Discipline. That's what this country was about. What Maputo and I were teaching them was that a little chaos could be extremely entertaining.

By now, we were through with the stunts. Maputo and I engaged, kicking, punching, parrying, setting a pace and gauging the speed of the other man. His kicks were just as quick and vicious as before, but against me they weren't landing with the same devastating effect. In South Korea, I'd sparred with true experts, and they'd taught me much. Mainly, they'd taught me how to survive.

The first round ended without any decisive points

being scored by either of us. We rested a minute and then were back at it. Maputo tried his side kick again, but I sidestepped it and caught him flush on the chest with a roundhouse of my own. Not a lethal blow but enough to score what might've been the first major point of the tournament. Frowning, Maputo attacked, trying combinations now. In each case I avoided his blow and managed to keep him off balance enough that much of the power of the kicks was wasted in trying to adjust his stance to keep up with my movement. But then, just as I was about to sidestep another kick, Maputo hopped in the air, switched to his other leg, and caught me with a short quarter side kick in the solar plexus. There was a gasp from the crowd. It was a clear blow, the best of the battle so far. I grabbed the lapels of his *dobok*, jerked him forward, and resisted the urge to punch his face in, only feigning the punch, scoring one or two minor points in the process. Then we were kicking again. His combinations were better than mine, and that one blow to the solar plexus had given him a substantial lead. Desperately, I tried another roundhouse, but at the last second he managed to parry and it glanced off his elbows. The whistle sounded. I returned to the sidelines. I stood by Hero Kang and, breathing heavily, placed my hands on my knees.

"Only one more round," he said. "Maputo is beating you."

"Yes."

"There are more security guards now."

I followed his eyes. The contingent had doubled in size. Still, no Senior Captain Rhee.

"Is there another way out?" I asked.

"There is no way out of here," Hero Kang told me, "except to win."

I looked at Maputo. He was limbering up, bending forward at the waist, long arms dangling toward the floor. Above, the old general beamed, enjoying the match immensely. Commissar Oh continued to smoke, staring pensively at the rows of uniformed young women on the far side of the gymnasium.

"All right," I said. "Then I must win."

"Maputo is ahead," Hero Kang said, "and he knows it. He will be cautious. He won't attack. He's afraid of your countermoves."

"Then I have to offer him something. Something to make him come out. Something he can't resist."

"Like what?"

"What do they offer the leopard to get him to expose himself?"

Hero Kang thought about that. "A goat."

"Yes."

"But you don't have a goat."

"No," I replied. "I only have myself."

The whistle sounded and we returned to the center. We bowed once again and the referee told us to begin.

Earlier, Hero Kang had explained the Joy Brigade.

Almost the entire country of North Korea was militarized, including a meticulously selected unit of young women. A cadre of operatives was sent into the country to audition middle school girls. Those who were most talented, and most beautiful, were brought to Pyongyang for additional training. After high school graduation, those who made the final cut were organized into something called *Kippum jo*, the Joy Brigade. The women who'd massaged Hero Kang and washed me were members of the Joy Brigade, although lesser minions. The most beautiful and charming young women entertained the elite Communist cadres of North Korea, all the way up to the Dear Leader, Kim Jong-il, and, it was rumored, to the Great Leader himself, Kim Il-sung. Some of the lesser members of the Joy Brigade, those who were maybe not so young or not so beautiful, or those who'd fallen into disfavor, entertained foreigners. This could include foreign diplomats or visiting dignitaries or even foreign athletes. A woman within the Joy Brigade had some weeks ago contacted Hero Kang. She was in possession of information concerning the plans to eliminate the Manchurian Battalion. This was the person I somehow had to find.

Doc Yong had warned me never to mention to Hero Kang what she was about to tell me.

"Why not?" I'd asked.

"Because it is a great shame. The woman who will contact you is more than just an acquaintance of Hero Kang. She is his daughter."

"She's the one holding the secrets?"

"Yes."

"Why is he ashamed?"

"Because she serves those who have betrayed the people. But you must never mention it. Even though she is his daughter, he refuses to acknowledge it."

"He's Korean," I said. "He can't turn his back on family like that."

"Here in North Korea he can. She is no longer his daughter. She is now a servant of the Great Leader. And a wife to whomever the Great Leader chooses."

"But now she's going to help save the Manchurian Battalion," I said.

"Yes. That is her redemption."

I launched a side kick that Maputo easily sidestepped. I launched another and missed again. But this time I feigned fatigue and allowed the kick to drift off to my left. When I regained my footing, my body was turned slightly toward Maputo, completely exposed. He didn't attack. Hero Kang was right, he was being very cautious.

In desperation, I tried roundhouse kicks. Again, Maputo warded them off easily, circling around me, seeming to want only to protect himself. I watched his eyes. There was still something in them, a hunger. A greed for glory, something that all young men have—at least those who are worth a damn. The audience was quiet now. Too quiet. This match, which had started off so well, had now become boring. Everyone knew the outcome. Maputo had scored some good points, he was ahead, and now all he had to do was hang on. I wanted to glance at Commissar Oh to see if he and the old general were bored, but I didn't dare take my eyes off Maputo. He sensed it too. He'd beaten all his other opponents decisively. Bloodying them. Humiliating them. He'd begun this third and final round probably thinking that he wouldn't be able to do that to me—I was too wary of his tricks. But he did think he'd win on points.

Still, the hunger for glory was there and I'd shown him how to get it. He saw that when I threw a side kick I would leave myself open. We stood with probably less than a minute left in the final round. I stared at him, sneering, and launched a side kick. He stepped back, his eyes igniting. When I launched the next kick, he sprang forward like a cat, his front foot raised. But I held the kick, lowering my foot, and, twisting to my right, I grabbed the heel of his raised foot and lifted it into the air, twisting his entire body skyward. I hopped forward, lifted my right foot, and brought it down to rest on his neck as he slammed to the ground. I held it there, making it clear that had I put all my weight into it, I could have snapped his neck like a twig.

The auditorium exploded in applause. Burning with rage, Maputo scrambled to his feet. We faced each other as the referee was about to wave us back into combat, but just then the final whistle sounded. Maputo groaned and stomped his feet and waggled his forefinger at me. In English he said, "I kill! In real life, I kill."

The referee ordered us to face the judges. They conferred and passed judgment, and the referee raised my arm in victory.

After he lowered my arm, I held out my right hand toward Maputo. He slapped it away, marched past me, and, grabbing a towel from a bench, stormed out of the gymnasium.

Hero Kang hurried toward the judges. Everyone glanced at the old general, who was being helped to his feet, shrugging off hands. He started to hobble out of the bleachers, heading toward the exit, Commissar Oh following.

Frantically, Hero Kang spoke to the judges. One of them, the senior judge, scurried across the floor and caught the attention of Commissar Oh. The two men talked, glancing back toward me. Commissar Oh shook his head and started to walk away. Hero Kang met the returning judge and received the news.

The commissar thought the match between me and Maputo had been amateurish, like a schoolyard brawl, and had not reflected well on the great tradition of Taekwondo, nor on the glory of the Great Leader. Therefore, even though I'd won the foreigner's tournament, I would not be invited back to the people's banquet activities this evening.

The old general and Commissar Oh had their backs turned toward us. Hero Kang stood with his arms at his side, defeated. The security guards at the exits started to advance. The beautiful Senior Captain Rhee Mi-sook reappeared out of one of the side doors. Hero Kang and I spotted her at the same time.

We would fight. I looked around for weapons. There were none, except for a rickety straight-backed chair. I could break it apart and make a club for each of us. We would go down fighting. That would be better than imprisonment, or torture.

Just then, like a man electrified, Hero Kang turned away from the approaching security people and walked toward the departing general. His booming voice filled the gymnasium.

"Wait!" he shouted. Everyone stopped and turned to listen. "The officer," he said, pointing back at me, "the officer from Romania, the winner of the foreigner's tournament, he wants to offer a challenge."

Commissar Oh raised his cigarette to his lips. It was an effeminate move, reminding me of a manicured housewife absorbed in her favorite soap opera. While everyone waited, Commissar Oh said, "Oh yes, Great Hero Kang? And what sort of challenge does this officer from Romania have to offer?"

"He was unable to display the full measure of his skills," Hero Kang replied, speaking so everyone in the hall could hear him. "He was forced to compete against an inferior opponent and under such circumstances true expertise cannot come to the fore."

I believe at this moment Commissar Oh had already anticipated what Hero Kang was about to say. A half smile twisted his fleshy lips.

"This officer from Romania," Hero Kang continued, "asks the permission of the great general of the people, and the permission of our Great Leader, for another match." Hero Kang waved toward the white-clad Koreans who were about to put on a display of true expertise for the assembled audience. "The officer from Romania challenges the champion of the People's Army First Corps!"

A murmur of disbelief rippled through the crowd. Commissar Oh smiled and then conferred with the general. Enthusiastically, the old man nodded his consent. Hero Kang exhaled deeply as General Yi and Commissar Oh returned to their seats.

A phalanx of Taekwondo experts approached the center of the gym. Their leader, a muscular man with a face and a body of stone, stepped forward. Hero Kang hurried to my side.

"His name is Pak," Hero Kang told me. "Fifth-level black belt."

"I have to beat *him?*" I asked.

"Yes. If the Manchurian Battalion is to survive, if you are to make Doctor Yong In-ja your wife, if you are to save the life of your son, then you must win."

"And if I don't?"

Hero Kang shrugged. "It is over." He glanced toward the beautiful Captain Rhee. She stood leaning against a wall, her arms crossed and the brim of her black leather cap pulled down low over her eyes.

I studied my opponent. Slowly, easily, he was limbering himself up, not bothering to look at me. Legs spread apart, he touched his forehead to the floor, and finally the champion of the First Corps raised his gaze. His eyes were black and I saw in them nothing but determination. Determination and death.

-5-

When First Corps champion Pak's foot came down on my forehead, I literally did not see it coming. Later, my mind recreated the blur of the foot rising and crashing down on me, but by then it was too late. Too late for a lot of things.

The referee allowed me to get back to my feet, but then the attack started again, unrelenting and impossible to stop. I was nowhere close to being in this man's league. I held up my arms, circled backward, did my best to stay out of his range, but all I was doing was running. First Corps Champion Pak could land a blow whenever the spirit moved him.

The gym was silent. This wasn't a competition; it was slaughter.

Finally, somehow, the round ended. Hero Kang rushed

to the center of the ring and pulled me to the sidelines. He slapped my face.

"Can you hear me?" he asked, staring directly into my eyes.

"I can hear you," I replied.

"He didn't take you out in the first round," Kang told me, "out of respect for General Yi. On the other hand, after one round of entertainment, it would be disrespectful to let this slaughter go on. As soon as you step back out there with him, he will carry you for maybe thirty seconds, then he will drop you."

"Yes," I said, nodding.

Hero Kang slapped me. Hard. Faces from the audience gawked. He leaned closer to me, embracing me, hissing in my ear. "You must win!"

"Win?"

"Yes, win. If you don't, the Manchurian Battalion will be doomed." He studied me, not liking what he saw. "If you don't win," he continued, "you will never see Doctor Yong In-ja again. You will never see your son, the one who carries your name, the one who carries the blood of your family. You must *win*."

The words seemed odd, alien to me somehow: first "son," then "win." Hero Kang twisted my head until I was gazing at Senior Captain Rhee Mi-sook and the fixers who were waiting, guarding the exits. "Look," he ordered.

"They'll capture us," I said dully.

"Yes."

"And we'll be tortured," I said.

"That too. But if you win, we will be under the

protection of Commissar Oh and the fixers won't be able to touch us. You must *win*."

I gazed at the twisted flesh of his perspiring face. "How?" I asked.

"How what?"

"How do I win?"

"Forget Taekwondo," he said. "Forget everything. Just think of getting out of here. Think of not being tortured. Think of life."

I remembered feeling like I felt now, once, long ago. There were bad boys in my neighborhood, bigger and meaner. They would waylay smaller kids and steal coins we might have squirreled away in our blue jeans. They'd twist our arms and pinch us until we cried. I hated them; I was willing to do anything, pay any price, to avenge myself and the other kids. And then I'd discovered the Los Angeles sheriff's athletic program at the Main Street Gym. A few good deputies took the time to teach us scrawny Mexican kids how to box. How to throw a left jab, how to counter with a right, how to hold our punches until there was an opening and then connect with our arms straight, our fists tight.

"You must *fight!*" Hero Kang hissed again. "Forget Taekwondo. Forget everything. Fight for your life."

The whistle sounded. I found myself back in the center of the ring. A kick came out of nowhere. And then I was flying.

Hero Kang had been fifteen years old when he joined the Manchurian Battalion. They gave him a rifle, cloth shoes, a down-filled jacket, and along with a group of new recruits, he was ordered south through the swirling Korean winter to fight the Yankee imperialists. Doc Yong told me the full story, both the official myth and the truth as best she knew it.

Hero Kang immediately fell under the guidance of Bandit Lee. His real name was Lee Ryong-un and he had led the Manchurian Battalion since the early days when they raided the Japanese Imperial Army and stole food, fuel, and medical supplies to distribute to the starving Korean communities in the hinterlands of the Manchurian wilderness. Years later, during the Korean War, Bandit Lee led a battalion of hardened foot soldiers—soldiers who faced the U.S. Army near the 38th parallel and suffered the brunt of vicious air and artillery assaults.

"The way we fight," Bandit Lee told the man who would become Hero Kang, "is we dig in like moles during the day and at night we creep close to the Americans. So close that they can't use their big guns or their airpower. Then we fight them with bayonets if we can, bullets if we have to."

Many American soldiers had expected to encounter push-button warfare in Korea. Instead they'd ended up fighting in muddy trenches in freezing weather, face to face with a desperate enemy, using basically the same weapons that had been used during the Stone Age.

On Young Kang's first nighttime raid, Bandit Lee was seriously injured. While they were creeping toward enemy lines, napalm was dropped on their advancing lines. Most of the soldiers were able to burrow into shell holes in the battlefield, but Bandit Lee was standing up, directing his men to take cover, when the first splash of napalm hit. He was burned so severely his men thought he was dead. After the assault, the Americans left their fortified positions and charged down the hill. A horrible battle ensued and it was only later, while licking their wounds, that Young Kang and the men of the Manchurian Battalion realized their leader had been captured by the Americans.

The future Hero Kang was so upset by the capture of his mentor that under the cover of heavy rainfall he slipped away from his own lines and found the Americans who were interrogating—and torturing—Bandit Lee. Young Kang attacked, killing five Americans, rescued Bandit Lee, and carried him to safety. That was the myth. And it was so impressive that it eventually earned Hero Kang North Korea's highest military honor, Hero of the Republic, and he was allowed to meet with and shake the hand of the Great Leader himself.

According to Doc Yong, what actually happened was quite different. It was Young Kang who was captured. Behind their sandbagged positions, the Americans tortured him. His howls of pain and pleas for mercy could be heard by his comrades hunkering down at the bottom of the muddy hill. Bandit Lee organized a rescue operation, just himself and a few trusted veterans. While the rain poured down, they attacked the Americans, killing all five and rescuing Young Kang. It was on the way downhill that the planes attacked. The wave of sizzling napalm was like a tsunami from hell. All of the soldiers in the patrol were incinerated, except for Bandit Lee, who was badly burned. Young Kang was spared because Bandit Lee tossed the almost unconscious youngster into a muddy pit and fell on top of him.

The reason for the lie was that Bandit Lee was covered from head to toe with burns and later his legs had to be amputated. In his horribly mutilated condition, he could no longer lead the Manchurian Battalion. Not officially anyway. Koreans, and especially North Koreans, are superstitious about the wounded and the handicapped and they hide them away. They don't allow them to be seen in public, and they certainly wouldn't allow a hideously deformed man to be the leader of one of the most important battalions facing the Americans. Young Kang was chosen as Bandit Lee's successor because he was husky and strong and had a marvelous speaking voice, and because he could carry Bandit Lee on his back. While Young Kang—Hero Kang—was given official leadership during the Korean War, Bandit Lee was the true commander, and he still maintained the position more than twenty years later.

"And this double life," I asked, "being considered a hero but not really being one, does it bother him?"

Doc Yong nodded slowly. "Yes. He owes everything to Bandit Lee and the Manchurian Battalion. That is why he helps us. That is why he is risking his life."

"Is that the only reason?" I asked.

"And also," she said, "because he faces a great shame." She paused. I waited. "In North Korea, even a hero, or the family of a hero, is not immune from the avarice of the Great Leader and the legions of party cadres who serve him. Hero Kang's daughter was systematically brainwashed like all the other young women who grow up in this country."

"Brainwashed?"

"Taught to believe the Joy Brigade is a place of honor when it is a place of shame."

When my senses returned, the referee was guiding me back toward the center of the floor. Hero Kang looked worried. The soldiers on either side of the gym were standing in the bleachers, pointing and laughing. All their lives, the government and the schools taught them to hate foreigners—especially Americans and the Japanese—but for entertainment purposes, any foreigner would do. I spotted Senior Captain Rhee, her arms still crossed and a look of disgust on her face. The experts of the First Corps all stood in a line, smirking and shaking their heads.

Fifth-degree black-belt Pak glanced up into the stands at Commissar Oh. The Commissar languidly removed his cigarette and nodded. Pak looked back at me, smiling. It was the cold smile of a predator. I turned to Hero Kang. His fists were clenched, his face puffed in a spasm of anguish. Pak was about to take me out. Kang knew it, Pak knew it, everyone in the stadium knew it. Senior Captain Rhee motioned for her security men to move in closer. Hero Kang and I would be arrested and tortured.

The referee waved us together. Suddenly, I knew what I had to do. It had nothing to do with the rules of this tournament, nothing to do with the martial spirit of Taekwondo, but everything to do with survival. If I could survive one kick, I would be able to take it from there.

Almost casually, Pak stepped forward, his back straight, not even crouching in the fighting position most often assumed by practitioners of the martial arts. He didn't need to. His kicks came out so fast he was confident I couldn't stop them. I was confident of the same thing. But stopping them wasn't my goal. I hopped forward. Pak launched a circular front kick that swiped my forehead. It didn't hurt me, but I pretended to stagger. The crowd was hooting. Pak followed. I backed up but stood my ground. Pak launched a vicious round kick to my midsection, which I partially blocked with my forearms, but still it forced me to bend forward. That's when I lunged. He countered with two more roundhouses to my head and my shoulders and for a second I thought I'd black out. Somehow I fought away the darkness until I could see his eyes staring straight into mine. He wasn't worried. As soon as we clinched, the referee—according to the rules of Taekwondo and the rules of propriety—would break us apart. We would pause for a second, the referee would wave us together, and then Pak could resume his assault.

As the referee stepped forward to break us from our clinch, I remembered the sheriff's deputies at the Main Street Gym. I remembered them coaching me to keep my left jab straight. "Don't get fancy," they'd tell me. "Just reach out straight, like you're reaching for an apple." While Pak was standing there—dropping his guard, backing up, complying with the referee's orders—I let him have it with a left jab. His head snapped back. My right followed.

Before fifth-level black-belt Pak hit the ground, he was out cold.

The referee screamed in outrage, shoving his arms in front of me. The men of the First Corps howled in anger and rushed toward me. Hero Kang shoved me from behind and I lost my footing, falling under a sea of rushing bodies. There were punches and kicks from every direction and I heard Hero Kang cursing above me. Out of the pile, a foot swung toward my head and suddenly everything went blank.

When I came to, I was lying facedown on stone.

I expected to hear the wet splash of the sponge and feel the cool dribble of soap on my skin, but instead all I felt was cold. A terrible cold. I tried to raise my head. A spasm of pain ran down my back. I controlled it and lifted my head as high as I could. The room was dark, no steam, no masseuse hovering nearby. There was only the sound of clanging metal far away and occasional distant voices. Flickering rays of light filtered through a high aperture. I studied the stone beneath me. It wasn't stone at all. It was brick. I lifted myself to my feet, but before I could stand fully my head hit the roof. I shuffled toward the light and peered through a small barred window that I only now realized was part of a thick wooden door. The brick hallways outside were long and silent and empty.

Prison.

I took inventory of myself. I was only wearing jockey shorts and a soiled T-shirt, and suddenly I realized I was shivering, my teeth chattering from the cold. The cell was only a few steps across in either direction, and the only appurtenances were a metal bucket and a wood-slat bench made of ancient lumber, splintered and filthy.

Still, it was better than the floor.

I sat on the bench, crouched forward, wondering what had gone wrong with Hero Kang's plans. I remembered the rage in people's eyes, their desire to kill me. No wonder they'd thrown me in here. Maybe they'd done me a favor. It was better than being torn limb from limb by an angry mob. Sort of.

I thought of the torture in my future. Would they tie my wrists behind my back and hang me from the rafters, popping my shoulders out of joint? Would they turn me upside down and pour water up my nose? Or would they just practice their Taekwondo on me for hours at a time?

How long would I be able to withstand it?

Not long, I decided.

Whether or not my cover story would stand up to scrutiny depended on how well it had been prepared by the Manchurian Battalion. I tried to think of a fallback cover story, in case the Romanian one fell apart. Some way to convince the North Korean interrogators that I wasn't an American spy.

Offhand, I couldn't think of one.

-6-

The wooden door swung open. Startled, I sat up on the bench.

A guard entered, armed only with a billy club. Two other guards stood behind him, one with a Russian-made pistol strapped to his waist.

"*Charyo!*" the guard said. Attention!

I stood as best I could, but I had to keep my head bowed because of the low ceiling. Candlelight from the hallway cast a dim glow into my cell.

The guards stood aside and a small man in a military uniform entered the cell. I recognized him immediately—the man in charge of the Taekwondo tournament, Commissar Oh. He was smoking furiously, as if to dispel whatever odor this room might have, an odor I could no longer notice. He wore a loose cape and smoked from an ivory cigarette holder. He had the darting eyes of a fashion designer on opening night in Paris.

"*Naimsei na!*" he said, wrinkling his nose and glancing toward the bucket in the corner.

One of the guards hustled forward, grabbed the bucket, and carried it out of the tiny cell. With the offending filth removed, Commissar Oh looked me up and down. His eyes lingered on my crotch, as if he were fascinated by something. I decided not to flinch, nor to look downward to see what he was looking at. If my fly was open, so be it.

Finally, he looked back at my face and said something in Russian.

I stared at him blankly.

He exhaled in exasperation. Then he started speaking in Korean. "What are you, stupid? A Warsaw Pact officer and you don't speak Russian. What the hell good are you?"

I continued to stare at him blankly, pretending that I didn't understand, keeping the muscles in my face immobile so they wouldn't betray me.

He puffed on his cigarette, squinting behind rising smoke. "Maybe I ought to chop you in pieces," he said, still speaking in Korean, "and sell your rotten foreign flesh to a hog farm."

A couple of the guards murmured in assent.

Commissar Oh glanced back at them angrily. "No one wants your opinion."

They lowered their heads and became quiet.

"You embarrassed us today," he continued, "attacking

our First Corps champion like that, knocking him down. With *trickery!* You couldn't have done that within the rules."

He paced to his left, studying me as if I were indeed a lump of flesh he was planning on carving. I tried not to respond in any way. Stoic, like the war hero I was supposed to be.

How good was the cover story Hero Kang had constructed for me? Had Commissar Oh checked me out with the Foreign Ministry? Was he still convinced I was a Romanian officer? If they'd had any inkling that I was an American spy, they would have already been feeding me to a hog farm.

"What to do with you?" Commissar Oh said. "I can't just let you go without punishment; it would be like covering our face with shit. You must make amends to our Great Leader." He stared at me, waiting for a response. When he didn't get one, he said, "You'll have to pay for your crime somehow. And dearly." He puffed mightily on the last of his cigarette until the filter glowed. "Foreigners. Always a problem."

He tossed the butt on the ground and stomped it flat. He swiveled on his high-heeled leather boots and stalked out of the cell.

"Punish him!" he shouted to the guards. "Make him understand that he's nothing but a miserable foreign beast. Less than human. Make him cry and kneel and praise the Great Leader." Then he stopped, pointing his finger at the lead guard. "But don't kill him."

The guard nodded. When the door closed, I was left alone.

Nervously, I sat back down on the bench.

Ten minutes later, the guards returned, bearing straps and chains and the same bucket they'd removed from my cell, still sloshing with filth.

It seemed like years, but I knew that only two or three hours had passed since Commissar Oh had left my cell. Every part of my body hurt and I could still feel the filthy water clinging like slime to my sinus cavities and the back of my mouth. In the middle of the water torture, I'd lost all sense of pride. It was too much. When you can't breathe, nothing is sweeter than the thought of air, of just being allowed the luxury of inhaling and exhaling. Finally, I blurted out in English, "No more!"

The guards who were torturing me were uneducated men and knew nothing of the language of their archenemy, America. Luckily for me. They probably assumed I was speaking Romanian. When I realized they weren't going to stop, I shocked them by speaking Korean.

"Let me talk to Commissar Oh," I told them.

By the way they stepped back and their eyes widened, you would've thought that an ape had just opened its mouth and recited a passage from Kim Il-sung's Juche philosophy.

The good part was they stopped torturing me. Someone was sent to fetch Commissar Oh. They kept me shackled but allowed me to hobble over to the splintered wooden bench. I collapsed and, luxuriating in the sweet air entering and exiting my lungs, soon fell asleep.

Commissar Oh's face loomed above me. I realized that his hand was on my belly and my stomach muscles clenched. I sat up, almost bumping foreheads with him. All the guards had disappeared.

"You wanted to speak to me?" he said in Korean.

I nodded. "I lied to you," I said, hanging my head, as if ashamed. "I didn't want you to know. I thought it might give me some sort of advantage, but the truth is that I've been studying Korean. A little. But I don't speak well."

Commissar Oh puffed on his cigarette, forcing a small gray cloud to rise in front of his eyes. "I can understand you well enough," he said.

"I apologize for punching the First Corps champion. I was wrong. He was too good for me. I didn't know what else to do."

Commissar Oh continued to puff and nod. "You've been lying to me," he said. "Not letting us know you speak our language. Where did you learn?"

"Here. Since I've arrived." I let my head droop, in total submission. That part, I wasn't faking.

"Repentance," he said, "isn't good enough."

"What?"

I pretended not to understand the word.

"Saying you're sorry," he repeated. "That's not good enough. You must prostrate yourself before the Great Leader, publicly. You must admit your crimes. And then you must make amends."

Amends? What sort of amends? But I didn't ask out loud.

"I will arrange it," he said, "but it won't be easy." New

energy came into his voice. "You must show your loyalty to the Great Leader with actions, not just words."

I dared to gaze up at him. "What sort of actions?"

"You're a military man," he said. "You must have some information on military equipment, supplies, that sort of thing." The ember of his cigarette flamed more brightly. "The Warsaw Pact consumes much of the weapons and material our socialist comrades in the Soviet Union so generously supply. Certainly you can find out what's budgeted for in your next five-year plan. It would help if we knew so we could adjust our own internal production accordingly."

The Soviet Union bleeds its own people to churn out military equipment in a mad attempt to keep up with the massive military-industrial complex of the United States. It also provides tanks and guns and ammunition to the Warsaw Pact countries in Europe and in North Korea. There's competition for the military aid. If North Korea knew how much had been committed to the Warsaw Pact, it would help in their negotiations with the top brass in the Kremlin.

Commissar Oh wanted to turn me into his personal spy.

I stared out the barred window of my cell into the bleak hallway. Impatient guards farther down the corridor shuffled their boots and murmured. I glanced at the half-empty bucket of filth sitting in the corner and wanted to give in immediately to all of Commissar Oh's demands. Instead, I fought the urge. I bargained.

"I want to be paid in dollars," I said.

Oh stared at me from behind the glowing ember of his cigarette.

"There's no pay. You must work out of loyalty to the Great Leader. Otherwise, I could keep you here forever."

"My embassy would find out."

He shrugged. "What could they do?"

"I want money," I said, putting as much stubbornness into my voice as I could. "Then I will work for you."

Commissar Oh lowered his almost-finished cigarette and flicked the burning tip onto the brick floor. It sizzled for a second and flamed out.

"Only after we confirm your information to be genuine," he said. "Then we will pay yen, not dollars."

Japanese currency would be good enough. "Yes," I replied, "but I want some money up front."

"Now?"

"Now."

Commissar Oh barked a laugh. Then his face hardened. "First, before you receive any money, you will prostrate yourself before the Great Leader. You will beg his forgiveness. You will ask him to cleanse you of your foreign ways and enlighten you in the path of his shining leadership. Do you understand?"

I nodded. "I understand."

Commissar Oh swiveled, flourishing his cape as he did so. On the way out the door, he shouted, "Get him cleaned up! I want him in the Great Hall in half an hour!"

I was being washed again.

The difference this time was that the woman doing the scrubbing was cute, and she wore only a bra and panties. After a couple minutes of sponging, I stood up, grabbed a bucket, and started pouring water over myself to wash off the soapy lather. The woman seemed worried and kept pointing for me to lie back down. Instead, I grabbed a towel and dried myself off. I sloshed across the moist floor and swung open a wooden door. A blast of cold air hit me as I stepped outside onto dry tile.

My body ached and I could see bruises on my arms and shoulders and legs. Nothing I couldn't survive.

I wasn't sure exactly where I was. The guards had kept the shackles on while we climbed three flights of stairs. In a holding area that reminded me of a South Korean police station, they unlocked my chains and allowed me to slip back into my Warsaw Pact uniform. Then they shoved me in the back of a quarter-ton truck. I sat huddled on a narrow wooden bench as we turned onto a long boulevard. I inhaled deeply. Fresh air, available even in the center of this country's most densely populated city. Still, I thought I could taste the filthy water in my throat and fought back the urge to vomit.

After a couple of miles, the driver turned off the main road and soon we were winding our way up into the forested hills. I wondered if Hero Kang and Doc Yong would ever figure out where I was. Maybe. But it was up to me to get myself out of this mess and find them. As we continued into the hills, the scene around us changed. In the distance, elegantly carved pagodas stood above walled homes, and behind them lurked hidden ponds, gardens, gingko trees, and crimson dragons guarding wood-carved gateways. Beverly Hills come to Pyongyang. Just reward for the self-sacrificing vanguard of the people's revolution.

Uniformed guards opened an iron gate and we pulled into a long driveway. Unceremoniously, I was yanked out of the truck and ushered downstairs, and for a moment I thought I'd be locked up again. Instead, I was treated to another steam bath.

Commissar Oh had called the building I was in "the Great Hall." It was a vast affair with elegantly carved wooden buildings and gardens and pleasure halls, like an ancient palace preserved as a museum that's not open to the public. Hero Kang had described it to me earlier: the main cadre's rest and recuperation area and the Pyongyang headquarters of the Joy Brigade. I'd ended up where I'd wanted to go all along. Not as an honored guest, but as a supplicant who was under orders to grovel in shame and prostrate himself in front of the Great Leader. And as a spy for Commissar Oh.

But at least I was here.

I didn't know the name of the woman I was supposed to find, or even what she looked like, but there was a password. She'd say it and then I'd respond. Although why I had to verify my identity, I wasn't sure. At the moment, I felt completely conspicuous, as if I were the only round-eyed foreigner in two provinces.

It was beginning to dawn on me that one of the reasons my identity as a Romanian soldier was holding up so well probably had to do with North Korean provincialism. In all the propaganda posters I'd seen so far, American soldiers—while performing various atrocities—were invariably portrayed as blond, blue-eyed, their narrow faces supporting enormous, grotesque proboscises. As a Hispanic male—with black hair and brown eyes and a nose that fit my face—I didn't match that stereotype. So far, this had worked in my favor.

I walked behind a wooden divider and found my clothes, which had been washed and pressed. Although the uniform was still damp, I didn't mind. My body heat would dry it off soon enough.

The half-naked masseuse helped me dress, even squatting in front of me to tie my shoelaces. She was a cute girl, very cute, with straight black hair tied in pigtails and a round, pleasant face. In other circumstances, I probably would've tried to spend more time with her in the steam room. But not now. I was too nervous. And the gaping maw of that dungeon was still fresh in my mind. All I could think of was finishing the job so Hero Kang and I could get the hell out of here and find Doc Yong.

When I was fully dressed, I combed my hair and pulled on my cloth cap and pushed through a pair of double doors that led out into a long gallery. Confused as to which way to go, I glanced back at the girl. She smiled and pointed to her right. I nodded and marched down the hallway.

Varnished wood slats squeaked beneath my feet, interspersed every few yards with wooden pedestals holding celadon vases stuffed with flowers. Oil-papered windows looked out onto well-tended gardens on either side, illuminated by a three-quarter moon and the soft glow of Chinese lanterns. Again I thought how well these party cadres lived. It pays to cozy up to the Great Leader.

Voices murmured up ahead, dozens of them. The hallway wound to the left and back to the right and finally I arrived at an ornate wooden door with large brass handles in the shape of fire-breathing dragons. The voices behind the door were louder now. I took a deep breath and pushed the door open.

It was a vast hall. Most of the space was filled by an elevated floor covered in tatami mats. Sitting behind a short-legged table on a dais were Commissar Oh and four or five political lackeys. All of them wore traditional silk pantaloons and red vests, looking like courtiers from the Chosun Dynasty. The venerable General Yi, Commander of the First Corps, was nowhere to be seen.

In front of the dais were many small tables, only a couple of feet off the floor, and sitting around them cross-legged were dozens of men, all of them young and athletic-looking. Before the tournament, Hero Kang had briefed me about what to expect if I made it this far. This was an awards banquet in honor of various teams—soccer, volleyball, and Taekwondo—that had won tournaments within the last few months. I recognized the athletes of the First Corps Taekwondo team. All of them glared at me. Except for the older men on the dais, everyone wore military uniforms. Each table held a charcoal brazier and sizzling atop it were succulent chunks of beef. The aroma of charred meat filled my nostrils, accompanied by the sharp tang of pickled cabbage and roasting garlic, causing me to salivate. A young woman knelt in front of each brazier, using shears to cut raw meat into edible pieces and chopsticks to flip burning morsels deftly atop the flames. The women were very young and attractive and they all wore the short-skirted uniform of the Korean People's Army.

All eyes were on me. None of them exactly pleased to see me.

I held my breath. With one word from Commissar Oh, these men would rise up and tear me limb from limb. I scanned the room. No Hero Kang. Another thing I noticed: fifth-level black-belt Pak wasn't here either. I hoped the erstwhile First Corps champion hadn't been seriously hurt, but even if he hadn't, the loss of face at being knocked out by a foreigner would be too much for him. It figured that he wouldn't make an appearance.

The young women serving the older dignitaries at the head table were not wearing military uniforms. Instead, they were decked out in the beautiful full-skirted *chima-chogori* traditional Korean gowns. Commissar Oh frowned and motioned with his chopsticks and one of the girls knelt next to him. He whispered something in her ear. She bowed and, keeping her head lowered, backed away respectfully.

All talking stopped. The only sound was of meat sizzling. I stood alone, not knowing what to do, feeling as out of place as a hunchback at a ballet rehearsal. Finally, a soldier appeared at my side, a frail young man, clearly not one of the athletes. He motioned for me to follow. I slipped off my shoes and stepped up onto the raised floor.

Off to the side, balanced on a varnished wooden easel, stood an enormous color photograph of the Great Leader. It was bedecked with sweet-smelling flowers, and red-wrapped gifts and bowls of fat fruit, which sat in front of the photo. The young man led me to a spot about twenty feet in front of this shrine and handed me a yellowed slip of paper filled with ink-smudged hangul.

"*Ilgo*," he said. Read.

He backed away and I turned to the expectant crowd.

Everyone had stopped eating—all eyes were on me. I held the paper in front of me and started reading. An enraged murmur rolled through the crowd. My young guide hustled forward, motioning with both hands downward. I knelt on one knee and he kept motioning. I lowered myself on both knees and then lowered my forehead to the ground. Satisfied, the young man backed up.

How the hell was I supposed to read the script with my head touching the ground? I raised my head a little, just enough so I could hold the note in front of me and still see the photo of the Great Leader. This time, when I started reciting it, there was a respectful silence.

Hangul is a phonetic writing system and I read the note verbatim. Parts of it I didn't understand. Still, the essence of it was that Kim Il-sung is stronger than Superman and kinder than Jesus Christ and the rest of us are less than maggots and all good things emanate from an absolute, unquestioning loyalty to the Great Leader. When I finished reading, the young man motioned for me to bow three times, which I did.

Finally, I was allowed to rise to my feet and back away respectfully from the smiling mug of the shining light of the people.

Although they were sitting flat on the floor in a cross-legged position, all the athletes in the room rose to their feet gracefully and started toward me. I braced myself, prepared to fight to the end. Instead, they started clapping and cheering, and soon I was being patted roughly on the back and punched playfully on the shoulder. One of the beautiful young ladies approached me with a smile and held out a wreath of flowers. I lowered my head and she placed it around my shoulders and bowed to me. Then I was escorted up on the dais where a short-legged table was set up for me.

My chopsticks were made of silver.

I was a hero again.

-7-

Commissar Oh and the young men in the crowd grabbed their chopsticks and started chomping away on marinated beef, pickled vegetables, and fluffy white rice.

The charcoal inside the metal drum suspended from the center of my little table was already glowing. One of the silk-clad ladies appeared and deftly laid slices of *kalbi*, deboned short ribs, on its hot wire grill. In seconds, the fat of the marinated beef was sizzling. She also set down a bowl of rice and three plates filled with turnip, cabbage, and cucumber kimchi. Then she departed. On my own, I used the shears she'd left behind to slice some of the meat and adjusted the slices over the fire with the chopsticks, keeping them out of the flames.

None of the men present knew that Commissar Oh had

locked me in a dungeon and had me tortured. But I knew. And I wasn't about to forget it either. Still, I was famished, and even though I wasn't happy about accepting his hospitality, I was going to eat my fill. It was mid-evening now. I tried to figure out how long I'd been locked up. At least twenty-four hours, I figured, although I couldn't really be sure. I wondered if I had a concussion from the beatings I'd taken or lung damage from the water torture. Probably, but no one had mentioned anything about medical attention and I certainly wasn't going to ask. I felt I was hanging on by my fingernails here, and as long as I was being fed and I wasn't locked up, for the moment, that was good enough.

Now that the foreigner had been shoved in his corner, everyone turned their attention away from me and resumed eating. Martial music burst out of tinny speakers. I figured I'd better eat quickly, because Koreans have a habit of clearing all tables at once, whether you're finished or not, and then beginning speeches or entertainment or whatever delights the evening might hold. I shoved beef, still bloody, into my mouth. I ate all the kimchi and all the rice, but no one appeared at my table to offer me seconds.

I watched Commissar Oh. He ate sparingly and listened intently to the conversation of the men around him. The pleased expression on his face told me that they were flattering him. The same young man who had guided me from the door to this spot appeared next to Commissar Oh. He knelt and whispered into the commissar's ear, and they both glanced at me. I stared back, my face impassive. The commissar turned back to the aide and said something, and the aide bowed and backed away.

I studied the young women who served the athletes. For the most part, they performed their duties in a business-like manner, but occasionally one of the young men said something to them and they looked up and smiled. Wire baskets containing clinking bottles of clear liquid were brought into the hall—soju. Soon the young women were pouring the soju into small shot glasses, holding the bottle with their right hand, supporting their forearm with the flattened palm of their left. The same elegantly dressed woman who'd delivered my food brought me a half-filled bottle of soju and a glass. She left abruptly. I poured it myself. In South Korea, she would have poured it for me. Not doing so was, if not an insult, at least a lack of propriety, but I was in no position to complain. When all glasses were full, Commissar Oh raised his in the air and started to speak.

Some of it I didn't understand because the statement was long and flowery, but it boiled down to this: Foreigners continue to flock to our country to bask in the glow of the teachings of our Great Leader. Even now his wisdom is spreading beyond our shores and all who hear his mighty words quake at his power and the single-minded resolve of his people to use their bodies as weapons to protect his glory and advance the cause of our Great Leader and kick the running-dog Americans out of Korea and reunite our country under his glorious banner.

Or something like that.

When he was done, I drank as heartily and as deeply as anyone, mainly hoping the 40-proof liquor would ease the aches and pains in my tortured body.

More meat was brought in, and more soju, and then a troupe of young women in flowing silk dresses, each a different color, began to dance to a music that was less martial and more traditional. The women swirled their huge skirts and banged on drums. They leaned against each other and sang lilting songs with sweet voices.

While I was watching the show, someone knelt in front of me, keeping her head bowed. A woman in a bright-blue silk dress, not the one who had been serving me previously. She cut my meat, placed some of it carefully on the brazier, and turned it with chopsticks. Then, using two hands, she poured me a shot of soju. After I sipped, she looked up at me.

I held myself steady, attempting not to gasp. Kneeling before me was Senior Captain Rhee Mi-sook.

Up close, she was even more beautiful than she'd seemed at a distance. Lips soft, complexion flawless, black eyes burning. I thought of something I'd read somewhere, about the Mongol Khan's advice when choosing a wife: Her face should be as flat as the grassy plains, her eyes narrow in order to keep out evil spirits, and her legs strong to make her husband happy. Except for the legs, which I couldn't see, Captain Rhee fit the requirements. Back at Eighth Army, some GIs would have found her unattractive. She didn't meet the traditional Western standard of beauty. Her nose wasn't pointed, her eyes weren't round, and she certainly wasn't blonde. She was strictly Asian, through and through, and that's what I found fascinating about her. Her straight black hair was oiled and pulled back and knotted in a bun, held in place by a single red peg.

She said something in a language I didn't understand. Was it Latin-based? It seemed to be. Romanian, I thought. I caught the words that were similar to the Spanish for "where" and "born." The problem was that I had no answer for her. I made something up.

"Moldavia," I said.

This seemed to satisfy her, and, luckily for me, she apparently had reached the limit of her ability to speak Romanian. She switched to English. "Who are you?" she asked. Her voice was sultry, like the voice of a lover tangled in satin sheets.

I gawked at her, trying to concentrate, lost in the beauty of her soft white skin.

She continued speaking quietly, intimately, in English, keeping her head bowed so no one would notice our conversation, appearing to concentrate on turning the meat.

"A Peruvian sailor named José Aracadio Medin," she said, "disappears from an Albanian ship. Then a Warsaw Pact officer turns up on a train unexpectedly, traveling north out of Nampo, but for some reason he doesn't speak Russian. Now that same Romanian officer wins a Taekwondo tournament." With her beautiful black eyes she peered up at me. "Who are you?"

Again, I didn't answer. I knew if she hadn't exposed me already, she wouldn't until she could figure out whether or not powerful people in North Korea were behind me. If she exposed me too early, she took the risk of also exposing the incompetence of her clients, the commander of the Port of Nampo and the security apparatus at the Pyongyang Train Station. And incompetence in North Korea can prove fatal. Mistakes are not tolerated by the Great Leader and are dealt with harshly. Therefore, bad news is suppressed; information flows downhill but never uphill. Senior Captain Rhee's task was to follow me, capture me if possible, question me, and keep everything quiet until she was sure of who, and what, she was dealing with.

"Hero Kang claims you are a hero of the invasion of Prague," she said, staring intently into my eyes, searching for any sign of understanding. "But the Romanians didn't participate in that invasion." She leaned even closer to me. I felt her fresh breath mingling with mine. "You are a liar," she said, pausing for a while to let the insult sink in. When I didn't react, she said, "In this country, everyone lies. It is how we live. But you are after something. What is it?"

Her hand reached out and touched mine. The fingers were soft, long, clinging.

"We are the same, you and I," she said. "You can trust me. Maybe we can do business."

The music ended with a rousing crescendo. The gorgeous young dancing women took a bow and started to back out of the room. Senior Captain Rhee Mi-sook leaned away, pulling her hand back quickly. She looked around. I couldn't help admiring her lovely profile. Her figure was full, and even under the covering of her silk tunic and high-waisted skirt, it was clear that Captain Rhee Mi-sook was all woman.

"I will talk to you later," she said. "Stay away from the women here. Anyone you touch will be cast off and sent to work in the rice fields."

Still, I didn't answer. She couldn't be sure I spoke English. She stood and gave me one last exasperated look. "Do you understand me?" she asked. But it was time for her and all the women to leave. She sighed in frustration and disappeared in a whoosh of swirling silk.

The lights lowered. Somewhere behind us, a movie projector clattered to life. A beam of light found a white screen and then we were feted with sports highlights of recent international events. In each clip, North Koreans competed and were victorious. Not one loss was reported. As the film flickered, the young women started to filter back into the room. However, they were no longer wearing their military uniforms. Now they were wearing skirts and blouses of either pure white or flowery patterned silk. Some of them went straight to a particular table and a particular young man. Other women held back, unsure of where to go, until one of the young men called to her. Then they bowed and scurried forward eagerly, taking a seat next to the man and almost immediately snuggling up next to him. The commissar had disappeared. Soon no one was paying attention to the sporting events on the screen and I realized that there was a lot of heavy breathing going on. Skirts were lifted, blouses opened.

I'd been in brothels before. Plenty of them. Even the worst of them offered a little privacy. But here, none of the young athletes were grabbing some girl by the hand and sneaking off into a back room. They all stayed where they were. It didn't seem natural. But this was North Korea. The bosses wanted to reward these young champions, but they didn't want to offer any of these young people privacy, where they might be able to form an even more intimate relationship, where they might talk about their hopes and dreams, where they might—by some fantastic stretch of the imagination—begin to plot against the Great Leader. I felt very uncomfortable.

And then a young woman appeared by my side. The flickering light of the newsreel fell on a round face and a mouth set in a determined line. She was still wearing a military uniform.

"Even in the harshest of winters," she whispered in Korean, "the *mugunghwa* blooms."

The purple *mugunghwa* is the ancient national flower of Korea. The sturdy blossom springs to life throughout the length and breadth of the Korean peninsula. In recent times, the North Korean regime designated the *mongnan*, a type of magnolia, the new national flower in its place—a move the South Koreans never agreed with.

She waited for my answer.

"Especially, I'm told, on the highest mountains," I whispered back.

She picked up a tray of cold meat and slipped a key in my hand. Without looking back, she carried the tray away through the side door of the hall. Holding it low so no one else could see it, I studied the key. It was large, old-fashioned, apparently made of brass. A number had been etched along its side: 444.

I stared at the key, twisting it in the dim light to make sure I was reading it right. There it was, three Arabic numerals: 444. I was surprised because I'd never before seen such a combination in South Korea. South Korean hotels don't have a fourth floor, or even a room number four, much less a room numbered four forty-four.

Still, there it was. I clutched the key in my hand. Everyone seemed preoccupied. I slipped into the shadows by the wall and edged through the rustling clothes and gasping breaths until I'd made my way out into the empty hallway.

In the moonlit courtyard, I crouched for a moment behind a tall shrub with sturdy branches.

I waited. No one was following. No sign of Captain Rhee Mi-sook. I crept away toward buildings that I hoped would be lodging for the cadres, still wondering about the curious numbers. Still wondering if I'd live through this night.

Four is the number of death.

In Chinese, the character for the number four is pronounced like the "su" in "surreal." In Korean, the same character is pronounced "sa." And in both cases the character for death is pronounced in exactly the same way. That's why hotels in the Far East skip the fourth floor. Some hotels, especially those catering to Westerners, also manage to do without a thirteenth floor, thereby covering superstitions developed on both ends of the Eurasian landmass.

So I wondered at a room numbered 444. Were the North Koreans actively trying to eliminate old superstitions? If so, that was laudable. One of the few laudable things I'd seen this government do since I'd arrived.

The woman who'd handed me the key wasn't after me for my body. In fact, a North Korean woman with any brains would avoid me like a cholera epidemic. Relationships with foreigners are nothing but trouble. Any sign of anything other than complete and utter loyalty to the Kim clan, any allegiance to any foreign power, could result in not only the offending person but also their entire family being sent to the North Korean version of the gulag. Conditions there were so bad that for most people a prison sentence was the equivalent of a death sentence.

So the woman who'd handed me this key had been very brave. It was my job now to find her without exposing her to more danger.

When I was sure no one was watching, I emerged from the shadow of the bush and strolled toward a tile-roofed building on the far side of a gurgling pond. It would be best to avoid people, to stick to the shadows, but not to seem that I was hiding. In case I was caught, I could play the role of the dumb foreigner—a role that every North Korean had been propagandized to accept—and claim that I was lost.

There were no lights on in the building. It was single-story, about twenty yards long. Above the doorway at the end, I searched for some sort of numbering system. Then I saw it, carved into an oblong wooden placard attached to the doorframe: 73. Building number 73. So this key probably belonged to building number 44. I gazed around me. Nothing moved, just dark buildings all about the same size as this one, moonlight glimmering off their tiled roofs. A lot of real estate, I thought, and a lot of well-maintained buildings not being put to good use. The Communist cadres could afford waste like this, while the working people, whom they were supposedly sworn to protect, lived in poorly heated hovels with one family crammed on top of another.

This country truly was paradise, if you had the right connections.

Would they miss me back at the main hall? Probably not for a while. At least not until the newsreels were over and the heavy breathing stopped.

Sticking to the shadows, I continued my search.

Just as I approached the building that I thought was number 44, I heard the whistle. It was low, so low that I couldn't be sure it wasn't only the gentle evening breeze wafting through the rose bushes. So low that I thought I'd imagined the sound and that it was no more than the quivering of my nervous system.

I froze, hidden behind a low rock wall.

There it was again, another low whistle.

Someone was trying to warn me. Of what?

I lowered myself almost flat on the ground, holding myself just off the grass in a push-up position. Carefully, I studied every shadow around me. Nothing. No movement. I rose slowly and slunk toward the entranceway of the building I thought was number 44.

It was unlike the others. In fact, it wasn't a proper building at all, just a grassy hillock with a stone wall on one side, like an ammunition storage facility. But as I approached, the moonlight glinted off stone carvings, faded from years of erosion, and then I saw the carved placard: 44. Building 44, door number 4. This was it. I realized why it had been given the number of death and why it looked so much like an explosives storage facility. It was a tomb. An ancient tomb. The door, however, looked modern, made of iron rather than the hand-carved stone that surrounded it.

The ancient kingdom of Koguryo had many tombs scattered throughout North Korea and what is now Chinese Manchuria. I knew that some of the most famous tombs were located near Pyongyang. This was one of them.

Fingers touched my elbow.

I spun, my eyes wide, ready to fight.

I had to look down to see her face. It was the woman who'd handed me the key. She held a forefinger to her mouth, warning me to be quiet. Then she held out her palm.

After steadying myself and releasing my breath quietly, I placed the key in her hand. She motioned for me to step into the shadow of the mound and then shoved the key into a hole in the iron door. She tried to turn it, but it didn't budge. She glanced back at me inquiringly. I stepped past her and tried the key. It seemed to be catching, but, predictably, the locking mechanism was rusted from disuse. I wished we had some lubricating oil, but we didn't, so I pulled the key out of the lock, licked my fingertips, and rubbed spit along the edge. I placed the key back into the lock and turned. It resisted, but I kept a steady pressure on it, not enough to snap the key but enough to force the stubborn connections to give. Finally, the key groaned and the handle of the door sprung upward. I pulled on the handle and the door creaked open, disturbing soil and grass.

Stale air rushed out, as if grateful to be free. We stared at the stone steps leading down into a black pit.

I still didn't know why I was here or what we were supposed to do. All I knew was that I had to trust this woman. She was my only hope of getting out of here in one piece.

She glanced behind us, then reached into the pocket of her wool jacket and pulled out a small flashlight. She stepped inside the tomb and I followed. Only when I'd pulled the big iron door shut behind us did she switch on the flashlight. At the bottom of a short flight of steps, a long stone hallway led away from the door. She inched forward, walking upright. I had to crouch to keep from knocking my head against low-hanging rock.

Her name was Hye-kyong. She didn't tell me her family name, but I already knew it. Kang. Doc Yong had told me that she was Hero Kang's daughter, something that was best left undiscussed. I spoke Korean to her freely. If she betrayed me, I'd never get out of here alive anyway, but I didn't think she would. Being a member of the Manchurian Battalion, and working with a foreigner like this, she was in as much danger as I was—if not more.

The smooth stone walls of the passageway were covered with frescoes. Ancient hunting scenes: men galloping on horses, letting loose arrows at magnificent horned creatures, dogs running at their side.

We hardly had time to admire them.

"Where are we going?" I asked.

"There are tunnels," she said, "all through this complex. Some lead to the ancient Koguryo tombs, some to bomb shelters. This one leads to the meeting room where Commissar Oh conducts his state security briefings."

"And we're going there why?"

"I want to show you something."

I decided to prod her a little, to get her to open up. The more information I had, the more likely I was to survive. "Are you a member of the Joy Brigade?"

She lowered her head. "That is my shame."

"I thought it was an honor to serve the Great Leader and the cadres who assist him in his great work."

She stopped and swiveled on me. "Do you mock me?"

"No," I said. "I'm just trying to understand."

Her small fists were clenched and her round face was bright red. "I am a proud woman," she said. "My father is a proud man. We believed that I would be serving the Great Leader when I was chosen for this job. And then I discovered our real purpose here."

I waited, afraid to speak. Hero Kang's daughter was about to explode.

In her effort to control herself, her entire body shuddered. "It is *vile!* These things they ask us to do. Always for the glory of the state, always for the good of the loyal comrades who serve the people and the Great Leader. But it's not right! We are women. We have pride. We have pride in ourselves, pride in our bodies, and pride in the husbands and children and families that we someday hope to have. And they ask us to do these *things!*"

And then she was crying, still standing at the position of attention, the tears rolling down her soft cheeks. After a few seconds I stepped toward her, my palm open, ready to pat her on the shoulder. At the last second, she backhanded my forearm away.

"No!" she said. "I don't need your pity. I am a soldier. A comrade of the Manchurian Battalion. Come," she said, pulling herself together, "we have work to do."

Hye-kyong swiveled and marched down the tunnel.

I realized why Hero Kang had risked everything to get me in here. He wanted more than just state secrets. If he was any kind of father, and I believed he was, he'd also want Hye-kyong out of here. But to run away, to defy orders, would be tantamount to bringing a death sentence down upon herself and her family.

We'd have to escape quickly and we'd have to escape together. With the secrets and, if possible, with our lives.

At the end of the tunnel we reached a hatchway, a few feet up from the floor, probably designed for quick escapes. I studied it. No keyhole. Just then, we heard voices. I froze. One of the voices I recognized: Commissar Oh. Hye-kyong patted me on the shoulder reassuringly and then climbed up on a rock shelf that hovered just to the right of the door. She peered into something on the face of the wall, then pulled back and motioned for me to come forward. I did. It was a tiny hole, about half the width of a dime, slanting downward into a room a few feet lower than where we lay. It was a well-appointed room with overhanging fluorescent bulbs and maps and chalkboards mounted on stone walls. In the center was a long mahogany conference table, one end of which I could see clearly. Legs and feet were visible beneath the table, but I couldn't see faces.

"Report!" a man barked. It was Commissar Oh.

Another voice I didn't recognize started droning on with all the verve a detailed government report deserves, listing facts and figures: how many men in a unit, how many men out sick or on leave, a breakdown of artillery pieces and their state of repair. It was difficult for me to follow because many of the Korean-language nomenclatures were unfamiliar. Still, it was clear that they were talking about military hardware.

When the report was finally over, Commissar Oh asked another man if everything would be ready. Of course, he agreed that it would be. Even at Eighth Army, no officer in his right mind ever admits, especially to the boss, that he won't be ready—for anything.

After about a half hour, the meeting was adjourned. We heard feet shuffling and chairs scraping and then someone spent another five minutes tidying up. The door of a safe slammed shut with a reassuring metal clang. Finally the light was switched off and another door slammed. I climbed down off the ledge and squatted next to Hye-kyong.

"We must enter," she said.

"How?" I asked.

"Tomorrow night, I will be serving at a logistical staff meeting." She pounded on the metal hatchway. "When no one is looking, I will open this door from the inside. Then, you will enter."

"What do you mean 'when no one is looking'? Won't they be watching you closely?"

"That is my problem," she said. "Not yours. At the conclusion of the meeting, they will make sure I leave. That is why we need another person—you—to enter through the escape hatch. There is no one else in this place we can trust to take on this job, only you. Once the lights go out, you will enter the conference room."

She briefed me on the information that was needed and the most likely places to find it. "Once you have what we need," she said, "you must escape."

"How?"

"Exit through the ancient tomb and head south toward the main entrance of the First Corps headquarters. There will be signs. Along the way, I will meet you."

"Where will we go from there?"

"All has been prepared. You will bluff your way out. A sedan will be waiting."

A sedan? Only one person could be so bold. Hero Kang. I knew it might be indiscreet, but I couldn't stop myself. We were too close to a resolution now. Decisions had to be made. All our cards had to be on the table. "Your father," I said, "he is Hero Kang."

She stood rigid, glaring up at me, and even in this dim light I could see that her face was red. She spoke slowly, enunciating every word. "You don't talk about that."

I held her eyes. "Will you be escaping with us?" I asked.

"Enough!" she snapped.

But I refused to back down. "He's your father. Regardless of what has happened, he will help you. You have one chance to escape, tomorrow night, and you must take it."

Her face was a bright crimson now. She swiveled and marched down the tunnel toward the entrance. As she did so, she spoke over her shoulder without looking back. "Return now, before you are missed. Tomorrow you will join in athletic training with the others. At night, when food is served, you must feign illness and slip away. Come here. Wait. You have the key!"

-8-

I consider myself to be in fairly good condition. In preparation for this mission, in addition to the intelligence briefings and the Korean-language drills and the survival, escape, and evasion training, I also embarked on a rigorous regime of physical exercise. But that was measuring myself against normal people. People like U.S. Army Green Berets and U.S. Navy Seals. Not North Korean athletes.

East of Pyongyang, dirt roads wound through beautiful rolling hills. The sun rose red and assertive, burning off the morning fog, as if it too had bought into the "long live Kim Il-sung" propaganda. The men running in front of me glanced back and smirked. I was staggering. We must've run three or four miles already, at a blistering pace, almost a sprint. It was impossible for any normal human being to keep this up. But somehow they did.

I remembered what an old NCO had told me about South Korean soldiers: "You can outwalk 'em, but you can't outrun 'em." Maybe it's their diet—or not growing up in the East L.A. smog—but young Korean men seem to have an endless capacity for aerobic exertion.

None of the Korean soldiers had broken rank. They were pulling away from me, inexorably. Finally, the leader barked an order and, like a gigantic centipede, the formation of forty highly trained athletes turned around in the road and came back. The men chanted something as they passed. Two of the taller, stronger men in the front ranks grabbed me by the elbows and started pulling me along at their pace. I stumbled forward, wanting to be let go so I could plop down in a puddle right there in the middle of the road, but their grips were unbreakable. Somehow I kept my legs moving forward, one agonizing lunge at a time.

We rounded a hill. The red sun was at our backs now; we were heading home, to the Joy Brigade. I'd only been there one day, but already I was starting to think of it as home. I'd started as a prisoner being tortured in a dungeon, risen to a partially-accepted participant in a liquor-and-sex orgy, and now I was an athlete in training. Tonight, if everything worked out all right, I'd become a thief.

After morning chow, Commissar Oh called me into his office.

An officious young woman stood next to him, wearing

a cloth cap with a red star that was pulled so far down on her head that it looked like a helmet. Apparently he'd found an interpreter. He spoke Korean to her; she spoke Romanian to me. I understood the Korean much better than the Romanian—which I understood not at all—but I let the charade play out.

"Your embassy will be missing you," he said.

"Tomorrow," I told him in Korean, ignoring the interpreter, "I must return to work."

"When you return to your embassy," he said, "we will expect results quickly."

I kept my face impassive.

"Charges have been prepared," he continued, "concerning your underhanded assault on First Corps champion Pak. If we file them, you will not leave Korea."

I waited for the interpreter to finish her translation and then nodded.

"Don't think of escaping on a Russian or Warsaw Pact flight," he told me. "We inspect them all."

I nodded again. "My first payment," I said. "When will I receive it?"

Commissar Oh placed a cigarette in his ivory holder, lit it, and inhaled with an air of self-satisfaction. When he let the smoke out, he said, "When you make your first report, you will receive money."

"Yen," I said.

He nodded. "Yen."

"When can I leave?" I asked.

"Not until this evening. Arrangements are being made. Until then, you are our guest."

Some guest. I'd never worked so hard in my life. Later

that morning, I was scheduled for Taekwondo practice, and if I lived through that—which was by no means certain—I'd be participating in a soccer match that afternoon.

As I rose to leave, the interpreter said something to me in Romanian. None of the words seemed familiar, nothing like Spanish. This was a test, of that I was certain. Both the interpreter and Commissar Oh stared at me. Waiting. If I'd learned anything from Hero Kang, I'd learned that when you're about to get caught red-handed, there's only one thing to do. Get angry. Get very angry.

I strode toward Commissar Oh's desk and leaned forward, looking down at him and the tiny interpreter.

"I want *money!*" I said in Korean. "A lot of it. Not a lot of lies. Not a lot of your silly nonsense." Then I pointed at him, tapping my forefinger on his chest. "Do you understand?"

Somewhere, there must've been a silent alarm. Four armed guards burst into the room. They grabbed me and we started jostling. When they finally pulled me a few feet from the desk, Commissar Oh waved them off. He puffed furiously on his cigarette. It smelled of something vaguely familiar, maybe cherry wood, not the foul-smelling Korean tobacco I was used to.

"You will be paid according to your work," he said. "And only after we see what you bring us."

I shrugged the hands off me, straightened my Warsaw Pact tunic, and stormed out of Commissar Oh's office.

Later, I thought about what the interpreter had said. I kept running the words over in my mind, comparing them to Spanish or English or the little bit of Latin I'd studied in school. And then I figured it out. "Who are you really?"

Even the interpreter knew I was a fraud.

I managed to survive the Taekwondo workout. Apparently the word had gone out: I was working for Commissar Oh now and I was to be left alone. That was fine with me. As I stood on the sidelines, stretching and occasionally hitting the heavy bag, I watched the real experts go at it, one on one. I was glad no one ordered me to spar with them. In the afternoon we chose sides and were treated to a two-hour game of soccer. After about five minutes, the Koreans realized that I was hopelessly inept at a game that I'd never played before and they let me stand on the sidelines and pretend that I was interested in the outcome.

Finally, the workday was over. As I showered I wondered if the interpreter had worked up the nerve to tell Commissar Oh she didn't believe I was in fact Romanian. Of course, telling him that would be tantamount to explaining to him that he was an idiot. Somehow, I didn't believe she'd bother him with such impudent information. Still, doubts about me must have been growing. After all, they played soccer in Romania, didn't they? No one would believe it was a game I had played as a child. I was much too hopeless at it. And Senior Captain Rhee Mi-sook had more than just doubts about me. She was certain that I was not who I claimed to be. How long until Commissar Oh picked up on all this? Probably not long.

What was keeping me afloat, I suspected, was the good work of the Manchurian Battalion. Obviously, they had a mole in the Romanian Embassy, someone who had confirmed to the highest levels of the North Korean government that a certain Captain Enescu was indeed a member of their embassy and working in their employ. That, coupled with the manic level of mutual suspicion that pervaded the Joy Brigade, made it possible for me to survive. No one was willing to compare notes; no one was willing to express an honest opinion; no one was willing to admit that they—or, more importantly, their boss—might be wrong. Welcome to the efficient functioning of the worker's paradise.

During evening chow, I wolfed down all the food I could hold, because who knew when I'd be able to eat again. When the lights dimmed and the propaganda newsreels flickered to life, I slipped out once again into the moonlit gloom of the garden. After making sure no one was following, I made my way quickly through the maze of monuments and manicured lawns.

As I neared my destination, I rounded an artificial pond and crouched behind a stone edifice I hadn't previously paid much attention to. It was about eight feet high, thick at the base and tapering to a point, and there appeared to be carvings along the side. I rubbed my hand over the etched lines, but in the pale moonlight I couldn't make out any design. Erosion had faded the original inscription into an indecipherable jumble. Amid the tufts of grass at the bottom, a few bits of intricately wrapped paper and some polished stones were hidden. Gifts, I supposed, left by the people who worked nearby; gifts to this ancient monolith and to the primitive gods who predated not only the regime of the Great Leader but also the medieval kings buried nearby. I left the sacred edifice and slipped down-hill toward the iron door of the Koguryo tomb.

On the way, I found a heavy branch from one of the nearby trees and carried it with me. The locking mechanism in the front door of the tomb had been loosened now and was relatively easy to open. I slipped into the darkness. Instead of closing the door all the way, I propped it slightly open with the branch, just enough so it wouldn't lock behind me. That way, if I had to make a quick exit, I wouldn't have to fiddle with the key. I suspended the branch two or three inches above the ground, so I'd know if anyone entered behind me and dislodged it. When I was happy with my little warning signal, I stepped into the gloom.

Without a flashlight or candle, I felt my way down the steps, touching ancient stone with my fingertips. A rotten odor filled my nostrils. Rodents squeaked in front of me and tiny paws scurried away. Something flapped its wings. I waved whatever it was away from my face. On my left, the darkness seemed thicker somehow and the air was full of the musty reek of fur.

Finally, like a friendly beacon, I found the dime-sized beam of light emanating from the wall next to the iron escape hatch. I peered inside. The room was empty and only one solitary yellow bulb glowed. I squatted down on the cold stone steps, hugging myself, beginning to shiver. I waited.

I awoke with a start.

I'd been dozing on the steps, my forearms resting on my knees. Even as I stood, I could feel my muscles and joints complaining about the ridiculous workout I'd been subjected to earlier. Come what may, I was glad I wouldn't have to go through all that tomorrow.

Ahead of me, the hatchway moved, groaning. Light flooded the tunnel. I grabbed the edge of the iron door and peered inside.

Kang Hye-kyong looked like a sculpted hero in her People's Army uniform, all the lines of her wool skirt and wool tunic pressed, her square face stern, like her father's. She touched a forefinger to her pursed lips.

"They will be coming soon," she said. "I will leave this unlatched, but you must not enter until I call you, not under any circumstances, no matter what happens. Do you understand?"

I nodded.

Footsteps pounded on the far side of the room. Hye-kyong glanced back and reached for the inner handle of the door, pulling it shut. Or almost shut. She left it open just enough so the metal latch wouldn't catch. When the time came, I'd be able to pull it open.

I returned to the dime-sized peephole and peered in. Doors opened and voices murmured, one of them Hye-kyong's. I imagined her bowing and helping the various officials with their coats and hats. Then brown shoes appeared beneath the conference table. Something tinkled. Glassware. Cups, maybe. Hye-kyong was serving tea.

Eventually, a deep-voiced man cleared his throat and the meeting started. I tried to keep up with what was being said, but most of the reports consisted of long lists of supplies and numbers and logistical timelines. It was clear this was a working meeting of men responsible for the day-to-day operations of the First Army Corps, one of the most important military organizations in the North Korean People's Army. It was responsible for protecting the capital city of Pyongyang and therefore also the life of the Great Leader and his heir apparent, Kim Jong-il, the Dear Leader.

Finally, my ears perked up. One of the First Corps armored brigades would be moving out. Tomorrow. There was much discussion of the other brigades that would be responsible for taking over defensive positions along the perimeter of the city that would be left unguarded after their departure. There was also talk of tanks and artillery pieces and infantry units, and discussions about the fuel required to move all that equipment south toward the Demilitarized Zone. The most efficient route was discussed. The roads leading directly to the DMZ were ruled fairly good, but the road leading to the Kwangju Mountain Range was in sore need of repair. Maintenance had been neglected because the Manchurian Battalion, guarding the eastern portion of the DMZ, was notorious for being self-sufficient; therefore, over the years, the scarce resources had been diverted to other units.

It was decided that the Red Star Brigade, which was the First Corps brigade chosen for this mission, would not take a direct route to the Kwangju Mountains. Instead, they would head first toward Hamhung, the largest port city on the Eastern Sea, mimicking what would happen if an enemy invasion force broke through with an amphibious landing and reinforcements were needed. Paper crinkled. Maps were being spread atop the conference table. Eventually it was decided that before reaching the outskirts of Hamhung, the Red Star Brigade would turn south and make their way at top speed toward the Kwangju Mountains.

The roads, one of the officers complained, were miserable in these areas. These were practical men who weren't worried about propaganda considerations or saving face for the regime. They called it like it was, at least here in the confines of this secret meeting. Since the roads were so bad, it was decided that various units of the Red Star Brigade would split up and take different routes. That way, if one part of the brigade were blocked by landslides or heavy snowfall, the rest would still reach its destination. Once they reached a town called Beikyang, they would regroup and start their climb over the ridge of the highest peak in the area, Mount O-song, and commence their final assault on the Manchurian Battalion.

Or at least that's what I thought they said. This type of detailed information would prove invaluable to a military unit fighting in defense, but if I were wrong about the particulars, it could lead to disaster. The entire conversation taxed the very limits of my Korean-language abilities and I cursed myself for not studying harder. So much was at stake.

There was more discussion of the strength of the Manchurian Battalion, how many men they had, what their fighting capability was, how many artillery pieces and how many armored vehicles. It turned out that the battalion was virtually all infantry. They had a few dozen old Russian artillery pieces, but those were on tracks, dug into the sides of mountains, and pointing across the DMZ toward South Korea. They could not be turned around and used against an assault force attacking from the rear.

"Will they fight?" one of the generals asked.

"Of course not," Commissar Oh responded. "Once we drop leaflets explaining that they are being decommissioned and replaced by the Red Star Brigade, they will lay down their arms. After all, it is the will of the Great Leader."

A gravelly voice I hadn't heard before spoke up. "Is Bandit Lee dead?"

"No," Commissar Oh replied. "He is still the commander of the Manchurian Battalion."

"If Bandit Lee is alive," the voice said, "then the Manchurian Battalion will fight. He will never turn over his command to anyone other than the Great Leader himself."

A long silence ensued. As honest and practical as this group might be, no one was willing to venture an opinion on what the Great Leader should or shouldn't do. They had their orders. But the implication was clear: If the Great Leader commanded this expedition himself, Bandit Lee wouldn't oppose him and lives would be saved. If the silence in the room was any indication, the Great Leader had no such plans.

More paperwork was shuffled, more tea was served, and finally, after haggling over the amount of petroleum reserves that would be issued to the Red Star Brigade, the meeting was adjourned. Footsteps pounded on a stone floor, glassware was removed. An overhead fluorescent light was turned off and only the single yellow bulb remained.

There were still two people in the room. They spoke softly to each other and I turned my ear to the opening, trying to pick out voices. Commissar Oh and Hye-kyong. She seemed to be protesting something, saying no, and then the edge of the table shuddered. The entire conference table had been shifted about a foot. She kept saying no and I heard a couple of slaps, hand to face. The table lurched again. Something heavy landed atop it. Now I could just see the black boots of Commissar Oh. Hye-kyong's brown loafers lifted a couple of inches off the ground. Her hands clung to the far edge of the conference table. He was working behind her, shoving her forward roughly at first and then in a steady, rhythmic way. Hye-kyong was still protesting, whimpering like a little girl being punished for something she didn't do.

I stood up and stepped toward the iron hatchway. Just as my fingertips touched the cold metal, I stopped. Hye-kyong had warned me. No matter what happened, don't enter until she told me to enter. She'd known Commissar Oh was going to do this to her. Probably it had happened before, many times, and if I entered now and punched Commissar Oh's lights out, I'd ruin everything.

Still, it was torture standing here. Just as it had been torture watching all these poor, confused people praising the very criminals who were abusing them. I wanted to barge in there and catch the arrogant protector of the working class with his pants down and put my size-twelve boot firmly up his ass. But how many people would die—including me and Hye-kyong—if I gave in to that temptation? I stayed my hand, still gripping the metal handle of the hatchway. My fingers trembled.

I stayed like that for what seemed a long time. Finally, I squatted down, burying my face in my hands and feeling the sweat on my forehead. At length, the iron hatch squeaked open.

"*Bali,*" a voice said. Hurry.

I stepped inside the room. Hye-kyong pulled the hatchway shut and locked it. No sign of Commissar Oh. The conference table still sat at an angle. Hye-kyong motioned for me to help her straighten it out.

Her face was red, her clothes disheveled, and the hair that had earlier shone like a black helmet was now sticking out in sweat-matted disarray, like an exploding nova. The worst part was that she wouldn't look at me. She kept her eyes staring firmly at the ground. Without looking up, she pointed to a wooden stand with flat panels. I pulled one of the panels out. It held a map.

"Here," she said. "Find the location of the Red Star Brigade. Make a note of it. And then study the routes they will travel to Hamhung and up into the Kwangju Mountains. Pay particular attention to the supply points along the way. But leave the maps undisturbed. They must not know what we are planning."

"What are we planning?"

"Never mind now. Just take down the information. Do you have paper and a pencil?"

"No."

She pulled a small notepad and a short pencil out of her front pocket and handed them to me. "We don't have much time," she said. "You will have to keep your notes brief and memorize as much as you can. Can you do that?"

"I'll try."

"Memorization would be better," she said. "That way, if you're captured . . ." She let her voice trail off.

As I studied the maps, Hye-kyong held a candle aloft. The Red Star Brigade would be traveling the main road from

Pyongyang to Hamhung. The crucial information was what military intelligence calls "the order of battle." That was the strength and capabilities of the component units of the Red Star Brigade and the routes they would be taking once they left Hamhung and headed up into the Kwangju Mountains. I jotted down the unit designations and the names of the towns and villages along the routes. Also, most importantly, how much military equipment each unit had—tanks, artillery pieces, armored personnel carriers—and how many infantry platoons to back them up.

"Hurry," Hye-kyong said. "The regular staff will be back soon."

I made the list as short as possible, using symbols and numbers mainly and relying on memory tricks they'd taught me at Eighth Army. I used words from English, Spanish, and Korean to form pictures that would stick in my mind. For example, the regrouping area for the final assault on the Kwangju Mountains was the village known as Beikyang. One of the meanings of *beik* in Korean is white, and *yang* can mean goat. So I imagined a white goat with the point of a flaming red star slamming into its butt. Try to forget that.

Hye-kyong all the while had been fidgeting behind me. Finally, she said, "Do you have it?"

I nodded and handed the pencil back to her. "Why didn't you just give the information to your father yourself?"

"I can't leave," she replied. "Ever. Once someone becomes a member of the Joy Brigade, we are watched constantly. It's only you, a foreigner, who can come and go."

"Why don't you come with me now?" I asked. "Escape?"

"I must stay," she said, shaking her head vehemently. "No time for all that now. Come."

She opened the escape hatch for me, gesturing out into the dark tunnel.

"A car will be coming for you," she whispered. "This evening. We had our man in the Romanian Embassy raise a fuss, and finally Commissar Oh has consented to let you go a few hours early. You will be picked up in less than a half hour in front of the First Corps headquarters. You must not delay for any reason. Leave as soon as you are able."

I nodded and started to climb through the hatch. Hye-kyong grabbed my arm.

"You won't tell anyone about what you saw?"

I touched her hand. "Don't worry."

"If something goes wrong," she continued, "you must use the same tactics my father uses. Act totally unafraid. If anyone questions you in any way, become enraged. Remember, you are a foreigner. Foreigners have to be handled very carefully because your superiors might be in close contact with the men who work for the Great Leader himself. If you are insulted or become angry, who knows what kind of lightning might strike the person who opposes you? The best protection is to act completely unafraid."

She knew her father well.

After I climbed into the tunnel, Hye-kyong slammed the escape hatch with a loud clang. Touching the wall with my left hand, I stepped carefully through the darkness. Occasionally, puffs of air from invisible wings hit my face. After climbing stone steps for what seemed a long time,

I finally reached the main door. From the crack I'd left propped open for myself, a glimmer of starlight greeted me. I knelt and studied the branch. It lay flush on the floor, no longer elevated two inches off the ground. I stood, looking around in the darkness.

Someone had entered the tomb.

Were they behind me? I didn't think so. If they were, they obviously weren't using light. Most likely, rather than venture into the tomb, they'd backed out and were waiting for me outside. Who were they? Commissar Oh's men? Or maybe Senior Captain Rhee Mi-sook's fixers? Either way, I couldn't afford to be taken now, so close to escape. Was there another way out of this tunnel? The bats and the rodents managed to survive down here; there must be another way out. In fact, there might be a network of caves connecting one ancient tomb to another, and Hye-kyong had mentioned bomb shelters. But I didn't have time to explore. The car would be waiting outside for me. I had to get there, somehow. Barging out of this door and trying to fight my way to safety with just a wooden club wasn't going to work. And then I had an idea.

Bats.

I knelt and carefully pulled open the door of the tomb just far enough to free the wooden branch. Hooking the crooked tree limb to the edge of the door, I slowly pulled the door open and let it swing free, backing away quickly into the darkness. By the time the door was fully open, I was crouched around a bend in the tunnel, out of sight.

I listened. Nothing. Even though a car would be waiting for me soon to transport me out of this hell, I had to force myself to be patient. Five minutes later, maybe ten, footsteps sounded on the stone walkway. Men in boots, two of them. As they cautiously entered the tomb, I backed even further into the darkness. Their footsteps seemed to speed up, as if they'd heard me.

After a few yards, I reached the darkest place, the place that smelled of musty fur, swathing myself in blackness so thick I could almost hear it breathe. A beam of light flashed around the corner. I waited a few more seconds, and then, when the men were almost on me, I lifted the wooden branch and started beating it against the roof of the tunnel. Tiny soft things pelted my arms and my legs and then the air was full of dust and fluttering and an eerie squeal filled the night. Bats. Millions of them. Like an enormous cloud, they soared toward the light. Keeping low to the ground, I started to run back toward the open door of the tomb. Ahead, I heard a man scream and fire a shot blindly into the darkness. I crouched reflexively but kept moving. And then I was on them, ramming my body into one of the men, slapping the wooden branch against the head of the other. An AK-47 clattered to the ground but I didn't stop for it. I couldn't. I was being shoved toward the open door by the swarm.

When I reached the big wooden door, I grabbed the edge, turned, and slammed it shut. I pulled the key from my pocket, jammed it home, and twisted until it locked.

Inside, furry bodies pelted the door. The bats that had escaped continued to swarm, swirling around me, then flew off toward the promise of juicy insects at the limpid ponds nearby.

I hurried up the walkway, wiping filth off my face, straightening my tunic. When I rounded a corner, she was standing there. Alone. Waiting for me. From her hand, a pistol was pointed right at my gut. She was beautiful in her high boots and long leather coat cinched at the waist. Her white face was luminescent, like the moon glimmering above, but grim and determined. I was defenseless against her, but I didn't allow myself to think of that.

Instead, I kept walking.

There comes a moment when you have to decide whether to live or to die. You have to decide whether it's better to raise your hands in surrender and enter a world of interrogation and torture—a world so full of pain that soon even death would seem preferable—or to take a stand and die.

I decided to die.

I kept walking, straight into the pistol pointed at me. I'd had enough. Enough of running and hiding and lying and living with constant physical agony and the unrelenting tension of thinking that every breath might be my last. I was finished. I'd done all I could do. If she pulled the trigger, it would be over quickly. There'd be no lingering minutes and hours and days and weeks of unbearable pain. It would just be done. I marched toward Senior Captain Rhee Mi-sook resolutely, staring right into her eyes, daring her to pull the trigger. In the glow of moonlight, she stared back impassively. Did I see a tightening in the arm holding the pistol, or was it my imagination? I kept waiting for the hot steel to rip into my stomach, for the jolt to knock me backward, but nothing happened. I was less than two strides away—it was now or never. I took one more step and reached out, viciously slapping the pistol out of her hand. It bounced on the stone steps.

And then I grabbed her.

She clawed at my eyes.

A man should never hit a woman. And I never have. I believe it to be cowardly, and the many men I've known who slapped their girlfriends or wives around were always—without exception—cowards. When faced with someone who can fight back, a man of equal strength and determination, they'd rather negotiate than fight. But when they're alone with a woman—or worse yet, with children—they're tough guys.

So I don't like fighting a woman. But Senior Captain Rhee Mi-sook left me no choice. Now that her pistol was gone, she leaped at me like a cornered Siberian tigress.

She hadn't shot me, I believed, because a dead Warsaw Pact officer would have been hard to explain. She'd have been the one on the defensive—the one put on trial. And no matter how convinced she was that I was not who I appeared to be, could she be 100 percent sure? What if she were wrong? It wasn't worth it to pull the trigger and find herself sent off to die in a North Korean gulag. So she hesitated, and that hesitation saved my life. But she wasn't hesitating now.

I dodged her sharp nails just in time, grabbing her wrists and twisting, but she responded in exactly the way a person of less weight and inferior upper body strength should respond. She became dead weight. She fell to the ground, yanking me down with her, and when she landed she started kicking me with her high-heeled boots. Off balance, I managed to avoid a vicious kick aimed at my groin, but it missed only by inches, slamming into my inner thigh. I cursed and stepped aside, still holding onto her wrists. I dragged her along the pathway, twisting her arms behind her torso and forcing her to flip over, and then rammed my knee down on her spine. She screeched and spit and I hoped to God no one could hear us out here. But she wasn't yelling for help. There was a rage in her, a viciousness I'd seen in few people—men or women— and I believed that she wanted only to win. Finally, pinning down her squirming body, I managed to loosen her leather belt. At the stone monolith, I pulled her into a sitting position and belted her arms securely around the stone. Quickly, I pulled off her boots and ripped off her socks, shoving one into her mouth. She almost managed to bite off one of my fingers. Luckily, I pulled my hand back in time. Before she could spit out the sock, I pulled off the other sock and used it as a gag, tying it securely at the back of her head.

Now she was helpless.

Her long black hair was in disarray, some of it mushrooming out of her gag, some of it hanging loosely in front of her face. I knelt and stared directly into her eyes. Hatred looked back at me.

In Korean, I said, "When you're angry, you're beautiful."

Her entire body jerked forward, but the bindings held. I touched my forefinger to the brim of my cap and saluted. Then I stood, turned my back on Senior Captain Rhee Misook, and hurried off through the still, deserted grounds.

The soldier at the First Corps headquarters checkpoint stood at attention. His eyes were wide—he didn't see many foreigners. I marched toward him, glowering, fists swinging at my side. The smooth flesh of his face quivered with indecision.

All armies are the same. After beating unquestioning obedience into their soldiers, they still expect them to make informed independent judgments. Usually, it doesn't work. I made my face even fiercer as I approached the guard. Finally, when I was only a few feet from him, he raised his right hand in salute. Smartly, I saluted back and strode past.

He didn't move and I didn't look back.

A complex of cement buildings stretched before me— the First Corps headquarters. I entered a side door and walked down a long hallway. Even at this late hour, there were signs of human activity.

I was in a fairly busy area now. The hallway was lined with offices with names that I didn't fully understand but that contained words such as "logisticals" and "security" and "explosive ordnance." Most of the people working here, both men and women, wore military uniforms and looked haggard, as if they'd been working many extra hours. Remembering Hye-kyong's admonition, I marched down the center of the hallway as if the whole world would soon bow to my will. When I reached the main entranceway, I stepped through two double wooden doors and stood at a semicircular driveway that was the drop-off point in front of the First Corps headquarters.

Two soldiers eyed me nervously. "Where's my car?" I barked.

They looked befuddled. I stood with my feet planted broadly in the center of the entranceway, hands on my hips, staring about impatiently for a car that I could only pray actually existed.

After what seemed like eons, an engine rumbled in the distance. As the car approached, I recognized it immediately. The same old Russian sedan Hero Kang had used to bring me here in the first place. White gloves gripped the wheel. Could it be Doc Yong? But my hopes were dashed—it wasn't a woman at the wheel, it wasn't even a chauffeur. It was Hero Kang. He was driving the sedan himself. In a country where human labor is dirt cheap, why did he drive himself? Probably, I thought, because he didn't trust anyone else.

The sedan pulled up to the front of the First Corps headquarters. A small flag of the DPRK fluttered in front. The armed guards saluted.

I pulled open the passenger door with a great feeling of relief and was about to climb in when I realized Hero Kang had shoved the sedan into park and switched off the engine.

"Where is she?" he asked. When I didn't answer, he said, "Where is my daughter, Hye-kyong?"

"I don't know," I said.

"But you saw her earlier this evening."

"Yes."

"Has he been at her again?"

"What do you mean?"

"You know what I mean."

Ashamed, I turned away.

Hero Kang's face flamed bright red. He climbed out of the car, shouting, "Wait here!"

And then he was running up stone steps, ignoring the salutes of the armed guards, storming through the front door of the First Corps headquarters. I waited for a second but knew I couldn't just stand there. I ran after him.

I followed him down a corridor that was new to me. At the end, a door was open. It led into the darkness of the surrounding gardens. After a few yards, hanging paper lanterns guided me along a winding flagstone walkway.

The thirty-foot bronze statue of the Great Leader was the most well-lit part of the grounds. Beyond, I spotted Hero Kang's hunched back, moving purposefully to the far side of the garden. Ahead, a group of men had paused in front of a fountain surrounded by hanging red lanterns. They looked back at Hero Kang. One of the men I recognized. Commissar Oh. The other men were military officers and I could only surmise that they were the men who'd been in the meeting below ground in the secure area. Apparently, they'd waited upstairs while Commissar Oh had finished his assignation with Hye-kyong.

Hero Kang never slowed his pace. He marched right up to Commissar Oh and did exactly what I would've loved to do. He punched him right in the snout. The commissar reeled backward. The other men protested, reaching their hands out to stop Hero Kang, but nothing short of a Mack truck could've slowed him down. He leaned over Commissar Oh, who had now retreated to the edge of the fountain, and punched the hapless apparatchik again. Kicking him, Hero Kang started screaming that Commissar Oh was the worst son of a bitch who'd ever defiled the uniform of the people's revolution.

Then Hero Kang grabbed Commissar Oh's throat, squeezed, and shoved the red-veined face into the scum-laced water of the fountain.

I suppose I shouldn't have been surprised. It was illicit sex with his daughter that Hero Kang and Commissar Oh were discussing at the moment. A one-way conversation, to be sure, since Hero Kang's massive paw was wrapped firmly around Commissar Oh's scrawny throat. The commissar's half-burnt cigarette floated in green slime, and his face was beginning to turn purple.

The other men flitted around Hero Kang, like bear cubs pawing at a grizzly.

Every now and then, he swung a fist backward, warning them off.

I thought of the car back at the entranceway, of our getaway, but if Hero Kang murdered Commissar Oh, I didn't see how escape would be possible. I stepped forward and grabbed his shoulders.

"Let's go," I said in Korean. "Leave him. We must go."

He didn't hear me.

The ambient light from the hanging red lanterns rippled on the water of the fountain. About six inches below the surface, Commissar Oh's eyeballs were as wide and round as a frog's. In seconds he'd be dead. If I punched Hero Kang, I could maybe stop this, but then what? Hero Kang was my only lifeline. My only chance of escaping from this place and my only chance of staying alive. As I pondered what to do, a figure launched from the shadows. Hye-kyong. She rammed into the back of Hero Kang, knocking him over, forcing him to release his grip.

"Abboji," she said. Father. "We must go."

When she received no response, she reached down and grabbed him by the lapels of his tunic. "The car," she said. "Now. You must go. And take him," she said, motioning toward me. "Now, Father. Now!"

Hero Kang seemed stunned, confused by what he'd just done. "What about him?" He glanced down at the spitting and coughing Commissar Oh.

I realized that the other men, the commissar's lackeys, had disappeared. Sensing more trouble than they ever wanted to be involved with, they'd all faded discreetly into the night. We were alone.

"You've ruined everything!" Hye-kyong screamed. "I was to stay here, monitor their plans. Now that's not possible. First, you go! I will follow." When Hero Kang hesitated, she said, "I will take care of him. Leave him to me."

Befuddled, Hero Kang seemed to agree. "You must come," he said.

"Yes," Hye-kyong agreed. "This changes everything. Go to the car. I will follow. Go now."

She turned her father around and shoved him hard. Like an enormous child, Hero Kang stumbled down the walkway, returning toward the entrance of the First Corps headquarters. I glanced at Hye-kyong. She motioned for me to follow her father.

As I hurried along the flagstone walkway, I glanced backward. Hye-kyong had lifted Commissar Oh slightly out of the water. She slapped him. Hard. The noise reverberated through the deserted garden.

Hero Kang and I wound through shrubs. When I looked back again, Hye-kyong was leaning over the edge of the fountain, facing down, like a woman at a stream churning laundry. As if she were soaking soiled rags, expunging them of filth. She stood like that for what seemed a long time.

-9-

Although, just moments before, the corridors of the First Corps office complex had been teeming with life, now they were deserted. Word must've spread like fire in a rice granary: trouble in the headquarters. People of great power were fighting, flinging lightning bolts like gods on Mount Olympus, and mere mortals had to flee for their lives.

Hero Kang's footsteps pounded down the tile hallway. I kept looking back, hoping that Hye-kyong would appear. She didn't. In front of the headquarters, the black sedan sat undisturbed. The guards had disappeared, except for one who crouched in his open-windowed shack. Hero Kang clambered behind the wheel of the sedan and started the engine. I opened the passenger side door but hesitated.

"Where is she?" he asked.

"Not here yet," I replied.

Hero Kang gunned the engine impatiently.

He was just about to reenter the building when footsteps clattered down the long corridor. Hye-kyong appeared, hopping down the stone steps, the sleeves of her uniform sopping wet, tears running down her cheeks. There was no time to talk. I opened the back door and she dove in. I climbed into the passenger seat and then we were off with a great lurching and grinding of gears.

There wasn't much internal security in North Korea, not of the type we're used to in the modern world. Not the type that responds to emergencies if someone is hurt or feels threatened, or the type that stands guard at the front gate of a government building. At first I wondered why. Gradually it dawned on me that the small trappings of security in the West were mainly there to protect people: the government worker from a terrorist attack, the average citizen from assault by a burglar, the middle-aged man from the threat of a heart attack. Those things weren't deemed necessary in the People's Republic. The entire country, in a very real sense, was a prison. Everyone was assigned a workplace or a place of study, and once the prisoners were securely locked away—and spies were in place to make sure they didn't plot against the Great Leader—they were otherwise ignored.

Hero Kang rolled onto the wide expanse of the central road leading past the Great Monument to the Victory of the People Against Foreign Imperialists. The statue of striving workers and farmers and soldiers holding up hammers and sickles and Kalashnikov rifles was as brightly lit as the red carpet at a Hollywood premiere, but the street was deserted. We zipped past, no one commenting on the waste of electricity.

Hye-kyong cried softly in the backseat. Hero Kang gripped the wooden steering wheel as if he were trying to strangle it.

"Where are we going?" I asked.

Although it was cold inside the car, sweat poured down Hero Kang's big forehead.

"Which brigade is it?" he asked. At first I didn't understand the question, so he repeated it. "Which brigade has been assigned to attack the Manchurian Battalion?"

"The Red Star Brigade," I said.

He grinned. "I thought so. That son-of-a-bitch Yim has been chosen to betray his own people. A good man for it."

I remembered the name in the material I'd reviewed in the secure briefing room: Brigadier General Yim On-pong, Commander of the Red Star Brigade. "You know him?"

"I know him. The bastard would sell his own daughter if it would earn him a promotion."

And then Hero Kang realized his poor choice of words. I turned. Tears flowed down Hye-kyong's face. We drove in silence. I watched Hero Kang's tortured features, listened to Hye-kyong's sniffling, and faced forward to watch the road for signs of trouble.

At dawn we ran out of gas.

As we had rolled through the countryside, there had been no roadblocks. Hero Kang explained to me that they wouldn't bother. Word would just be sent out from

Pyongyang to the commanders in the field and the provincial police forces to keep an eye out for us and arrest us on the spot. They would wait for us to fall into their net. He went on to verify what I'd already surmised: A rapid response force, standing by armed and ready to do someone's bidding, was not an institution that the Great Leader trusted. Armed men sitting around with nothing to do would inevitably turn their thoughts to sedition. Besides, nothing was a true emergency in the Democratic People's Republic of Korea—except, of course, a threat to the Great Leader. Everything else could wait.

Hero Kang and I climbed out of the sedan and pushed while Hye-kyong—now admirably recovered from last night's trauma—steered the car into the central road of a small farming commune. Although the sun was just coming up, work teams had already marched far out into the fields, carrying hoes and rakes balanced on their shoulders. Doors remained shut. Not only did no one come out to greet us, no one so much as peeked out a window.

"They're frightened," Hero Kang said. "Of such a big car. Of men in uniform."

"And of a foreigner," I said.

"Especially of that."

Past the main buildings of the commune, the dirt road veered right and ran sharply downhill. Hero Kang and I stepped back and Hye-kyong steered around a bend into a narrow valley that held an old straw-thatched animal pen, except there were no animals inside. Momentum carried her halfway into the front entrance, and when we caught up, Hero Kang and I pushed her all the way inside the pen. After Hye-kyong climbed out of the car, we grabbed pitchforks and tossed straw over the black sedan until it was mostly covered.

"You planned this," I said.

Hero Kang's eyes widened. "Of course. Everything's been planned."

I paused for a moment, studying his face. He was happy tossing the straw over the car, happy having something definite to do.

"You didn't plan to attack Commissar Oh," I said.

Hero Kang tossed his pitchfork into a pile of straw. "No. That came upon me suddenly." He pulled a ring of keys out of his pocket and shuffled through them until he found the correct one, which he used to pop open the trunk of the old Russian sedan. Inside sat a wooden crate, next to it a crow bar. He pried the crate open and pulled out the equipment inside.

My breath caught involuntarily. I recognized it from my training. A Soviet-made RPG, a rocket-propelled grenade with a high explosive projectile.

"What are we going to use that for?" I asked.

Hero Kang grinned, hoisting the weapon to his shoulder. "To stop the Red Star Brigade," he said.

Hye-kyong reached inside the trunk and pulled out two canvas satchels. One she strapped over her shoulder, the other she handed to me. It was heavy. Additional projectiles. Then she took the keys out of her father's hand, relocked the trunk, and finished covering the car with straw.

Five minutes later, we were marching along a narrow dirt path through a pear orchard.

We spent the night in the open, shivering and squatting next to one another for warmth. Before dawn, we were up and walking again.

"We must stay on the ridgelines," Hero Kang told me. "Away from the cultivated valleys. Unfortunately, the Red Star Brigade is stationed the farthest away from Pyong-yang. In about thirty *li* we should be there."

Thirty *li*, or about fifteen miles.

By midafternoon we lay atop a hill looking down on a military compound, which was surrounded by a wooden fence topped with concertina wire. A few trucks and armored vehicles were lined up near sheds, as if awaiting maintenance. Still, there wasn't as much activity as I would've expected for a unit preparing to move out within hours, heading toward the eastern coast of the Korean peninsula.

"They haven't received their petroleum yet," Hero Kang told me.

Hye-kyong said, "Do you remember the part of the briefing about fuel requirements?"

"Yes," I said. "That was the most boring part. Very precise calculations of how many kilometers per liter each type of vehicle could receive; how many kilometers to Hamhung; how many kilometers from there, by the various routes, to Beikyang. And then calculations on how many more kilometers it would be up the slopes of Mount O-song."

"They want to issue just enough diesel fuel," she replied, "to allow the Red Star Brigade to reach a refueling point outside Hamhung."

"The shortage of fuel is that great?" I asked.

During my briefings in Seoul, I'd been told that the

Soviet Union was generous in providing the North Korean military with petroleum products.

"It's not a shortage," Hero Kang told me. "It's part of the method of control. The Great Leader keeps each military commander on the shortest of leashes as far as how much ammunition he is provided and how much fuel he is allowed to move his unit throughout the country. He doesn't want any commander getting any ideas about overthrowing the government."

"As an additional precaution," Hye-kyong chimed in, "their families, including their wives and children, are housed in Pyongyang, supposedly for the better schooling and more luxurious lifestyle. But actually they're held as hostages so the commander doesn't get out of line."

"In Yim's case," Hero Kang added, "they even keep his mistress in Pyongyang."

Hye-kyong turned her face as if stung.

Once again, Hero Kang realized his mistake. He clenched the binoculars he held in his hand so tightly I thought they might bust. Abruptly, he shoved them back up to his eyes and studied the compound below.

After a few minutes, in a timorous voice, Hye-kyong said, "The diesel fuel delivery will come through that pass. We must attack them there."

"Us?" I asked.

Hye-kyong nodded. "Since the Red Star Brigade is under orders to move out in the morning, the delivery will be made tonight."

"No earlier than absolutely needed," I said.

She nodded again, somberly.

We crawled back down the hill.

▪ ▪ ▪

Hye-kyong found apples.

We feasted on a ridge overlooking the narrow pass through a series of hills leading to the valley that was home to the Red Star Brigade. In the fields below, farmers worked, but none of them looked up our way. Even if they had, we were hidden behind clumps of wild shrubbery. I sat on a rock.

Gingerly, I removed the brown low quarters that were standard issue for Warsaw Pact military officers. They were made of thick leather, not very pliable, and stitched together with wire-like thread. My feet were red and tender and most of the flesh on the Achilles tendon had been scraped raw. The backs of my socks were stained with blood. I used a little precious water from our one canteen to wet them and wring them out before slipping them back on my aching feet. Then I put the shoes back on, leaving them unlaced so they wouldn't hurt so much.

After devouring a third apple, I tossed the core away and waited for Hero Kang to resume his briefing. The plan was that he would fire the RPG at the second fuel tanker in the convoy. Then he would fire the other two rockets we had at the fourth and the sixth tankers. Hopefully they'd be clumped close enough together that some of the other fuel-laden vehicles would join in the conflagration.

"Won't they attack us?" I asked. "Won't the guards assault this hill?"

"There won't be guards," Hye-kyong said. "Only party minders to make sure that no one stops and sells fuel along the way."

"But the drivers," I said. "They'll be armed."

"Yes," Hero Kang replied. "They'll be armed."

I shook my head at the lack of convoy security. In South Korea, the U.S. Army MPs spend much of their time escorting valuable cargoes around the country. But with the population here in North Korea being so tightly controlled, the Communist regime seemed unconcerned about hijacking.

"Surely they must be worried about us," I said. "And after an armed assault on a fuel convoy, they'll finally send forces after us, won't they?"

Hero Kang stared off into the valley below. "Yes. They will. But like I told you before, since the moment you set foot in this country, everything has been carefully planned."

"Good. I appreciate that. But all of this you could've done on your own. Why do you need me?"

"You have the most important part of this mission," Hye-kyong said.

I turned to her. "What is it?"

"The tunnel," Hye-kyong said.

I sat back, surprised. "You know about the tunnel. What do you know about it?"

"You must help the Manchurian Battalion to survive," Hye-kyong said. "You're an American. Only you can do that."

"Enough," Hero Kang said. "When the time comes, you will be briefed."

Darkness had fallen three hours ago. I had spent much of that time sweeping away the pebbles on the hard ground beneath me and rolling from side to side, trying in vain to get comfortable. My wool Warsaw Pact uniform wasn't doing much to keep out the cold.

My teeth felt gummy, my beard itched, and when I lifted my arms, a blast of fetid air assaulted my nostrils. How I longed for a hot shower, a shave, and a warm bed with crisp white sheets. Not to mention a bowl of hot oatmeal to fill my stomach. So much for dreams.

In the distance, a low groan turned into a roar. Engines.

Hero Kang lay next to me behind a pile of rocks we'd set up as our gun position. He hoisted the RPG onto his shoulder. My job was to hand him the next rocket after he'd fired the first one, help him reload, and then prepare the third and final one for launching. Hye-kyong, against my protestations, had taken a position at the base of the hill. Neither she nor Hero Kang would tell me what she was planning to do.

In the distance, the first set of headlights appeared. More followed. The convoy rumbled toward us. I scanned the shrubbery behind us and the valley below, expecting at any moment to spot a squad of light infantry.

When the trucks were about two hundred yards below us, Hero Kang carefully sighted the rocket launcher. I held my breath. He waited for what seemed a terribly long time, until I thought he had lost his nerve and the convoy would pass beneath us unmolested. For the briefest of seconds, I was relieved that on this night we wouldn't be firing this rocket, or blowing up fuel trucks, or killing innocent drivers. And then the night exploded.

Searing air blasted my face as the rocket whooshed off into the night. The darkness was illuminated by the explosion, and we felt the heat from our position on the hill. Someone was shouting at me, calling for the next round. I regained my senses and lifted the rocket into the hot weapon. I found the groove in the metal casing and clicked it sharply into place. Hero Kang fired again. This time I was ready, and without thinking I shoved the final round into place.

The night was ablaze.

"Let's go!" Hero Kang tossed the equipment aside. As I rose to my knees, I spotted a figure dart from the rocks and head toward the first blazing truck. Hye-kyong. She reached an open door on the passenger side and grabbed a man by the arm, yanking him to the ground. When he landed, she knelt over him and seemed to be loosening something. After dragging him farther from the inferno, she started back toward our position. She was halfway up the hill when they opened fire. She screamed.

Hero Kang darted forward, and I followed.

The sound of automatic gunfire was constant. Flames leapt from blistering paint. As Hero Kang had hoped, one or two additional trucks caught fire. Still, there were maybe a half-dozen fuel tankers that were untouched. Their drivers had the presence of mind to back them away from those that were engulfed in flame. The lead truck had darted forward and was already well down the road, heading for the Red Star Brigade compound.

When we reached Hye-kyong, I could see that her leg was shattered.

"Here," she said, handing me an AK-47. That's what she'd risked her life for. More gunfire was headed our way. We crouched behind the rocks.

"Help me," Hero Kang said.

He was trying to hoist Hye-kyong onto his shoulders. But she was in so much pain that it wasn't easy to do without hurting her. As I grabbed her hips, she screamed. I lifted her onto her father's back. In seconds, Hero Kang was running up the hill, sprinting from boulder to boulder like a pirate absconding with a bag of gold. The sharp crack of small-arms fire landed all about us. I crouched low and followed, a few yards between us, the AK-47 slung over my shoulder.

Hero Kang and Hye-kyong had almost reached the top of the hill when the lethal round slammed home. Kang collapsed, sliding back down the hill. On all fours, I scrambled toward him, grabbed his arms and pulled. Using all the strength I had, I managed to drag them over the crest of the hill and behind the safety of our rock barricade.

"Where?" he asked. "Where am I hit?"

I checked. The blood was gushing out of his stomach. I ripped off my cap and pressed it against the wound.

"There?" Kang said, laughing. "Not good. How's Hye-kyong?"

I examined her. She was alert but grimacing in pain. "She will recover," I said. "Only hit in the knee."

Hero Kang nodded. "Okay," he said, using the English word. "Here's the rest of your mission. You must reach the Manchurian Battalion on the side of the O-song Mountain. Do you know how to get there?"

"I have a general idea."

"Get there," he said. "And then they're going to have a job for you to do, having to do with the tunnels of the wild man. Do you understand?"

"I understand."

"It is vitally important. You must convince the Americans to reinforce the Manchurian Battalion. That's the only way they'll survive the onslaught coming their way. We need you to go south, through the tunnels, and bring help. You're the only one who can do it and it must be done. Do you understand?"

"I understand."

I didn't really. I didn't see how it would work. The Eighth United States Army was much too cautious to commit to such a plan, a plan that might embroil the entire Far East in another Korean War, but now, while he was bleeding, was not the time to tell this to Hero Kang.

"Good," he said. "Go now. Leave us."

"I can't leave you."

"You *must*. Think! What's the alternative?"

He was right. They were both badly in need of medical care. In fact, even if every effort were made to immediately transport Hero Kang to a hospital, it was doubtful he'd survive that vicious round to the stomach. Even now the blood was spurting out from between my fingers. Hyekyong would live, unless she bled to death in the interim. While I thought about what Hero Kang was telling me, I whipped off my belt and tied a tourniquet around her leg. The bleeding slowed.

I heard shouts down below. The soldiers were regrouping, preparing to assault the hill.

"No time," Hero Kang said. "You must go. Take the rifle with you."

"I can't," I said.

"You *must*," he repeated, grimacing as he spoke, the pain becoming too much.

And then I was crying, so profusely I was blinded by tears. The emotion that overcame me was nameless. It seemed to include everything—everything I'd ever thought and everything I'd ever felt and everything I'd ever heard or suffered or longed for in my entire life. All of it coalescing right now, right here, with these two brave, doomed people who'd chosen to live, if only for a moment, as free souls. People who were now choosing to die as heroes.

A hand touched my face. Hye-kyong. "Find the village of Neibyol," she told me. "It is east of here, not far. Wait there. A man called Moon Chaser will contact you."

"Moon Chaser?"

"Yes. He is waiting for you. He will guide you to the Manchurian Battalion."

"How will I find him?"

"He will hear of this." She nodded toward the mayhem below. "And he will be watching for you. Do not approach the village directly. Wait on the outskirts. Word will spread soon enough."

I hesitated, looking at the two of them. With a retching cough, Hero Kang spat up blood.

Hye-kyong struggled to a sitting position. She cradled her father's head in her arms. "Go," she said.

I grabbed the rifle and popped off a few rounds at the drivers below. They scattered. Then I handed it to her, wrapping her fingers around the cold metal.

"I won't need this," I said.

Below us, on the side of the hill, gravel spattered against stone. Voices cursed.

"They're coming," Hero Kang said.

I knelt before them. I kissed Hye-kyong's forehead and then kissed Hero Kang's hand. Then I rose and strode away. In seconds, I was running, gravel scattering under my feet. Before I crossed the valley, gunshots sputtered across the hill. A fiery conversation ensued. Finally, after a half-dozen exchanges, all was quiet.

Perspiration covered my body as I jogged along pathways separating night-shrouded rice paddies. Ahead loomed another ridge, illuminated by a three-quarter moon. Beyond that, in the invisible distance, the Kwangju Mountains brooded, sheltering Mount O-song, the home of the Manchurian Battalion.

-10-

A dirty-faced boy startled me awake. He stared down at me, his mouth partially open, narrow eyes impassive. His bamboo-thin body was clad only in a flimsy tunic and loose pantaloons, more like rags than clothes.

"*Koma-yah*," I said, "*mul isso?*" Boy, do you have water?

The boy turned his head slowly and pointed. "*Choggi-isso.*" Over there.

"*Katchi ka*," I said. Let's go together.

Last night, I'd found refuge in this small shed that must've once been used to house an ox. All valuable farm animals, of course, had long since been confiscated by the collectives. However, individual livestock pens like this one, high up in the hills on the fringes of arable land, still stood. This was the third shed I'd slept in in as many nights.

Strangely, the boy wasn't afraid of me. He reached toward my beard and grinned.

"*Halabboji dok-katte.*" Just like a grandfather.

"*Nei,*" I said, rubbing the rough stubble. "*Halabboji pissut hei.*" Yes. The same as a grandfather.

From a rusty pump, the boy poured me water in a dented metal pan. I drank it down. Then I asked him, "*Pap isso?*" Do you have food?

"*Jom kanman,*" the boy said. Just a moment. He ran off.

I estimated his age, at first glance, to be about eight or nine, but with malnutrition rampant in these mountains, he could've been two or three years older. If he brought me something to eat, that would be good, but if he brought adults, I'd have to flee. I squatted next to the drafty walls of the animal pen and squinted out into the overcast daylight. I'd slept late. It had to be an hour past dawn. I should've found a better hiding place before the sun came up, but the night before I'd been making good time through the hill country and hadn't wanted to stop until I stumbled into this splintered refuge. I wasn't sure how far I was from the Kwangju Mountains. When the boy returned, alone, I asked him.

"Forty *li,*" he told me, pointing toward the east. He said there was a bus that ran from the village to the town of Sokdei. I could take that.

"*Tone oopso,*" I told him. I don't have any money.

His mouth fell open. "But you are a foreigner."

"Some foreigners," I explained, "don't have money."

While he chewed on that amazing thought, I chewed on the *ddok* he had brought me. A thick, glutinous cylinder of rubberized rice powder. Awful stuff. In South Korea,

I'd often turned my nose up at it. Here, after three days of eating only the occasional rotten turnip or wilted cabbage leaves, it tasted like four courses at a five-star restaurant. In seconds it was gone. The boy brought me more water.

As I drank, he asked, "Are you a soldier?"

"Yes," I said, although I wasn't going to tell him in which army.

"And you're going to the Kwangju Mountains."

I nodded.

"Why don't you ride in a truck?"

"Not all soldiers ride in trucks."

"Yes they do. They all do. I saw them, between here and Sokdei. Maybe five trucks."

"Where were they going?"

"Many places. Each truck went in a different direction."

They were setting up a line, I thought, between me and the mountains. How much did the North Koreans know of my mission? How important did they think I was? Important enough, anyway, to send five truckloads of infantry. In the last three days, I'd searched in vain for the village Hye-kyong had told me about, the village called Neibyol. I decided to risk asking this boy.

"It's over there," he told me, pointing. "To the south. On the other side of that mountain."

Sokdei, where the boy had seen the soldiers, was to the east. It made sense for me to travel south toward Neibyol. Still, my strength was fading and it would only be a matter of time until the soldiers closed in on me. Now was the time to take a chance.

"Have you ever heard of someone called Moon Chaser?"

"Moon Chaser?" The boy's eyes opened wide. "You know him?"

"We've never met," I said.

The boy started shaking his head. "My mom never does business with the Moon Chaser. She loves the Great Leader. She would never do such a thing. The Great Leader provides everything for us."

The boy was nervous now, stepping away from me.

"What's your name?" I asked.

He shook his head. Then he turned and ran.

I moved out, heading south.

A red sun cast long shadows by the time I reached Neibyol. It was the most unprepossessing cluster of shacks I'd seen during my entire three-day sojourn in these hills. The buildings were made of rotted wood, some of the planks knocked loose; the thatched roofs had turned rust brown and looked as if the bundled straw hadn't been replaced in years.

I was well hidden in a stone grotto, with escape routes both ways, because I was worried that the boy had alerted someone to my presence. But even if the army knew about me, they would have trouble navigating their way through these hills. The countryside looked as if it hadn't changed since the Chosun Dynasty. The massive roads and trains and canals leading into and out of the capital city of Pyongyang were not to be found here. There was little arable land in North Korea, so all the big agricultural communes were located in the Taedong River valley, to the northeast. Neither were there any mining activities that I'd seen. I knew from my briefings that massive amounts of copper, zinc, lead, and iron ore were found in North Korea, but those deposits were located in Hamgyong Province, far to the north. These hinterlands, between Pyongyang and the DMZ, were like a land that time forgot. Soldiers in trucks would have a lot of ground to cover and poor roads to do it on, which would be good for me. My goal was to reach the Manchurian Battalion somewhere on the slopes of Mount O-song. If I kept moving, I had a chance.

A white fluffy dog, a common breed in Korea, was chained to a stake outside a hovel on the edge of Neibyol. Smoke rose from metal tubes that jutted out of a few of the homes. At a stream less than a mile away, women squatted, hammering laundry with sticks. I contemplated knocking on a door, startling the homeowner, and asking for Moon Chaser. The odds of anyone here owning a phone and being able to notify the authorities were slim to zero. Still, I decided to remain hidden, to observe. Food was on my mind. Inside one small fence, earthenware kimchi pots were half buried in the ground. I could lift the lid, rip off the cheesecloth covering, and shovel handfuls of the fiery-hot fermented cabbage into my mouth. Just the thought caused saliva to form at the edge of my dry tongue. But I wasn't a thief. There must be a better way.

A door slid open. An old woman in a baggy skirt and tunic stepped off a wooden porch, carrying a pan that she placed in front of the dog. The dog wagged its tail gratefully and immediately stuck his snout into what looked like rice gruel. The woman left the dog and puttered around in a small garden. Nothing was growing at this time of year, but still she squatted through the rows, pulling out weeds where she found them.

Her hair was gray, her face covered with liver spots. Certainly, she'd been an adult two decades ago during the Korean War. The experiences she'd lived through, I could only imagine. I decided to take a chance on her. I rose from my hiding place and walked slowly into the village. As I approached, she looked up and I greeted her.

"*Anyonghaseiyo, halmonni?*" I said. Are you at peace, grandmother?

To my surprise, she didn't seem shocked at the sudden appearance of a foreigner. The wrinkles on her face deepened as she smiled.

"*Anyonghaseiyo,*" she replied.

She seemed delighted to see me. There probably wasn't a lot to do in this sleepy village of Neibyol. Even a filthy foreigner emerging suddenly from the hills was a welcome diversion. I apologized for my appearance and told her that I'd been traveling and asked her if she had any rice gruel she could spare.

Still smiling, she nodded and told me she had. Placing both hands on her knees, she rose stiffly and walked with her back bent into the house. Two minutes later, she returned with a pan that looked very much like the one she'd given the dog. I bowed and thanked her and squatted near her porch, shoveling the delicious rice gruel laced with what I believed to be turnip greens into my mouth with the pair of chopsticks she'd furnished. When I was finished, I bowed and handed the pan back to her, using both hands, as was the custom.

She was still smiling. "You're very hungry," she said.

I nodded, wiping my mouth.

"Where are you going?" she asked.

"I'm searching for someone."

"Who?"

I decided to risk it. "Moon Chaser," I said.

Her expression didn't change.

"Are you a Soviet?" she asked.

"Romanian," I replied.

The word apparently meant nothing to her. "Why are you alone?"

"I got lost. Moon Chaser will help me return to my unit."

She nodded at that. "Do you know what Moon Chaser does?"

"No," I replied. "Not exactly."

"He's a capitalist," she said. "He exploits the people, sucks their blood. And worst of all, he doesn't follow the precepts of our Great Leader." Her face broke into an even broader grin and she was cackling madly, as if at some great joke. "A capitalist," she said, slapping her knee with the mirth of the statement. "A *capitalist*." She was almost choking on her laughter now. "Can you imagine those idiots? Here they almost starve us to death, work us to the bone, steal our sons to spend their lives in the army, and then they tell us to beware of *capitalists*. Capitalists who would exploit our labor. Capitalists like that skinny idiot, Moon Chaser!"

She was beside herself with laughter now. I was grinning too, keeping up with her.

"And what has Moon Chaser ever done," she asked me, "except maybe make a little extra money for his mother and his grandmother? Except maybe build a new grave-stone for his father. 'Exploit the workers.' *Bah!*"

Then she glanced around, realizing she'd said too much. She turned back to me. "Are you going to turn me in?"

I shook my head. "I am a simple soldier. I only want to talk to Moon Chaser."

She squinted at me, suspicious for the first time. "Why do you speak Korean?"

I shrugged. "Practice."

"You are a soldier," she said, "but not so simple." She studied me pensively, her mind reaching back in time. "During the war, I saw many foreign soldiers. They all looked like you. Dirty, dark beards, filthy clothes. But to us they looked like princes. They had food. They had medicine. At night, when there was no fighting, they'd sometimes set up tents and fire up diesel-fuel heaters. They lived like kings."

She was staring off into space, conjuring up ghosts.

"The Great Leader wants us to hate them," she continued. "I suppose I should—two of my brothers were killed in the war—but I can't bring myself to hate them. They were just doing what their leaders forced them to do. Like us. Always under the thumb of the emperor."

In all my time in North Korea, no one—not even Hero Kang—had spoken so boldly.

"You are very brave, grandmother," I said.

She cackled. "What are they going to do? Shoot me? I'm old. They'd be curing the ache in my bones. Still, I don't normally talk like this. Not to these nosey old bid-dies here in this village. But you are a foreigner. No one listens to a foreigner. I can say whatever I like."

"What kind of man is Moon Chaser?"

"Smart," she replied immediately. "Despite what the people around here say. He does business. He survives. He takes care of his mother and his grandmother. Isn't that what a son is supposed to do?"

"I thought you said he was an idiot."

"An idiot to take the risks he does. But smart to get away with them."

"How can I find him?"

She glanced around the village. "They're all out working now. Go hide somewhere. When I see him, I'll tell him to go to you."

"Where should I hide?"

The old woman thought. "Are you afraid of ghosts?"

"Ghosts? No."

"Good. Just ignore them. They won't harm you. You're a foreigner. Wait at the grave mounds, on that hill over there. Stay well hidden. I'll send Moon Chaser to you."

Before I left, she handed me a few rubbery lengths of *ddok*. I bowed and thanked her gratefully.

It must've been nine or ten p.m when the army trucks pulled into Neibyol. I lay flat on a grass-studded grave mound, my *ddok* long since eaten, wondering when—or if—Moon Chaser would show up. There were two trucks, Soviet-made, judging by the triangular shape of their engine compartments. Had the old grandmother betrayed me, or was this just part of their regular search pattern? Actually, it didn't make much difference. Either way, the smart move was for me to canvass the area. Still,

I waited. I wanted to find out as much as I could about this patrol.

Shadows leapt off the backs of the trucks, about a dozen from each. They fanned out toward the flickering candlelight from the straw-thatched hovels. Voices were raised in fright and in protest. More voices shouted them down. Soon the entire village had been searched and people were lined up to be questioned. My eyes were well adjusted to the moonlight by now, but only by listening to the quavering tone of children's voices could I imagine the tears on their faces. And then one woman was screaming. The soldiers were taking something valuable from her, an heirloom of some sort. The gruff voice of the officer in charge accused her of harboring contraband and hoarding wealth against the will of the people. She screamed that the heirloom belonged to her grandmother, but she was smacked down, and except for her whimpering, the village became deathly quiet. Using lanterns confiscated from the villagers, the soldiers started searching the outlying barns.

I contemplated trying to steal a truck. My feet were raw and the soles of my shoes were about to fall off. I wasn't sure how much longer I'd be able to march through these mountains. In the end, I decided that letting them know that I was here would be the worst thing I could do. Reluctantly, I backed away from the grave mounds, leaving the ghosts behind, disappointed that I hadn't been able to make contact with the man called Moon Chaser.

When the sun rose ahead of me, I was still walking. No matter how painful each step was, it was better than stopping and allowing the cold to seep into my bones. There was little frost on the ground, so I figured the temperature was just above freezing, but that didn't mean that my teeth weren't chattering. It seemed that my upper and lower jaw had been clacking together for eons.

Following the contours of the terrain, I traveled as close to the top of the ridgelines as I could. In the valley below, I glimpsed the occasional pair of headlamps during the night, moving east, as if the soldiers searching for me anticipated that I would continue my march toward the Kwangju Mountains. Or did those headlamps have nothing to do with me? I couldn't be sure, but I had to assume they did.

Before the sun burnt off the morning mist, I found a spot amongst a clump of rocks that provided some shelter from the wind. Storm clouds rolled in, dark and enshrouding. I prayed that they wouldn't do what I knew they were going to do. But they did. The clouds opened up and as the first splats of rain hit me on the forehead, I searched for shelter. There was nowhere to hide. The best I could do was huddle with my back against a large boulder, arms crossed, legs pulled up. In minutes I was sopping wet and shivering more than ever. No need to stay hidden behind rocks now; the overcast sky would protect me from prying eyes. I rose to my feet and continued walking, rain pouring off my hatless head. I thought of Hero Kang and how my soft cap had stanched his stomach wound and how he'd died a true hero. And I thought of his daughter, Hyekyong, and the way she'd gone down fighting like the heroine she truly was.

They were the smart ones. I was still alive, suffering through this. Like an idiot.

By the time night was about to fall, I'd reached such a state of exhaustion that it was like being in a coma and swimming through a sea of pain. I stumbled down muddy ravines and back up again until somehow I reached a rocky precipice enveloped in mist. The rain had stopped but the valley below was stuffed with clouds. I glanced up and that's when I saw it, clinging on the ledge of a plateau—an old wooden pagoda. A few broken tiles lay at my feet. Stone steps led up to the holy place. At the side of the cliff, I began to climb. The stone was slippery and there were few handholds, but by not looking down I managed to reach the plateau before the last of the sunlight had faded. With clouds floating across the sky, the world was intermittently enveloped in pitch darkness. Still, I managed to grope my way to the old wooden building and step up on wooden flooring. I slid back a rotted door. From what I could see in the little starlight that seeped in, the place seemed to be deserted. I flopped down on the floor, my back pressed against a wall, and collapsed into sleep.

Later, in the middle of the night, the shriek of a banshee startled me awake.

When I was a kid growing up in East L.A., there was much talk of ghosts. The old Mexican neighborhoods seemed to be crawling with *brujas*, old Indian women steeped in the lore of the ancients, who scared away the gangs of young toughs by threatening to cast spells on them. Although the fledgling criminals laughed off such threats, they studiously avoided the *brujas*. They had no fear of the Los

Angeles Police Department, with its square-jawed officers and wooden cudgels. But witches, that was something
else.

Still, I never bought into any of these superstitions.
Moving from foster home to foster home taught me that
reality, not supernatural forces, was what I had to worry
about. I studied hard in school, finding the logical worlds
of science and mathematics to be a refuge from the chaos
that surrounded me. My science textbooks taught me that
the *brujas* were charlatans. That's what I believed then.
That's what I believe now.

Still, when I sat up, cold and wet and hungry, in that
abandoned Buddhist temple in the hills of North Korea,
for that moment, and that moment only, I was a believer.
If anyone could have seen me in that dark pagoda, I'm
sure they would have noticed my filthy hair standing on
end.

The screech was unearthly, like an old crone's scream
of terrible pain. And then I saw her eyes, huge and green
and gleaming, fixed right on me. I'm not sure if I yelled,
but I was aware of a massive amount of air suddenly being
expelled from my lungs. The eyes lunged straight toward
me.

I dodged, raising my arms, and then I felt the warmth
of the creature and its feathery caress. I was scooting backward, sliding against the wall, willing myself away from
whatever insane creature of the night had launched this
attack. The wings swooped low and became black clouds
before me. Finally, they settled high up on a rafter and, as
if by magic, melted into a lantern shape. The green eyes
were staring at me again.

I straightened up, breathing very fast now.

It was perched on the old wooden rafter above me. An owl. Not a ghost, not a witch, not a creature from hell. Just an owl.

A long, low "*Whoooo*" sounded from the valley below.

Sweating, keeping an eye on the owl, I rose to my knees and peered out the open window. The sound floated up again. "*Whoooo.*"

That wasn't a bird.

Keeping low, I left the pagoda, slithered off the edge of the wooden porch, and moved to the edge of the cliff. Cautiously, I peered down into the valley and saw the silhouette of a man, out in the open. He raised his hands to his mouth and the sound floated upward again. "*Whoooo.*"

There were no trucks behind him. No other movement. He appeared to be alone.

He crouched, as if he'd heard something coming up the dirt road behind him, and melted into the night. There appeared to be some sort of pack tied to his back.

I continued to stare at the spot he'd been standing in, wondering if I was imagining things. And then I heard the sound I dreaded even more than the screech of a banshee: a heavy diesel engine coming up the hill.

The headlights appeared around a curve in the distance below. They disappeared suddenly and reappeared again. A large truck, probably military, was making its way uphill along a winding road. Soon, assuming the road was open, they would arrive here. I broke off a branch from a shrub and used it to sweep the gravel beneath my feet, hoping to eliminate any sign of footprints. Then I returned to the pagoda and did the same thing in there, raising dust as

I did so. The owl kept a wary eye on me and flapped its wings. When I had done my best, I hopped out the back of the old building and climbed straight uphill for twenty minutes, until I stood on a rocky promontory. The clouds had pulled back and the moon had risen. Enough light shone down on the valley for me to see the roof of the old pagoda and the canvas-covered truck chugging its way toward the open gravel area in front. I crouched and watched.

Soon the truck stopped in front of the old building, right where the man had stood. Soldiers hopped out, cursing and switching on electric torches. I'd seen enough. Carefully, I started to climb down the far side of the mountain.

I was halfway down when someone grabbed me.

I stared into a bearded Korean face, slathered in sweat. His lips were pulled back, white teeth revealed, and the man said, "*Whoooo!*" He was laughing.

After a few seconds, when I realized he wasn't going to cut my throat, I was laughing too.

Moon Chaser was a merchant. *Changsa-gun* was the term he used, a purveyor of business. People who dabbled in business had never been high on the social scale in Korea. Confucius classified people into four ranks: scholars, farmers, craftsmen, and, lowest of all, merchants. So in the Chosun Dynasty, people who sold things door-to-door didn't get much respect, no matter how much money they made. Today, under the Communist dictatorship of the Great Leader, the stigma was worse. The *changsa-gun* were classified as criminals, exploiters of the people, and, more importantly, dangerous men who lived free and independent lives, disdainful of the largess of the Great Leader. Still, Moon Chaser was proud of his status.

"Nobody tells me what to do," he told me, jabbing his thumb into his chest. "I make my own money and earn my own rice."

"Why aren't you arrested?" I asked.

"Corruption," he replied. "The cops are on the take. It's like paying taxes. I have to give them something, 'a gift' they call it, every time they catch me. Then they let me go, after popping me upside the head a few times with their batons. The bastards."

But there was no bitterness in the Moon Chaser's voice. He was simply describing the world as he saw it. He led me quickly downhill, away from the soldiers searching the pagoda. We crossed a narrow valley where we were soon hidden by an orchard of apple trees. Moon Chaser moved fast, as if he knew exactly where he was going, and I struggled to keep up, occasionally having to duck to avoid being conked by a low-hanging branch. A heavy wooden A-frame dangled from Moon Chaser's back. He moved so surely through the woods, over and around shrubbery, that the long-legged carrying rack seemed to be part of his body. Finally, we waded through a narrow stream and then climbed atop a grave mound overlooking a bend in the waterway. He sat down and told me to rest.

"What about the soldiers?" I asked.

"They won't come this far," he replied. "They're tired and hungry and cold. Just like us."

It was still dark, but by the dim moonlight I could tell

he was a youngish man, probably not yet thirty. He cultivated his beard in a fringe around the edges of his face, probably to make himself look older. He wore soiled white pantaloons and a white tunic, but they seemed to be made of a sturdy material. His canvas shoes were rubber-soled and I longed for something as comfortable.

The sole of my left shoe was flapping now as I walked, like the lolling tongue of an exhausted dog. I flipped it open and stared at the raw toes beneath.

"Go wash in the stream," he told me. "It's cold but you'll feel better. When you finish, I'll have a razor and some soap ready for you."

Although I was exhausted, I did as Moon Chaser said. I stripped at the edge of the stream, splashed freezing water all over my body, and then vigorously washed my face. Moon Chaser tossed a knotted hand towel to me. After drying off, I put my clothes on and squatted by the edge of the stream, shaving with the straight razor and soap he provided.

When I returned to the grave mound, he had set up his wooden A-frame. A canvas pack was tied securely to its crossbeam. The two long legs of the A-frame had been propped upright by his walking staff, forming a man-high tripod. From out of the pack, Moon Chaser pulled some food. More *ddok*, because it was so portable, and one tube of *kimpap*, seaweed-wrapped rice enveloping a string of pickled turnip. I devoured it all, ravenously.

When I was finished, Moon Chaser rose to his feet. "Come on," he said. "We have to make more distance before sunrise."

Wearily, I stood up. Moon Chaser grabbed his staff

and slipped his arms through the harness of the A-frame. Bending at the knees, he hoisted the heavy load, balancing it expertly on his back. Two hours later, the sun was starting to rise and I was about to pass out on my feet. Moon Chaser let me rest. He rested also, standing with the long legs of his A-frame touching the ground. After what seemed like only a few minutes, he roused me and made me follow him up into shrub-covered hills.

"Isn't it dangerous to travel during the day?" I asked, hoping for a chance to ease my pain-wracked body.

"The army won't come up here," he told me. "They're there." He pointed. "Waiting for us."

In the distance, a mountain range rose higher than any I'd seen. "Those are the Kwangju Mountains?" I asked.

"Yes. The peak on the far right, that is Mount O-song."

I was about to ask him how he knew my specific destination but thought better of it. He'd tell me if I needed to know. Moon Chaser kept me moving all day. Finally, I couldn't take it any longer. I flopped down and told him I had to rest.

"Every minute we delay," he told me, "the First Corps puts more soldiers between us and the Manchurian Battalion."

That was the first time he'd mentioned those words.

"And," he continued, "they move more of their armored units into attack position."

My body was screaming for rest, my toes bleeding, my calves and thighs quivering with exhaustion. Still, I got to my feet and plodded on, following Moon Chaser blindly, concentrating all my attention on the wooden A-frame on his back, the one that held his canvas pack and apparently all his worldly possessions. I'm not sure how long we walked.

The next thing I remember is being shaken awake. It was nighttime now. I must've collapsed without even being aware of it.

"They're here," Moon Chaser hissed.

"Who's here?" I asked.

He covered my lips with his forefinger. "Quiet. They're nearby."

I sat up. Earlier on this long, grueling march, I'd sworn that I didn't care if I were captured. At least I'd be able to rest. Now that arrest was imminent, suddenly I was terrified. And ready to run.

-11-

Moon Chaser grabbed my wrist and pulled me to my feet, motioning for me to follow. I stayed close to him as he moved through underbrush, keeping low. Finally, we stopped and knelt. He pointed. Below, three snub-nosed trucks were parked in a row. Beside them stood a woman. A tall woman dressed in a long, black leather coat and long, black leather boots, her straight hair hanging down beyond her shoulders.

Senior Captain Rhee Mi-sook—fully recovered now, hair glistening, looking like what the Paris fashion world would imagine a female Communist officer should look like. She stared up in the hills, right at us.

"Do they know we're here?" I whispered.

"No, it's not possible. No one's ever caught me in

these hills. This way," he said, pulling my wrist again. "Keep low."

Soon we reached a ravine. Moon Chaser guided me through it. A half hour later, we'd left the soldiers far behind.

Before dawn, we caught a few hours of sleep. Just before the sun came up, we crawled to the edge of a precipice and looked down.

"There it is," Moon Chaser said. "Imjingang." The Imjin River.

The narrow valley stretched south, as far as the eye could see.

"It reaches the DMZ," Moon Chaser said, "and beyond."

I knew the Imjin River well. It flows southeast where it crosses the DMZ, not far from the truce village of Panmunjom, the place where the North Koreans meet the South Koreans and the United Nations Command Military Armistice Commission does its work. Eventually, the Imjin empties into the Yellow Sea.

"To the south," Moon Chaser said, "the river is heavily fortified. So if we're going to reach Mount O-song, we have to cross here."

The banks of the river were flat and strewn with gravel. Water rushed rapidly through a central channel.

"The river is higher than normal," Moon Chaser said. "Normally we could ford here, but it would be dangerous with such a deep flow. Look."

I followed where he pointed, to a clump of bushes I'd barely noticed. I looked more closely. Shapes emerged: sandbags, camouflaged headgear.

"Machine guns," I said.

"Yes," Moon Chaser replied. "They're planning to stop us here."

We spent the morning searching up and down the length of the Imjin and spotted gun emplacements every two hundred meters or so, depending on the terrain.

"There must be roving patrols also," I said, "on our side of the river."

Moon Chaser agreed. We decided to hide until evening. He led me up the side of a rocky cliff to a cave that overlooked a bend in the river. From there we waited and watched. We chewed on the last few dirty chunks of *ddok*. I asked Moon Chaser how we were going to cross the river.

He shook his head. "They're really after you now." After thinking a while, Moon Chaser said, "There's only one place to cross."

"Where?"

"Eat your *ddok*. I'll show you"

Two hours later, after night had fallen, we crawled to the edge of a cliff and stared down at the Imjin far below.

"There," Moon Chaser said, pointing. "That's where we'll cross."

It was an earthen dam. Crude, not fortified with cement, but Moon Chaser assured me that the Great Leader had plans to construct an enormous modern dam and a hydroelectric power plant at this site. A huge volume of water was stored behind the earthen berm, forming a man-made lake. Through sluices lined with lumber, water rushed into the Imjin River. As part of my briefings, I'd learned about this planned network of dams north of the DMZ. The purpose, according to my Eighth Army briefers, was not only to control the flow of water reaching South Korea, but also to use the dams, if necessary, as a weapon. It was thought that once all the dams were constructed, the North Koreans would be able to open a half dozen or so and allow water to gush into South Korea, damaging crop production by allowing the Imjin and Han Rivers to overflow their banks. Eventually, if the Great Leader's plans were fully realized, the volume of water rushing down across the Demilitarized Zone into South Korea would be of biblical proportions. Water as a weapon of war.

I studied the primitive dam. A string of dirty light-bulbs, hung on poles, reached from side to side. The dam itself contained an enormous amount of dirt and seemed fairly new. Across the flattened top was a wood-slatted roadway. What worried me were the fortified wire gates at either end, protected by armed guards and multiple gun emplacements.

"How are we going to cross that?" I asked.

"Walk," Moon Chaser told me. When I looked at him skeptically, he said, "Well, at least I'll walk. You'll ride. Come on."

We waited until the middle of the night. The guards on either side of the dam had changed once and now these soldiers were listless and crouched near their weapons, doing their best to keep warm in the frigid night air. Many of the lights strung across the river had been turned off. Only half a dozen bulbs illuminated the entire expanse. No floodlights. No well-lit guard shacks.

Moon Chaser slid back the side panel of the wooden

cart he'd borrowed. It was a coffin-like box, large enough to hold a full-grown hog. "Get in," he said.

"I'll never fit," I replied, studying the small opening.

"You'll fit," he replied. "It's the only way across."

We'd spent the earlier part of the evening making our way to the village of Five Pines on the edge of the road that led to the dam. If there had ever been five pines in the village, they'd long since been chopped down for firewood. Now it was a barren spot with half a dozen shacks that provided the most basic types of amenities to the workmen and guards who manned the dam. All this activity was kept hidden, of course, since normal commerce was not allowed in North Korea. Supposedly, the grain and vegetable rations provided by the Great Leader were enough for hardworking men to survive on. In reality, everyone wanted more.

The elderly man whom Moon Chaser talked to was called Beggar Ryu. He dealt primarily in bowls of thin turnip soup fortified with dumplings made of rice-flour dough and laced with pig's blood; hearty fare for the workingmen who carried, by hand, the earth from the hills to the river valley below. The old geezer also sold cigarettes on the side and soju in clear bottles with a picture of the beaming face of the Great Leader on the label.

It was the soju and cigarettes that Moon Chaser was counting on to get us to the far side of the dam.

I had to curl up so tightly inside the cart that my knees were pressing up against my cheeks. The splintered wood reeked of dried pig's blood. Moon Chaser shoved my feet farther inside the cart and then slammed the door shut. What I was worried about most in here was cramps. If my muscles tightened and started to knot on me, there'd be no way to get out and stretch—or to run, if it came to that. I willed myself to relax, thinking of faraway places, like the day when I was in middle school and I lived in the home of Mrs. Aaronson. She packed me and half a dozen other foster kids into her old Plymouth and drove us over to Redondo Beach where we could swim and frolic in the waves. I'd suffered a sunburn that day, but I didn't mind. As a kid who'd known only the harsh summer streets of East L.A., a day at Redondo Beach had been a day in heaven.

The cart rolled into the night. There were no springs on it, so at each rock and pothole I was jarred so roughly that my molars knocked together.

It was a good half-mile to the first checkpoint. As Moon Chaser pushed the cart, he started to sing some ancient Korean song that was indecipherable to me. It seemed to make him happy though. As he marched, his voice rose and gradually became more lusty. The soju bottles packed above me rattled.

Finally, someone shouted, *"Shikuro!"* Shut up.

The cart rolled to a halt.

"Don't we have enough trouble," the voice said, "without having to listen to your shrieking, old man?"

It was the voice of a young man, one of the guards at the first checkpoint. In my mind, I saw Moon Chaser smiling and bowing, his omnipresent A-frame still strapped to his back.

"You don't appreciate fine culture," Moon Chaser replied. "My voice was trained in the People's Music Institute in Pyongyang, overseen by the Great Leader himself!"

"*Bah*. Shut up, old man. Do you expect anyone to believe your drivel?"

"Ah, but the truth is hard to swallow. Maybe this would better meet with your approval?"

Moon Chaser slid the door of the cart halfway open. Yellow light flooded in, blinding me. His hand reached in and pulled out a bottle of soju and the door quickly slammed shut, returning me to darkness.

"Only two won," he said. "The perfect way to warm this long evening."

"Two won?" The young man was incredulous. "Beggar Ryu charges us half that."

"Ah, but Beggar Ryu doesn't buy from the finest distillery in the capital city itself."

"Nonsense. His soju has a picture of the Great Leader on it, just like this one."

"Counterfeit!" Moon Chaser said with assurance. "Any thief can print a label."

They haggled like this back and forth for what seemed a long time. The young man on guard duty and the three or four voices I occasionally heard behind him weren't going anywhere and had nothing better to do than haggle with an itinerant merchant. Finally, after enduring an elaborate string of insults, Moon Chaser came to the point.

"I have a sick mother in the village of Oh-mok," he told the guard. "If she dies before I get there, I would never forgive myself, but if I walk north to Unification Road, it will take me two days." He offered the guard a bottle of soju and two packs of cigarettes if they'd let him venture across the dam. "I'll save a full day from my journey," he told them.

The men conferred amongst themselves and finally a price of two bottles of soju and three packs of cigarettes was decided upon. "But watch out for those thieves at guard post number three," Moon Chaser was told. All the guards laughed. "They'll steal your last bottle of soju."

Moon Chaser pushed the cart across the bridge.

Still curled up into a tiny knot, I sweated inside the cart. The wood was old and splintery but solid, probably an inch thick. Because I willed myself not to think about cramps, cramps were, of course, all I could think about. I felt the big muscle in the back of my right thigh start to tighten. Desperately, I willed it to relax. It did. By now, although it was desperately cold outside, sweat was pouring off my forehead and puddling in my armpits, flowing down my ribcage. Moon Chaser had pushed me a long way, clattering along the wood-slat road, but still we hadn't reached the end of the dam. The men at the final guard post must have been watching him approach. Did they notice the cart sitting low on the wheels? Thinking about that terrified me enough that, for a moment, I stopped thinking about the quivering muscles in my legs.

Finally, the cart rolled to a halt.

"Comrades," Moon Chaser said. "The men at the first guard post hold you in high esteem. They say you are men of discernment who appreciate the finest gifts from our Great Leader."

This time, I didn't hear any laughter.

Moon Chaser slid back the door, reached in, and grabbed two liter bottles of soju.

As he talked, the muscles in the back of my right leg tightened like a clutch of snakes. I tried to straighten my bent leg, but it had nowhere to go. My foot pressed hard against the wood, my mouth open in a silent scream. I waited for the muscles to loosen, for the pain to stop, but it just got worse.

A gruff voice snarled at Moon Chaser. "No one's allowed on the bridge, least of all a blood-sucking capitalist. Why did those bastards at guard post number one let you cross?"

Although I couldn't see him, I imagined Moon Chaser smiling and bowing and I heard his apologetic voice. He explained at length about his sick mother in the village of Oh-mok and how if he didn't cut across the river here, he might not reach her before she breathed her last. He explained how she'd been a long and faithful follower of the Great Leader.

"She fought with him against the Japanese imperialists," he said finally.

Apparently, this explanation had some effect on the snarling man. He said, "What about the Great War of Liberation? Did she fight the Yankees?"

"Oh, yes," Moon Chaser said. "She hates the Yankee dogs. Killed three of them with her kitchen chopping knife."

I couldn't control my leg now. The spasm was so strong that I had no choice but to try and straighten it. My foot thumped against the wall, pushing with all its might, and if this cart hadn't been fastened by interlocking bolts, I believe I would've kicked it apart.

Moon Chaser seemed to be aware that something was wrong inside the cart. He opened and banged the door loudly and it sounded as if bottles were being tossed and then caught in rough hands. Feet shuffled and I heard the guards cursing and Moon Chaser telling them that his price was only two *won* per bottle.

"You would charge us?" the snarling man said. "We who protect you from the bloodthirsty imperialists to the south?" There was incredulity in his voice. "You would come here in the middle of the night and ask us for money? For something as worthless as this cheap soju?"

Self-righteously, Moon Chaser defended the quality of his soju. The banter went back and forth for what was probably only a minute or two, but flush in the agony of muscle spasms, it seemed like years. In the last few days, my back and arms and chest and legs had been driven beyond their capacity. Exhausted and dehydrated, the quivering tissues screamed for relief. Finally, Moon Chaser reluctantly agreed to allow the soldiers to keep the soju free of charge—in honor, he said, of his ill mother.

With a note of triumph in his voice, the snarling soldier assured Moon Chaser that his service to the defenders of the country would bring good luck to his ailing mother. We were rolling.

I tried. God knows I tried. But every joint in my body was knotting in sympathetic response to my thigh muscles, which were now clumps of pain. I screamed, clasping my hand over my mouth as I did so in a vain effort to muffle the noise. Moon Chaser must've heard me because he shoved the cart forward faster, trotting now, but it was too late. I lost control.

Without even realizing what I was doing, I slid open the door of the cart and my right leg kicked out of its own volition, straightening until my foot dangled in the cold air. Moon Chaser cursed. The cart was rolling faster than ever.

Behind us, someone shouted. Moon Chaser was now pushing the cart forward at a flat-out run and it was clear that the angle of decline had increased. We were heading downhill.

A shot rang out.

Moon Chaser gave the cart one final nudge and then I felt the thud of his weight on it. We were rolling now, picking up speed. Another shot was fired.

The blacktop and gravel and rocks by the side of the road whizzed by at a tremendous speed. The cart was nothing more than a heavy square box with two bicycle wheels supporting it. There was no steering mechanism and no brakes. At this speed, we were sure to veer off the side of the road, but somehow we didn't. I felt little jerks, first to our left and then to our right. Something was steering the cart.

Moon Chaser was lying flat atop the cart now, his A-frame still strapped to his back, but he must've been using his staff to jab forward at the ground and give us not only a little breaking action but also some steering control. It wasn't much. Just enough to keep the rolling cart from careening off the edge of the road, into what I imagined to be an abyss below.

The gunfire had stopped. Still, we kept rolling faster down the ever-steepening hill. We were out of range of the men who guarded the dam now, but still in mortal danger of becoming a statistic by dying in your typical soju pig-cart crack-up.

Moon Chaser jabbed his staff hard to the left. The

entire cart lifted, threatening to tip over, but still Moon Chaser kept jabbing his staff. We veered to the right but left the dirt road, one of the wheels kicking up dust and gravel on the side. After attempting to steer for a few more seconds, he suddenly gave up altogether. I felt his body shift above me as if he were curling himself into a ball, and then he screamed.

We flew off the edge of the road.

Moon Chaser slapped me alert.

"Where are we?" I asked.

"Speak Korean," he said.

I asked the same question in Korean.

"Never mind." He pulled me roughly to my feet. "Come on. Those guards at the dam can't leave their posts, but their officer of the guard has a radio. They'll call this in."

One of the legs of Moon Chaser's A-frame had been broken. "Are you all right?" I asked.

"Yes. Quickly now. Up the hill."

We climbed. And we kept moving throughout the night. I surveyed my body as we moved. A few bruises and a world of soreness, but other than that I was healthy enough. Exhausted, hungry, and the back of my leg still throbbed from the cramps, but I was still in one piece. The thick walls of the soju cart had protected me from suffering any permanent damage.

It must've been maddening for the people hunting us to learn that we'd managed to cross the Imjin River, after all the precautions they'd taken. Still, they'd regroup quickly.

Moon Chaser shouted back to me as we hopped across

rocky ridges. "No stopping now. All speed. If we can make it to the Eastern Star Commune before they do, and get into the Kwangju Mountain Range proper, we'll be safe."

"How far?" I asked, my tongue already lolling out of my head.

"Don't ask," Moon Chaser shouted. "Just move!"

At dawn, we gazed down on a flat plain that stretched about four miles to a mountain range rising jaggedly into the sky.

"The Kwangju Mountains," Moon Chaser said. "There, the one capped with snow and mist, that's Mount O-song."

Just by examining the terrain, I could see how the Manchurian Battalion, with an independent leadership and the protection of a massive mountain range, could maintain its position as a formidable independent power, even in the midst of one of the world's most repressive Communist dictatorships. And I could understand why Commissar Oh had chosen to send the entire armored might of the Red Star Brigade up against them. By holding the dominant geographic position, the Manchurian Battalion would be difficult to dislodge.

"We need water," Moon Chaser said. "And food. I'll get us some there."

He pointed to the rows of low barracks-like buildings in a neat geometric pattern in the center of the valley.

"What's that?"

"The Eastern Star Commune."

"You'll be caught," I said. "They must've been notified."

"But you must eat. And drink. Even after we reach

the mountains, it will be a long climb to the Manchurian Battalion."

"I can get by without," I told him. "Better if we go around the valley, to the south, and cross there."

"No. Too close to the DMZ. It's crawling with soldiers. Better to go straight across the valley."

"They'll spot us."

"They'll spot you. Not me. If I go into the commune, attract their attention, you can make your way along that irrigation canal." He pointed. "It zigzags across the valley and eventually reaches the mountains. I'll join you at the far end, with food and water."

"How will you pull it off?"

Moon Chaser grinned and patted me on the back. "Don't worry. That's my department."

I gazed back down at the valley. The sky was overcast and even through the day the weather would remain cold, close to freezing, but there still could be some bright sunshine by noon.

"I'll be too exposed," I said. "Wouldn't it be better to wait until dark?"

"Yes. It would. But this valley will be full of soldiers before the morning is out. Right now, they're probably sending trucks out to pick them up from their gun emplacements along the river. Then they'll bring them here and form a line between us and the mountains. We have to take the chance."

Moon Chaser unlaced the pack strapped to the center of his A-frame. He rummaged around and pulled out what looked like a role of hemp material. He untied it and tossed it to me.

"Strip off that uniform," he told me. "Put this on."

I did as I was told. It was the traditional hemp panta-loons and tunic of a Korean farmer, slightly soiled. Then he tossed me a hat that had been similarly folded up in his backpack. It was made of straw that spread out slightly when I untied it, but it still held an odd, bent shape.

"How do I look?" I asked, when I was fully decked out.

"The legs are too short," Moon Chaser said. "The cuffs only reach halfway to your ankles. And the tunic is tight across the chest." I'd knotted the string holding it together tightly. "If anyone sees you up close," Moon Chaser said, "they'll spot you for a foreigner immediately."

"But from a distance?" I said.

"If you keep your back bent, staring at the ground, and stay low within the irrigation canal, you might not be noticed."

Moon Chaser turned and studied the main road lead-ing into the Eastern Star Commune from the north. "Nothing yet," he said. "No time to lose. Let's go."

He pointed out a plateau at the foot of the Kwangju Mountains on the far side of the valley as our rendezvous point. He also told me that if he didn't arrive by nightfall, I was to make my way to Mount O-song on my own.

"I'll wait for you," I said.

"No. Your mission is too important. If I'm not there by nightfall, climb farther into the mountains, find shelter for the night, and continue on without me."

We climbed down to the floor of the valley together. Then we shook hands, Moon Chaser grinning at the odd-ness of this Western tradition.

He continued on across the cabbage fields. I made my way south to the irrigation canal.

The edges of the canal were made of mud. I kept sliding down into the two- or three-foot-high runoff. I had to wade my way through the sludge until I found solid footing and climbed back up on the side of the canal. As I proceeded, I spotted the work groups and kept low as I crept past them. The water in the canal reeked of human waste and some sort of chemical that reminded me vaguely of ammonia. Probably toxic. In thirty years I'd be stricken by cancer and wonder how I caught it. Thinking of this—getting sick thirty years from now—kept my courage up as I made my way through the valley.

At one point, I climbed up out of the canal and lay down near some piles of hay and a metal pipe where runoff poured into the canal from the fields. The work groups seemed absorbed in their tasks, so I was mostly worried about the occasional groups of farmers, pushing carts laden with hand tools, making their way toward the fields. But with the valley as flat as it was, I was able to see them coming and slide down into the canal before they could spot me.

I gazed at the central buildings of the commune. I forced myself to stop worrying about Moon Chaser and the possibility of capture and concentrate on making my way across the valley.

I was more than halfway across when the old woman spotted me. I hadn't noticed her because she was squatting down on the edge of the canal, apparently hunting for sour weed, the wild herbs that Koreans often add to soups and stews. She had a bundle of leafy greens shoved into the loose pockets of her full skirt. The material was folded above her knees as she squatted, her lower body swathed in long underpants made of linen.

She smiled at me quizzically. "You're dirty," she said.

I nodded, bowing obsequiously. "Yes," I replied.

My pantaloons were rolled up above my knees and I'd been wading through a particularly noxious stretch of the irrigation canal, watching my footing as I went. I was less than ten yards from the old woman before she spoke and woke me out of my reverie.

"I'm sorry to bother you," I said.

She stared at me, her half-smile not fading. "What are you doing here?"

I searched my mind for an answer. In the distance, I heard the singing of a work crew making their way to the fields. They were getting closer.

Like a bullfrog on its haunches, the old woman sidled away from me.

I sloshed quickly through the water and grabbed her. She started to scream, but I shoved my hand over her mouth and pulled her halfway down the edge of the irrigation canal, pressing her body against the mud. Her eyes were wide now, the thin eyebrows threatening to pop off her head. Here in front of her was the embodiment of the dirty, hairy, long-nosed Yankee that she'd been propagandized to hate—and fear—all her life. The bogeyman come to life, staring down into her face, foul body odor and bad breath. She struggled to kick herself free, but I leaned all my weight against her, holding her still.

The work crew's singing grew louder.

There was a footbridge about twenty yards ahead. Luckily, it was just on the other side of a bend in the canal, so they wouldn't be able to spot us—if I could just hold this struggling old woman still. Should I kill her? Hold her head beneath the filthy water until she gurgled her last? Or, once the work crew was past, should I threaten her and make her promise to stay quiet, at least until I made my way to the far side of the valley? But then she'd alert the others, and once they knew I was nearby, they would turn on Moon Chaser. After all his heroic efforts, they'd torture him and kill him. But if I left her body here floating facedown in the muck . . .

I stared into her terrified eyes, felt the warmth of her old body struggling against mine, and knew—with absolute certainty—that I couldn't hurt her. No matter what the cost. I wished that somehow I could convey that certainty to her, so she wouldn't be so frightened, but there was no way.

The work crew passed. Their singing faded.

I told the old woman that I was going to take my hand off her mouth, but if she screamed I would shove her head beneath the water. I asked her if she understood. She nodded. I took my hand off her mouth.

She just stared, open-mouthed.

"If you don't betray me," I said, "I won't hurt you. Do you understand?"

She nodded again.

"You're going to come with me a way," I said. "If you do as I say, I'll let you go once we are far enough away." Before I could ask if she understood, she nodded vehemently. Evidently, she'd lost the ability to speak.

With me propping her up against the slanted wall of the irrigation canal, we made our way slowly around the bend that the work party had just passed and continued on our way to the far side of the valley. After about a half-mile of this, I decided that I was moving too slowly. I stopped, knowing I had to let her go.

"I'm going to let you climb up on solid ground," I said. "But I want you to sit there and make no sound. Do not move for at least thirty minutes. Do you understand?"

She nodded.

"If you don't promise to sit there quietly for thirty minutes, I won't let you go. Do you promise?"

She nodded again.

"Say it," I said.

"*Yaksok*," she croaked. Promise.

I helped her climb back up the muddy slope until she was perched on the ledge of the irrigation canal. She gazed down, clearly terrified. I smiled and told her I was sorry for muddying her dress. She said nothing. Then I turned and sloshed my way down the canal.

I had gone somewhat less than a hundred yards when I heard footsteps pounding away in the opposite direction. Probably her, I thought. She hadn't kept her promise. Still, she was a long way from the nearest work party. Then I heard the thin, whistling scream wafting along the valley floor.

I climbed up to the edge of the irrigation canal. It was the mud-spattered old woman, running and screaming— sour-stemmed herbs falling out of her pockets—alerting the entire commune of the Eastern Star about the presence of a Yankee imperialist.

I stepped up on solid ground and started to run.

They caught me before I reached the Kwangju Mountains. A work party of young farmers, all armed with hoes and rakes and wickedly curved scythes. I fought, but the sheer weight of them overwhelmed me.

One of them produced some hemp rope and they trussed me up and tied me to a thick pole and carried me like a dead boar back to the main square of the commune. In the central administrative building, they shoved me into an iron-barred cell that looked just like a Hollywood hoosegow. It was furnished only with a low straw-covered bunk and a metal bucket for a toilet.

After they untied me, I sat on the straw for about an hour, standing as often as I could because of the bugs practicing their broad jump. Finally, two uniformed men arrived. They shackled me with proper metal handcuffs and metal ankle bracelets and perp-walked me down stone steps into a basement. Actually, it was made of hewn rock and looked more like a dungeon. A single yellow bulb hung from the center of the ceiling. They sat me on a metal bench and then left, the iron-reinforced wooden door clanging shut behind them. I studied my surroundings. Nothing here except the bench and a barred window overhead with the glass painted black.

I sat and waited.

It seemed like days. Finally, the door opened.

Leather boots appeared on the stone steps. Soon her face came into view: Senior Captain Rhee Mi-sook, the woman who'd been haunting me since I first arrived in North Korea.

Her eyes were sad, and her full lips pouted.

"Now," she said in English. "At last."

She slipped off her leather coat, revealing a statuesque figure clad in tight black pants and blouse. From the pocket of the coat she pulled out a short leather whip. Then she turned to me and smiled, flicking the whip in front of her.

"Are you ready for some fun?" she said.

-12-

Senior Captain Rhee Mi-sook set the whip aside and reached into the deep pocket of her leather coat, pulling out an ivory-handled knife. She pressed a button and the blade popped up with a snap. Heels clicking, she crossed the brick floor and stood in front of me.

"You're *filthy*," she said, loathing in her voice. "Stand!" she ordered in Korean. I did. She didn't move away. Our bodies were practically touching. I was a head taller but she gazed up at me angrily, her soft lips curled in disgust. Deftly, she sliced my hemp tunic and pantaloons. With the long nails of her left hand she ripped the clothing off me. Finally, after she'd peeled off the last of my undergarments, I stood naked.

With the gleaming tip of the blade, she touched my

chest. Pressing only hard enough to slice the first few layers of skin, she ran the tip of the blade down my body, across my stomach, stopping just as she reached my pubic hair. As she held the point of the blade there, ready to jab, she gazed into my eyes—searching, I believe, for fear.

She found it. Then she stepped back and hollered for the guards. Two men entered, both carrying wooden pails sloshing with water. Without hesitation they tossed the water on me. It was freezing. Before I could regain my breath, more men entered. They doused me with more water and rubbed my back and chest with some sort of harsh-smelling soap. Someone produced a thick-bristled brush, scrubbing my flesh, scratching it, almost peeling it off. I tried to shove them back, but there were too many of them.

They kicked the straw-covered cot out of the way and I fell to my knees. When they were done, I lay in a bloody mass of suds on the cold stone floor.

When I awoke, it was night. A metal lamp with a soft red bulb had been brought into the chamber. The tip of an insistent boot roused me awake. With a start, I sat up.

Senior Captain Rhee Mi-sook gazed down at me. She wasn't wearing her uniform now but rather a loose blue smock made of some sort of diaphanous material.

"*Irrona*," she said. Get up.

I did.

She stepped closer and in the dim red glow examined the bruises and scratches on my body.

"Did they hurt you?" she asked.

"No," I replied.

Since my capture, she'd spoken only Korean to me. I wasn't yet ready to admit that I understood English. It was foolish, I suppose. Eventually she'd find out that I didn't speak Romanian and she'd figure out who I was, but all my training told me to stall for time, to give away nothing until I had to.

She stepped closer to me.

"You smell like lye," she said in English.

I didn't reply.

She leaned in so close to me that the tip of her nose was almost touching my chest. "But you're clean," she said in Korean.

Again, I didn't respond.

Her lips parted, a moist tongue slithering out. And then she was kissing me, starting at my neck, working her way down.

Upstairs, a man screamed.

"Who's that?" I said.

"Your friend," she replied dreamily.

Moon Chaser.

He screamed again. And it was indeed him.

As the soft lips and probing tongue of Captain Rhee Mi-sook explored every part of my body, Moon Chaser's screams of agony grew louder.

"You're torturing him," I said.

"Yes," she murmured.

"You must stop."

"When I'm ready."

"When will that be?" I asked.

"When you tell me everything."

I didn't answer. Moon Chaser kept screaming. Captain Rhee Mi-sook's soft tongue kept probing.

In the morning they fed me noodles. That night, a bowl of rice laced with turnip greens. In between, I was allowed all the barley tea I could drink. The purpose, I believed, was to keep me healthy. Captain Rhee and I engaged in two sessions a day, for three days. I told her nothing. All the while, during each assignation, Moon Chaser was tortured. It was a technique the North Koreans had used before: torture one man and let the guilt grow in another. Eighth Army had taught me to keep my feelings compartmentalized. Never blame yourself for what someone else was doing, in this case torturing a man who had risked his life for you. I tried, but it didn't work. After one particularly hideous session, I broke down.

In English, I said, "That's enough. You hear me? That's enough!"

Captain Rhee's eyes widened in mock surprise.

"I want you to stop torturing him." When she didn't respond, I took a deep breath and said, "I'm from Eighth Army."

Unconcerned, Captain Rhee toyed with the sparse hair on my chest. "I know that," she replied.

"Will you stop torturing him if I confess?"

"I'll think about it."

Moon Chaser was still screaming, so I confessed. Rapidly. Most of what I said bored her. About Hero Kang and Commissar Oh and Hero Kang's daughter, Hye-kyong, and how they'd both died heroically. About the Manchurian Battalion and how they were seen as being too independent and how the Dear Leader was set on destroying them. All the while, she tried to distract me with her long fingers and her nibbling at various parts of me. I wondered what they'd done to her to make her this way. And then she told me.

She'd been selected from among thousands of girls, for being smart, for being pretty. A cadre of apparatchiks had traveled around the country, checking school records, listening to talent recitals of little girls singing and dancing and praising the glorious work of the Great Leader.

"I played the violin," she said. "A composition written by the Great Leader himself, although my music teacher let slip once that it had actually been written by Bach. At the time, I didn't believe him. I was only fourteen. They took me to Pyongyang for training and more education. When I was seventeen, the Great Leader visited me himself."

"Alone?"

"Very alone. I didn't know he was coming. He appeared suddenly in my room. Everything was quiet. I believe the entire dormitory had been evacuated. Outside, a ring of cars and soldiers protected the area."

I studied her, looking for signs of outrage or sadness or even pride. I saw nothing. But she answered my unspoken question.

"I was a virgin," she said. "He was old. Things didn't work out so well."

"You were expelled from the Joy Brigade?"

"Put in the army. The Great Leader wanted to make sure that if I talked, I knew I would be shot."

"Did you talk?"

"Never."

"Then why are you talking to me?"

"You are a foreigner. No one understands you and no one believes you. You don't count."

"Also," I said, "I will die soon."

"Yes. That's another reason." She stared up at the stone ceiling, lost in thought. Then she said, "In the army, every man used me."

I waited, not moving.

"All the old colonels first, they each had their turn, with their weak bodies and their cold hands. And then the junior officers. I was lost, not knowing what to do. Shocked that I, who had dedicated my life to the Great Leader, was being betrayed like this. I knew that if the Great Leader were aware of their treachery, he would stop them and punish them all. But he wasn't there. I was alone."

"You had no one to turn to?" I asked.

"No one." She seemed slightly astonished. "A woman alone in the army, purposely kept away from other females. I was told to follow orders, to keep my mouth shut, that was all. I thought of killing myself. Of pulling out my pistol and ending it all, but I knew that would be seen as a direct insult to the Great Leader and my family would be punished. I couldn't do that. Finally, I found some inner strength from somewhere and I decided to change. Not to change the men who were using me but to change myself. If they loved me, if they loved my face, my hands, my body, I would use that as my power. Once I made that decision, I felt free—and strong. I became more aware of my surroundings and started to search out the men who made the real decisions, the men with power, the men who could protect me."

"The commissars," I said.

"Yes. And that's when I started to get what I wanted. Better working conditions, promotions, jobs with more authority."

"And now you're a fixer," I said.

"Who told you that?"

I shrugged.

"No matter," she replied. "Someday, I will be a commissar myself." She turned to me and smiled, her sweet, beautiful smile. "But first, you will help me take down the Manchurian Battalion. All the things you've told me so far, I already know. I need you to tell me more. Why did the Manchurian Battalion bring you here? Who was your initial contact? What are their plans?"

Most of the questions she asked, I wouldn't have been able to answer even if I wanted to. But I also knew that in the intelligence business a little information from one source could be pieced together with information from another source to create a comprehensive picture of the whole. When I claimed ignorance, sometimes honestly, she used the whip on me. I did my best not to cry out.

They were still torturing Moon Chaser. His screams had been reverberating through my skull for days. It was my fault he'd been caught. It was my fault he was suffering. Finally, I couldn't take it any longer. I broke down and told Captain Rhee about the manuscript of the wild man. She sat up as I spoke. I knew I'd caught her interest.

"Stop torturing him now," I said.

She snapped her fingers. A guard came in. She barked the order, and two minutes later the screaming stopped.

"Tell me," she commanded.

I told her of the tunnel through the Kwangju Mountains, impossible to discover except by the "wild man" who seemed to have some sixth sense that guided him through the bowels of the earth.

"It leads where?" she asked me breathlessly.

I was about to tell her when a bomb went off.

Quickly, she slipped back into her clothes, pulled on her boots, and ran outside. I sat on the metal bench, listening to the gunfire all around me, men shouting in anger and in terror.

A half-hour later, armed men burst into the dungeon. Some of them were spattered with blood. All of them were dirty and perspiration dripped from their foreheads. One of them held a ring of keys and he knelt and unshackled me. I was still naked.

Doctor Yong In-ja, holding a Kalashnikov rifle across her chest, strode between the men. "Find him some clothes," she ordered. "Then bring him."

Without saying a word to me, she swiveled and returned to the fight.

The redoubt high on the edge of Mount O-song was carefully camouflaged. Canvas netting strewn with weeds covered most of the buildings and some of them were sheltered beneath natural rock overhangs.

Doc Yong personally supervised my recovery. It didn't

take long. Most of my wounds were superficial. The avaricious Senior Captain Rhee Mi-sook had merely exhausted me. It was Moon Chaser who'd been methodically ripped to shreds. The soldiers of the Manchurian Battalion rescued him from the Eastern Star Commune but he hadn't survived the retreat up into the Kwangju Mountains. His body was carried the rest of the way and buried, with honors, within one of the grave mounds reserved for the martyrs of the Manchurian Battalion.

When I was well enough, Doc Yong introduced me to Il-yong, the First Dragon, my son. My first glimpse of him was like an awakening in my soul. Now I lived for him, not for myself. He was a bright-eyed boy who loved to smile. I thought he looked like her. She said he looked like me. He noticed everything and I told Doc Yong that that part was definitely like her. I prayed that he'd inherited her brains.

The raid on the Eastern Star Commune had killed a few North Korean soldiers and chased the rest away, including, presumably, Senior Captain Rhee Mi-sook. Immediately, I told Doc Yong everything I knew about the plan to deploy the Red Star Brigade first to a village near Hamhung, and then from there up into the Kwangju Mountains for the assault on the Manchurian Battalion. She nodded gravely. That matched intelligence they'd already gathered.

I spilled my guts about the order of battle and the notes that I'd taken in the catacombs of the Joy Brigade. Somehow, in all the madness since then, the notes had been lost.

"Here," Doc Yong said, sitting me at a wooden desk and handing me a pencil and a pad of paper. "Put down everything you can remember." She poured me a cup of barley tea and left the room. The silence grew. I remembered Beikyang and the red star hitting the butt of a white goat, but after that, not much.

Eventually, I gave up and found Doc Yong.

"Keep trying," she said. "Maybe in your dreams some of it will come back to you."

I also told her about Hero Kang and his daughter, Hye-kyong, and the holding action of assaulting the petroleum transport convoy.

Another ceremony was held, honoring them. A single carved memorial was erected.

At night, Doc Yong and I lay in bed together. Beside us, on a small mat, Il-yong breathed softly. I lay awake, staring at the moonlight seeping through an oil-papered window, my happiness complete. Or almost. Thoughts of Senior Captain Rhee Mi-sook remained, like a she-demon stalking me.

During the day, with Il-yong strapped to Doc Yong's back, she gave me a complete tour of the grounds. To the north, twin peaks protected the mountain valley from the cold winds. To the south loomed Mount O-song. Thus sheltered, the valley had a surprisingly temperate climate that allowed the men and women of the Manchurian Battalion to work the land and raise many of their own crops. Not rice but cabbage and turnips and carrots and even a small grove of pear trees. The streams provided some fish, and for the rest of their sustenance, they traded with the collective farms in the valley below. Sometimes, when out of political favor, they had to travel far afield to purchase the rations that the central government supposedly provided free. But they had allies everywhere; people who secretly admired not only the valiant history of the Manchurian Battalion but also their independence.

Everywhere I went, people bowed to me and smiled. Doc Yong had been raised in South Korea and knew the truth about the government down there. It was corrupt and had its faults, and the southern economy was still suffering from the devastation of the Korean War, but fundamentally people were free. Doc Yong had spoken of these things at village meetings and reassured the leadership that the Americans were no longer the enemy of the North Korean people. Compromises could be reached. Peace negotiated. The United States, she promised everyone, was reasonable. Most importantly, the U.S. might be able to help the Manchurian Battalion maintain their independence.

That's why I received so many smiles.

I thought of these things as I lay in bed next to Doc Yong. My belly was full with roast mackerel and *kokktugi*, pickled turnip, and heaping white bowls of steamed rice. I was satisfied, for once in my life, worried only about how I could provide help to these people. And how I'd be able to get Doc Yong and Il-yong back to South Korea.

Outside, wood clumped on stone. Rhythmically. I sat up in bed. Carefully, so as not to wake Doc Yong, I stood and slid open the small wood-paneled window.

A dark figure stalked away, like a fat blackbird with long, skinny legs. I stared at the figure in the glimmering moonlight, figuring that my eyesight must be going. Had Captain Rhee Mi-sook hit me so hard that she damaged my ocular nerve in some way? I rubbed my eyes and looked again. Still the same husky figure with stick-like legs. Then it rounded a corner and disappeared in shadow.

When I slid shut the window, Doc Yong, wearing her cotton nightgown, sat on our sleeping mat, eyes wide, waiting for me. I sat down next to her.

"What was that?" I whispered.

"Our leader," she said.

"Your leader? That was a man?"

"Very much a man," she said. "Tomorrow you will meet him."

Bandit Lee, the commander of the Manchurian Battalion, wore his wool uniform draped with metals from the campaigns against the Japanese colonialists and the war against the Yankee imperialists. His name had been acquired when he fought the Japanese Imperial Army in the vast wilderness of Manchuria and in the northern mountains of Korea. In those days, his enemies had thought of him not as a revolutionary but as a bandit.

He had broad shoulders and a thick waist, but at the knees his legs stopped. He stood on two wooden stumps. Doc Yong had told me earlier that he could've replaced the wooden stumps with more expensive prosthetics, or simply covered them with his trouser legs, but Bandit Lee eschewed both options. He wanted the world to see what had been done to him.

But the worst damage was not done to his legs. After all, war veterans without limbs were commonplace throughout the world. The most hideous part of his body was his face. Every inch of flesh had been charred, melted by American-manufactured napalm. North Korea—from coast to coast, from the DMZ to the Chinese border—had been saturated with the burning chemical during the Korean War. Bandit Lee had been one of its tens of thousands of victims. One who had survived. His face was not capable of expression. His nose was like a charred lump of coal, his mouth a wrinkled ebony slit. Red eyes stared out at the world as if from behind a mask. When he spoke, the words seemed burnt, escaping from a charred throat. His tongue flicked red, like a serpent emerging from a blackened hole.

"Beikyang," he said

The sound was so rough, like a reptile hissing, that at first I didn't understand him. He repeated the word and then said, "According to your report, the Red Star Brigade will rendezvous there prior to the final assault."

I nodded.

"We need to know which units will be proceeding where so we can attack them after they leave Beikyang. Have you been able to remember anything else?"

I had, and I pulled the notes out of my pocket. The names of a few petroleum refueling points and which units would be using them.

"Are you sure of this?" he asked.

"The petroleum points, yes," I replied, "but not of which units will be where."

Bandit Lee turned away and started giving orders to his waiting officers. Reconnaissance units would be sent out to gather information. Doc Yong was one of the officers who'd be going. The meeting was about to end when I spoke up.

"I will go with her," I said.

"No," Bandit Lee said. "You are too important. When

the time comes, we will need you to relay information to the Americans."

I knew better than to argue with him directly. Instead, I said, "My memory is coming back to me gradually. If I can see the units, if I can see the terrain, maybe I will remember more."

One thing we all knew for sure was that if an order of battle was devised in Pyongyang, the Red Star Brigade would not dare to deviate from it. In the North Korean Army, commanders are given no discretion for independent action. The guidance of the Great Leader is everything.

"If you can remember," Bandit Lee said, "that would be helpful." He turned to one of his subordinates. "See that he's properly outfitted."

It was an infantry unit with a few armored personnel carriers. They were refueling at a North Korean Army depot two kilometers outside the village of Jong-chol. Doc Yong and I stayed low, hidden behind rocks and shrubs on a hill overlooking the narrow valley. We had been traveling all night across rough terrain, and although Il-yong had been left behind in good hands, Doc Yong seemed more worried about him than she was about the enemy. Now, just after dawn, we counted the soldiers and the vehicles.

"Three platoons," I said.

Doc Yong stared through binoculars. "With climbing gear," she said. I took the binoculars from her. She was right. Two soldiers were pulling metal hooks and ropes out of the back of one of the vehicles, checking them, and stuffing them back inside.

"That's why they have so little armor," I said, "and no big guns. They'll try to assault the Manchurian Battalion from the rear."

Doc Yong jotted down a few notes. "Maybe this is the 7044th Mountain Platoon you mentioned."

"I'm not sure about the number."

"Don't worry. The point is we will have someone waiting for them when they make their way behind Mount O-song."

We pulled back from our position. We were halfway over the hill when the first shot rang out. I dived for dirt. Doc Yong did the same, landing beside me. We low-crawled toward nearby boulders.

Another shot rang out.

"Sniper," I said.

I peeked around the boulder, searching for someone on the promontory above us. I saw nothing. Doc Yong looked. After she pulled her head back to safety, she said, "There, at the very top. Beneath some shrubs."

I looked where her finger pointed and saw him. Just as I pulled back to safety, a third shot rang out.

It was then that it all came back to me.

"Quick," I said. "Paper!"

"What?"

"Paper! Pencil!"

Quickly, she rummaged through her canvas backpack and pulled out a short pencil and a pad of tattered pulp. I started jotting furiously. It was all there in my mind: unit designations, personnel strength, number of guns and armored vehicles, and, most importantly, which routes they would be taking up into the Kwangju Mountains.

Two more shots rang out.

"There's more of them now," Doc Yong said. "Come on. We have to go."

"Fire back," I said. "I'm almost done."

Doc Yong unstrapped the Kalashnikov from her back, lay down next to the boulder, aimed, and fired. Then she sat back facing me. "Not even close. That won't hold them long."

I continued to scribble.

"You'll be able to read that?" she asked.

"When we get back, I'll recopy it."

"If we get back."

Finally, I was done. The firing had stopped.

"They're trying to get closer," I said.

We hurried off, crawling through the brush. Unfortunately, not being able to stand up, we weren't sure where we were going. Only when it was too late did we discover that we'd gone in the wrong direction. A cliff loomed before us.

"We have to go back," I said.

Doc Yong grabbed my arm. "Too late," she said. "They're too close." She pointed through the shrubbery. In the early morning gloom, I spotted two dark shapes sliding down the slope behind us, no more than a hundred yards away. "If we crawl, it will take too long," she said. "If we run, they will pick us off."

I looked down over the cliff. After about twenty feet of rock, a sandy slope tapered steeply to the ravine below.

"We have to jump," she said.

I glanced back at the snipers. They took turns changing positions, so the stationary one could provide covering fire.

"Okay," I said, "I'll go first."

"No, me."

I wanted to argue with her, but before I could speak she was already over the edge. She dropped along the jagged rock and landed with a thump on the sand below, immediately tumbling down the hill. A shot rang out, missing me by a few feet. No time to wait. I slid over the edge. All I remember is slamming into about a thousand protuberances until I finally hit the sand. Fifty yards later, I rolled to a halt, stunned but still conscious. I sat up, searching for Doc Yong.

She hissed at me, waving her arm. "This way."

I stood up unsteadily and staggered toward her. This time I didn't hear anything. All I knew for sure was that someone must've swung an iron rod with all his strength, slamming it into the side of my calf and knocking me down.

And then Doc Yong was firing, her Kalashnikov on full automatic, and the next thing I knew, her hand was in my armpit and she was pulling and screaming at me to get up. I did, leaning on her, and we stumbled forward. Another round zinged past my head and then we were behind a rock.

It took us the better part of that day and into the late evening to make it back to the first guard post surrounding the Manchurian Battalion. I'd lost a lot of blood. All I remember is being carried by stretcher up a steep pathway. Then I passed out.

Il-yong sat on the floor next to me, playing with a ball of yarn. Doc Yong squatted next to my bedding, holding my scribbled notes in her hand.

"I can make out some of the numbers," she told me, "and some of the words, but do you think you're well enough to decipher it now?"

I held the paper unsteadily in my hand, staring at it. My eyes wouldn't focus.

"Never mind," she said, taking it from me. "We'll try again after you rest."

In the distance, an artillery round boomed.

"They're getting closer," I said.

"Never mind. You rest now."

I did.

It had only been a shard of rock that hit my leg, kicked up by the round fired by the sniper. Fortunately, an artery hadn't been severed, and what with antibiotics and the bandages being replaced regularly by Doc Yong, I felt alert by the next day.

The artillery rounds now fired almost every minute. I rewrote the entire order of battle, explaining it to Doc Yong as I did so. She seemed worried.

"What's wrong?" I asked. "This should help us."

"Yes." She nodded. "But the Red Star Brigade has made quicker progress than we hoped. Most of these places," she said, pointing at the slip of paper, "have already been overrun."

Nevertheless, she took the newly reprinted order of battle with her and told me she'd be back. While she was gone, I slipped into my clothes. Il-yong looked up at me and gurgled—as if he knew more than I did.

▪ ▪ ▪

I was ushered into Bandit Lee's presence. He wasted no time.

"We need ammunition," he said.

I sat before him on a simple wooden chair, Doc Yong next to me.

"You must enter the tunnel," Bandit Lee told me. "Our good Doctor Yong In-ja has memorized every word of the ancient manuscript. She will be your guide. It will be very dangerous. You might die. But if you survive, you must ask the Americans for resupply: ammunition, medicine, food. We will accept that from them, but we will accept nothing from the Japanese collaborators."

To Bandit Lee, the Japanese collaborators were the colonels and generals, including President Park Chung-hee, who now ran the South Korean government. In fact, many of them had been young officers in the army of the emperor when the Japanese had ruled Korea. Bandit Lee might have been engaged in a deadly competition with the Dear Leader, the son who would replace his former comrade, Kim Il-sung, but he was mortal enemies with the men who ran South Korea. Americans, although enemies in the past, could be negotiated with.

"I have allies throughout the country. They are silent now, and afraid to act, but if the Americans help us, they will rise up and support the Manchurian Battalion. We will take over this government and a peace treaty will be signed. We will renounce Soviet-style communism and create a democratic socialist government with free elections. Then we will cooperate with the Western world. But only if you help us now, in our hour of need. That is your mission. You must convince the Americans to help us, or die trying."

I bowed to the inevitable. He ordered us to depart within the hour.

As Doc Yong and I stood to leave, artillery roared in the distance. Units of the Manchurian Battalion were already on the attack, assaulting elements of the Red Star Brigade in the lowlands before they could fully deploy.

The entrance to the cave on the side of Mount O-song was well hidden. "This is why it has remained intact so long," Doc Yong told me.

We had to climb for an hour to reach it and even then it was concealed by a rocky overhang no sane person would have any reason to explore. But the ancient manuscript, the one Doc Yong had memorized, gave exact directions to the cave.

Crawling flat on our bellies, we entered. I carried the heavier backpack, with a full day's ration of beef jerky and my favorite traveling food, *ddok*. Doc Yong and I each held a flashlight and I had two spares in my pack, along with spare batteries and extra clothing wrapped in plastic. We didn't carry water. According to the manuscript, there'd be plenty. Maybe too much. Doc Yong carried the most precious cargo strapped to her back: our son.

He was quiet as we entered the cave, his eyes wide, studying everything. Doc Yong and I also had claw hammers, looped metal nails, and ropes tied to the front of our chests.

We had left the compound of the Manchurian Battalion alone, no escort. Bandit Lee wanted the secret of the tunnel held closely.

The first part of the tunnel was fairly easygoing. It was about four feet high, sloped downward gently, and by crouching and watching our footing, we descended what I estimated to be a couple hundred feet. At the bottom, we had to scale a ten-foot-high cliff, crawl across shale, and then slide through an opening that was filled with a universe of freezing air. Doc Yong stopped and pulled out an extra blanket to cover Il-yong and ordered that we both slip on canvas coats we'd brought along. When we were warmed, I aimed the flashlight at the opening beyond.

It was a vast cathedral, with twenty-foot stalactites and stalagmites projecting like dragon's teeth. It was so vast that the light didn't reach the far end. We sat quietly for a moment. In the distance something rumbled, like the voice of a giant.

"What's that?" I asked.

"The underground river." Looking worried, she adjusted Il-yong on her back.

"Will we have to cross it?"

"We'll only be in the water for a short distance. We will have to swim. That's why we brought the extra clothing wrapped in plastic."

Doc Yong was a brilliant woman who'd risen from poverty in South Korea to become a medical doctor by dint of her quick thinking and ability to anticipate all possible scenarios. I had no doubt that she'd thought of everything we'd need.

I rose to my feet and held out my hand to help her to stand. I lifted the edge of the blanket and kissed Il-yong on the forehead. He gurgled with delight. Still holding hands, we started across the floor of the cathedral.

The river was more formidable than I imagined.

"The runoff is greater than described in the manuscript." Doc Yong played the beam of her flashlight over the rushing waters. "The wild man and his pursuers must've come when the flow wasn't as violent."

I imagined they had. This river was a raging torrent. There was no way I was going to allow Doc Yong and Il-yong to enter it. I'd rather face the wrath of the Red Star Brigade artillery than face this.

We searched along the rocky shore, looking for a narrow spot to cross.

Finally, the river disappeared into a tunnel.

"Here," Doc Yong said. "This is where we must enter."

"What do you mean?"

"You assumed that we'd cross. I never said that."

"If we don't cross it, then what will we do?"

"We dive in here, as the wild man did when he was being pursued."

"Dive in? Are you out of your mind?"

"I'm not out of my mind," she snapped. "We must reach the Americans in the South. You've seen the Manchurian Battalion, you've seen how desperate we are. You've seen that we are willing to lay our lives on the line to oppose the tyrant who has taken over our country. Only you can testify to what you've witnessed. Only you can convince the Americans to send us ammunition. To send us what we need to fight and to win. If we don't go now, the people of the Manchurian Battalion will perish."

"If we go now, we all might perish."

"Maybe."

I swiveled on her. "What do you owe them?"

"Everything. My education. My life."

"Your parents were members of the Manchurian Battalion," I said.

"Yes. But what difference does all that make now? If we turn back, without American assistance, we will die anyway."

I wasn't so sure of that. When the fighting broke out, I thought there might be enough confusion for Doc Yong and me to slip south with our son, and with luck, make our way across the minefields of the Demilitarized Zone. If I could just reach one South Korean patrol, we'd be safe.

I was about to tell her all this, to reveal my plan, when somewhere behind us rocks clattered. We turned. From her belt beneath her jacket, Doc Yong pulled out a Russian-made pistol. Without hesitation, she fired into the darkness.

"Come on," she said, and pulled me to shelter.

The voice that emerged from the darkness was that of Senior Captain Rhee Mi-sook.

"Where are you running away to?" she asked in Korean. "Why are you so anxious to leave your homeland behind? Have you no loyalty?"

Crouching behind rock, Doc Yong clutched my arm. "Did you tell her about this tunnel?"

I lowered my eyes. "I started to. They were torturing Moon Chaser."

She nodded solemnly and then tilted my head back up

with her hand and stared into my eyes. "There was something between you two, wasn't there? That's why you were naked."

"I had no choice."

I expected her to be angry and she was, but not at me. "She's notorious. And now she follows us down here. But not for her country."

"She's a North Korean officer."

"Yes. But she never does anything for her country. Not if she can help it."

"Then why did she follow us?"

"Because she wants to escape too."

"Into South Korea?"

"Yes. Or better yet, America. She will use you. Do you understand that?"

I did. There was no need for her to tell me.

"And she will kill me. Do you understand that too?"

"I won't let it happen," I said, suddenly angry.

"And," she said, gesturing toward Il-yong, "she will get rid of him."

"Never," I promised. "Not while I'm breathing."

"Neither one of us will be breathing, once she knows the way out of here."

"Surrender, Captain Rhee shouted, "or we will attack!"

Armed men scurried from boulder to boulder.

"They will take us," Doc Yong said. "We must swim. Now!"

"Right," I said. "I'll take the boy."

Doc Yong hesitated but quickly realized that I was the stronger swimmer. She untied Il-yong from her back and strapped him to me, spread-eagle, facing my chest.

"Keep his head above water," she said.

"Okay."

"You go first. I will cover you." She still held the pistol.

I slipped down behind rock to the edge of the water. It was freezing. Quickly, we rubbed black grease on our faces, arms, and the lower calves beneath our pants. Doc Yong gently slathered Il-yong's face and arms and hands. We should've covered our entire bodies but there wasn't time.

A rifle shot pinged above us. We crouched. She kissed Il-yong and then shoved me forward into the water.

The shock of the cold sucked all breath out of me. It had the same effect on Il-yong. He leaned away from me as far as he could, his eyes wide open, but he didn't cry. There wasn't enough air left in his lungs for him to cry. I floated on my back, keeping Il-yong's head above water, the current carrying me quickly toward the tunnel. Another shot rang out, water splashed as we entered enveloping darkness. Safety. But now I was worried about the stone ceiling above me. Only about three feet of clearance, then two, and now one. Suddenly I realized that the entire tunnel was flooded. There would be no air. We would drown. But the current was much too strong for me to resist. I'd never manage to swim back. I focused on what Doc Yong had told me. The tunnel stretched for maybe fifty yards, and I'd already covered half that distance. Once we were underwater, if we could just hold our breath long enough to traverse the rest of the distance, we might survive. Before I could think about it further, my skull bumped rock, I took my last long breath and went under.

Il-yong squirmed in panic. I craned my neck and pulled

him up and placed my mouth on his. Gently, I breathed air into his lungs. He sputtered and coughed but then came back for more. We were still drifting downstream but not fast enough. I started grabbing rock outcrops above me to pull myself along. Il-yong wanted more air. I kept hoping that we'd reach the end of this tunnel any second, but when I realized that we wouldn't, I bent forward and tried to blow more air into his mouth. It didn't work. He was squirming now in total panic. The last of my air escaped upward and bubbled away. I clawed forward—cursing the people who'd written that ancient manuscript, cursing Il-yong's mother for taking me down here, cursing Eighth Army for sending me to North Korea—and then finally, grasping forward for the next handhold, I missed. No rock. I panicked, but then I realized that there was nothing left to grasp. The tunnel had ended.

I kicked forward and finally got my head above water. It was pure darkness, but at least I was breathing. I rolled on my back, floating. Il-yong wasn't moving. Desperately, I swam toward the side of the current and finally hit rock again. I pulled myself up as far as I could, tilted Il-yong's head back, and gently blew air into his mouth. Nothing.

Something splashed behind me. I stuck out my leg, a body rammed into it, and then hands clawed up my pant legs. I couldn't see her face, but from the feel of her body I knew it was Doc Yong.

"Light," I shouted. "Quickly. We have to get him on shore."

She clambered over me, kicking and shoving, not worrying about hurting me. I heard her hands shuffling through her backpack and a light switched on. At first I was blinded, but I recovered quickly.

"Here," I said, "take him."

She reached down and pulled him up. I clambered after them and reached a gravel-strewn beach. I ripped Il-yong out of Doc Yong's hands and held him by the ankles upside down. Water cascaded out of his throat. Then I cradled him in my arms and gently blew air into his lungs.

Nothing.

"Do something," I said.

Doc Yong ripped him out of my arms, turned him over, and pressed her fist into his stomach. More water poured out. She blew into his lungs, again and again. After what seemed like a lifetime, he coughed.

Then he was crying.

Doc Yong hugged him and cried and finally reached out one hand and enveloped me with her arm around my neck and we were all crying.

-13-

The cavern was honeycombed with tunnels. There were dozens of dead ends that fell precipitously into rushing waters, tunnels that climbed up and then down and appeared to have no end, and tunnels made of loose rock that could fall and crush the unwary explorer. In fact, many people had been mangled in this nightmarish underworld. We spotted skeletons, probably half a dozen of them, some surrounded by brass studs and amulets that must once have been fastened to leather garments. When we swiveled the beam of our flashlights, skulls grinned up at us. Daggers and swords lay rusting. One of the skeletons was so ancient that when I touched it with a stick, it crumbled to dust.

Before leaving the underground river, we had dried

ourselves as best we could and changed into the dry clothes Doc Yong had kept wrapped in plastic. Despite the darkness and freezing cold that enveloped us, Doc Yong's mind was as sharp as ever. She had committed to memory the instructions contained in the ancient manuscript and slowly, painfully, we made our way through that unholy pit. The turns never seemed to end. Sometimes we were climbing up, sometimes sliding down. I wondered if we'd lost our way, if she was just afraid to tell me. With an effort, I pushed such thoughts away. We trudged forward in silence.

Occasionally we stopped to rest. And when we did, I watched and listened. No sound behind us. No traces of light. Senior Captain Rhee Mi-sook and her minions hadn't followed us into the underground river. None of them wanted to commit suicide. She probably assumed we were dead. When I was sure no one was following, we resumed our trek.

Finally, we saw starlight, glimmering through a small opening. It took us two hours of steady work, hoisting jagged rocks and tossing them aside, to finally expose a passageway wide enough for Doc Yong to climb through. Once she was out, she started pulling away rocks from her side. When we thought it was safe, we shoved Il-yong through, and I followed.

At last, the three of us stood on steady ground, breathing fresh air.

"Mount Daesong," Doc Yong said.

Above us loomed jagged granite. Below, a valley glowed with a thousand lights. Electricity everywhere. A ribbon of road snaked off into the distance, automobiles and buses crawling along it like illuminated insects.

South Korea. We'd made it. We were safe.

Il-yong cried for a while, but eventually, tied securely to his mother's back, he fell asleep.

We made our way downhill, Doc Yong bracing herself by leaning against me when possible. When we finally reached the outskirts of the first village, people looked away, afraid that we were spirits of the dead emerging from the mountain.

In a way, we were.

The voice of the Charge of Quarters at the barracks was barely audible through the phone lines. He said, "Who is this again?"

"Sueño," I shouted. "Staff Sergeant George Sueño. I need to talk to Bascom. He's in room 15-A."

"Hold on, I'll check." Footsteps clomped down a noisy hallway.

I was exhausted, barely hanging on. The wound in my calf throbbed painfully. During the excitement in the tunnels, I hadn't felt it at all, but now it was back with a vengeance. For a second, darkness clouded my vision, but I fought it off. Five minutes later, the CQ came back. "Not in."

"What?"

"Bascom's not there. His roommate says he's out in the ville."

I should've known. Still reorienting myself now that I was out of the tunnel, I realized that it was Friday night.

"How about Riley?" I said. "Staff Sergeant Riley."

There was a long sigh of exasperation. "Hold on. I'll get him."

Three minutes later, a gravelly voice came on the line. "Sueño, is that you?"

"It's me."

"You son of a *bitch!* Where the hell are you?"

"In a village called Daesong-ri."

"In North Korea or South Korea?"

"South, you idiot. You need to have Ernie hop in the jeep and come out here and pick me up."

"He's out in the ville."

"So go get him."

"Okay."

Riley was befuddled. And not sober. I gave him directions and made him write them down. I told him I'd be in a *yoguan*, a Korean inn, called the Inn of the Righteous Dragon. "You got all that?"

"Got it."

Sober, Staff Sergeant Riley was one of the most efficient men I knew. Half-looped, he was hopeless.

I hung up, thanked the woman who owned the inn for the use of her telephone, and returned to our room. It was a warm *ondol*-floored cubicle and Doc Yong had already rolled out the sleeping mats. Even though we had no South Korean money, Doc Yong had concocted a story of us hiking on Mount Daesong, getting lost, losing our money when we fell into a stream, and borrowing these tattered clothes from farm folk. She spoke Korean in such a cultured way that the proprietress had been sure she was talking to a woman of substance. She consented to hold our bill until our friends arrived with money from Seoul.

We'd already eaten in our room, a warm bowl of *udong* noodles accompanied by steamed rice and cabbage kimchi. Il-yong played with a metal spoon while I told Doc Yong that Ernie would probably make it out here by about noon tomorrow.

"I don't want anything to do with the South Korean police," she said.

"I know that," I told her.

She loathed the South Korean authorities, seeing them as true traitors of their people. The people who ran South Korea now were the same people, literally, who'd worn Japanese military uniforms and hunted the Manchurian Battalion through mountains and valleys during the Japanese colonial period, when Doc Yong's parents had dedicated their lives to freeing Korea from foreign oppression and slavery. Although as an orphan she'd grown up in South Korea, Doc Yong had never lost her disgust for the Japanese collaborators.

Another complicating factor was that Doc Yong was wanted for murder.

Shortly after the Korean War, a group of thugs had taken over Itaewon, the red-light district of Seoul, and ordered the murder of those who opposed them, including Dog Yong's parents. She'd been six years old. Almost two decades later, Doc Yong and other sympathizers from the Manchurian Battalion took their revenge. One by one, the thugs, who were now prosperous businessmen, were found hacked to death and lying facedown in pools of their own blood. That's why Doc Yong had been forced to flee to North Korea.

But now we were back. Somehow I had to get her off the hook for that crime and at the same time convince the United States to reinforce the Manchurian Battalion before they went under. I wasn't sure how I would do it. I just knew I had to.

The next morning, I was standing outside the Inn of the Righteous Dragon when Ernie's jeep rounded the corner.

Ernie was driving slowly, unlike him, peering out the side of the jeep, searching for addresses. I ran forward, waving my arms. Ernie turned off the ignition and hopped out. We stared at each other.

"What the hell happened to you?" Ernie asked.

"What do you mean?"

"You look like shit. Your face is sunburnt, your arms and legs are all cut up, and even from here I could count your ribs."

"I lost a little weight."

"I'll say. Didn't they feed you up there?"

"Sometimes."

Ernie turned back toward the jeep. "Come on. Let's go."

"There's a couple of people I want you to meet."

I led Ernie into the inn.

Il-yong liked him right away. They played a game where Ernie hid a coin and Il-yong squealed with delight when he occasionally managed to grab it. Doc Yong knew Agent Ernie Bascom from before, when she'd been in charge of the women's health clinic in Itaewon. As part of our duties as Criminal Investigation agents, we'd worked with her on many cases, mostly involving young women who were raped or otherwise abused. In the past she'd been cold to Ernie, barely tolerating him in fact, but this time she ordered him to sit down in front of her and made him swear never to report her presence to anyone in the South Korean government. He swore.

After paying the bill, we hopped in the jeep and headed back to Seoul. Doc Yong sat in back, clutching Il-yong, terrified—I thought—by the opulence she saw around her. The neon signs, the whizzing traffic, buses full-to-bursting with people commuting to and from work. The noise, the honking, the whistles. The shops packed with food and radios and televisions. The gaudily painted movie marquees. None of this was part of life in North Korea. In the "people's paradise" workers stayed put, living either near their factories or in them. Nobody commuted. Nobody had cars. Traveling was considered suspicious activity. Disloyal. Here, everyone was on the move. The bustling city of Seoul was disorienting to me too. People hurtling this way and that. There didn't seem to be any order to this society. I wasn't sure I could get used to it.

That afternoon, we found a place in Itaewon for Doc Yong and my son to stay. After they were settled in, Ernie drove me to the Yongsan Compound. First we stopped at the emergency room of the 121 Evacuation Hospital and a medical aide there redressed my wounded leg and gave me a shot of something to keep the swelling down. Then we went to my room in the barracks where I was greeted by a few of the guys I knew. I showered and changed into my dress green uniform.

A half hour later, I reported to the J-2, the Chief of Military Intelligence for the Eighth United States Army, U.S. Forces Korea, and the United Nations Command. Within minutes, a meeting was convened and a row of officers sat on a dais before me. One of them was Major Bulward, the man who'd led my briefings before I'd departed for North Korea. The senior officer was Colonel Yancy, Chief of Intelligence for Eighth Army.

"They want what?" Colonel Yancy peered at me, his blue eyes incredulous in his puffy red face.

"Ammunition," I repeated. "Weapons. Medical supplies. It's an insurrection, sir. The Manchurian Battalion wants to lead the fight against the Dear Leader. They don't want him to inherit power from his father. Others will join them, like the Second Corps commander in the Hamgyong Province."

"And how do you know this?"

"Bandit Lee told me."

"Who's he?"

"The leader of the Manchurian Battalion."

My debriefing continued like this for hours, Eighth Army wanting mainly to know where the tunnel was, but I refused to tell them. Not until I was promised two things. First, a commitment that they'd supply ammunition and medical supplies to the Manchurian Battalion. With helicopters, the supplies could be flown right across the DMZ and dropped near Mount O-song. This suggestion was received with resounding silence. Second, that Eighth Army would obtain a full pardon from the South Korean government for the charges that had been lodged against Doctor Yong In-ja before she'd fled north.

Naively, I expected immediate compliance. Maybe they'd court-martial me later for trying to run my own foreign policy, but right now they were under pressure to act.

After all, any delay could endanger the first armed uprising that Kim Il-sung's regime had faced since taking power in 1948. Surely, if they practiced what they preached, if—as we'd so often been told—the godless North Koreans were the worst threat to Western civilization since the Black Plague, the anticommunist honchos of the Eighth United States Army would want to help. When they dissembled, I was appalled.

"They're dying up there," I told them. "Maybe they can hold out for a few days. Maybe only a few hours. We have to act now."

"We understand your concern," Major Bulward said.

"It's more than concern," I said. "They'll be slaughtered." I thought of the men of the Manchurian Battalion who'd risked their lives to rescue me from torture. I thought of the people who'd so generously nursed me back to health, who'd taken care of my son, who'd protected his mother from harm. "We have to do something!" I said. "We have to act now."

But no one acted. Negotiations dragged on. Gradually, it dawned on me that they weren't going to act. Instead, they kept hammering me for information on the tunnels. I kept refusing. Demanding now, in writing, the two things I wanted. Resupply for the Manchurian Battalion and freedom for Doc Yong. I was threatened with not only court-martial but also being charged with every crime in the Uniform Code of Military Justice. Still, I'd been around military law enforcement long enough, and the uses and abuses of power in the Eighth United States Army, to know that when you have a bargaining chip, you don't give it up. Not without ironclad guarantees.

And I had the tunnels.

Enraged, Colonel Yancy restricted me to the compound. For security reasons, he told me. But the real reason was that after having spent so much time in North Korea, and after having expressed views sympathetic to the Manchurian Battalion, the honchos of Eighth Army no longer trusted me. If they ever had.

Now, with the suspicion that had so unexpectedly turned my way, I wouldn't have left the compound anyway. I didn't want anyone following me to the hooch where Doc Yong and Il-yong were staying.

I did manage to break free from my briefings for long enough to make it over to Eighth Army Finance and collect the back pay that was due me. I'd never had so much money in one chunk in my entire life. Some of it I converted to won.

At night, Ernie took the money I'd converted and a few things—baby oil and fruit juice and cartons of powdered milk—out to Il-yong and Doc Yong. He took a circuitous route and promised he'd watch for anyone tailing him. I longed to go with him but dared not. Who knew what spies were lurking? It was too dangerous. Not only could I be court-martialed for violating my restriction, but, without a pardon, if Doc Yong were arrested, she might spend the rest of her life in a South Korean prison.

After two days, it was apparent that Eighth Army wasn't going to budge. They weren't going to provide ammunition and medical supplies for a group of fighters whom they considered to be Communist bandits and enemies of their allies in the South Korean government.

Still, they wanted the information on the location of

the tunnel. I refused to give it to them. They eventually did what I'd been expecting, formally threatening me with court-martial.

"That's why we sent you up there," Major Bulward told me. "To gather intelligence for the United States of America. You're under orders to provide that information."

Still, I refused.

The federal penitentiary at Fort Leavenworth was a long way away. In the wheat fields of Kansas. But if I had to go there to protect Doc Yong and my son, I'd do it.

Strange told us to meet him at the "snatch bar." It was actually the Eighth United States Army Snack Bar. GIs called it the "snatch bar" because occasionally a young soldier managed to form a liaison with one of the American female civilians or dependent teenage daughters who frequented the busy cafeteria. Of course, when one did, he'd blather the news all over the barracks.

Strange was the NCO in charge of classified material at the headquarters of the Eighth United States Army. I didn't believe he was one of those lucky GIs. Not with his potbelly, receding hairline, and cigarette hanging limply from a plastic holder. Still, he thought he was Mister Cool.

"They're not buying it," he told me.

"Buying what?" Ernie asked.

"Sueño's bargain. He wants his girlfriend let off . . ."

"She's more than my 'girlfriend,'" I said. We'd been through too much together for our relationship to be brushed off so easily.

"Okay," Strange said. "Whatever she is. And you want

the tunnel used to send weapons and ammunition to this Mongolian Battalion . . ."

"The Manchurian Battalion," I corrected.

"Okay, whatever you call 'em. You want ammo sent up there with no guarantee that these guys, whoever they are, will overthrow the Commies."

"The leaders of the Manchurian Battalion are communists themselves," I told him. "But they believe in a humanistic form of communism. A socialist democracy, actually."

"Whatever you say. But Eighth Army ain't going for it."

"Is there anything they will accept?" I was hoping that there was still time to save the Manchurian Battalion.

"They want to know the location of the tunnel," Strange replied. "Not to transport arms across the DMZ, but to enlarge it and reinforce it and use it as an invasion route if the North Koreans ever attack us."

"If I tell them, what do I get in return?"

"You don't get court-martialed."

"They have nothing on me. They can't court-martial a GI for not knowing something."

"But they believe you *do* know," Strange said. "You've as much as admitted it. After all, you escaped through the tunnel."

"It was at night. I was disoriented. There's no way I could lead them back."

"And that's your story?"

"That's my story."

Strange glanced around the busy snack bar, making sure no one was listening. Silverware clinked on porcelain. He leaned forward.

"They're going to burn her," he said.

"Burn who?" Ernie asked.

"Sueño's girlfriend." When he saw my face, he waved his hand as if to ward off anger. "I mean your associate or whatever she is. The South Koreans are out there now, doing everything they can to track her down."

"Why?" Ernie asked.

"First, she's wanted for murder. But more importantly, they figure that once they have her in custody, they'll have some leverage over our good friend Sergeant Sueño here."

I sat back. Not stunned by what Strange had just told me—I'd expected it—but filled with rage at the way, after all we'd been through, they still treated Doc Yong as a criminal. A woman who had dedicated her life to fighting for the freedom and dignity of the Korean people.

Ernie noticed my reaction and shifted his seat a little closer, as if to intervene if I reached across the table and grabbed Strange by the neck.

"How do you know all this?" Ernie asked.

Strange mimicked lifting the edge of a "Top Secret" cover sheet and peering at the document below. "I look out for my fellow NCOs."

Ernie sighed. "Okay, Harvey. Thanks for the information. What do you want in return?"

Strange leaned forward. "Had any *strange* lately?"

Ernie made up a story of erotic intrigue. As he listened, Strange's cigarette holder bobbled.

All I knew for sure was that Doctor Yong In-ja and our son were in danger. The problem was that, other than stay away from them, I didn't know what to do to protect them. Eighth Army had refused my deal. I had nowhere else to go.

■ ■ ■

I was sitting alone in the barracks, wishing I could see Doc Yong and Il-yong, when Ernie entered my room.

"Here," he said, handing me a note.

It was written in Korean and I had to pull out my Korean-English dictionary to decipher it. The meaning was what I had been expecting but dreading: *We are leaving*, she wrote. *Don't search for us. All we will do is rip you away from your own country. We will survive. I will teach Il-yong never to forget you.*

There was no signature.

I crumpled the note and looked up at Ernie.

"Where'd she go?" I asked.

He shrugged. "I don't know. She was already gone when I got there. All her stuff was cleared out. Only this note taped to the center of the floor."

Ernie walked with me down the hill to the NCO Club.

A Korean show band was playing that night. The Locks and Keys, I think they were called. I ordered a straight shot of Old Overwart with a beer chaser. After four of them, I didn't hear a word they sang.

Major Bulward ordered me to report to his office. He sat at a table across from me and slid a classified document my way. The cover sheet was red. It said "Top Secret."

"Read it," he said.

It was a report gleaned mostly from aerial reconnaissance, concerning the area near Mount O-song. It wasn't good. I slid the report back to him. He shoved the document into a leather briefcase and locked the metal hasp.

"The Manchurian Battalion no longer exists," he said. "The forces of the Dear Leader overran them two days ago. There were few survivors."

"How about Bandit Lee?"

"He died fighting."

I felt as if an AK-47 round had slammed into my gut.

"We could've saved them," I said.

Major Bulward was silent for a moment. Then he said, "That's a decision that was made above our pay grade."

I didn't answer.

"Are you going to tell us about the tunnel?" he asked.

"You don't need me. You'll find it eventually."

"I'm sorry about your girlfriend," he said.

"She's not my girlfriend," I said. "She's more than that."

"Your wife?" he ventured.

"Not now." I glared at him. "You ruined that."

I stood and walked out of his office.

Two months later, Ernie and I were back on black-market detail. Because we hadn't arrested enough housewives for exceeding their rationed purchases out of the commissary and PX, our statistics—as usual—were lousy. As a result, we'd drawn a nighttime security detail: escorting the Eighth Army J-2, Colonel Yancy, to a soiree at the ROK Ministry of National Defense.

We followed his sedan in Ernie's jeep, down the brightly lit streets of Seoul and through the big iron gates. We watched as his sedan pulled up in front of the huge cement-block building and uniformed South Korean soldiers opened the back door for him. Looking sharp in his dress blue uniform, Colonel Yancy marched up the cement steps toward the main hall of the ministry. Ernie parked in a lot out back and, after flashing our badges to more uniformed soldiers, we entered through a side door.

The hall was softly lit and there was a twelve-piece military orchestra on the balcony. Officers and diplomats and South Korean dignitaries of all types were enjoying canapés and hors d'oeuvres and bubbling champagne in fluted glasses. The women, like the men, were mostly middle-aged, but a few of the younger female South Korean officers caught Ernie's eye.

"Come on," he said. "Let's grab some of those crackers."

"We're on duty," I said.

"They won't miss 'em."

We walked along the edge of the hall until we reached the double doorway leading back to the kitchen. When a white-gloved waiter came by, Ernie managed to snag some snacks off a silver platter. The man ducked away and kept moving.

"Now for some champagne," Ernie said.

"Forget it, Ernie. You'll get us in trouble."

He stopped suddenly and elbowed me. "Get a load of her."

Across the hall, wearing a tailored uniform of a short skirt and a matching tunic, stood a statuesque woman.

"She's looking at you," Ernie said, munching on his cracker. "Man, she could be a fashion model. What a doll." He swiveled his head to study me. "Do you know her?"

I didn't answer. Instead, I stared into the haunting eyes of Senior Captain Rhee Mi-sook. At first, I had the impulse to run, but I controlled it. She wasn't wearing the uniform of a North Korean officer; she was dressed as a major in the South Korean Army. And she wasn't trying to hide. Not at all. She seemed perfectly at home in this crowd. She held my gaze boldly, a half-smile on her lips.

Then she raised her champagne glass in a toast and sipped.

Continue reading for a preview of

NIGHTMARE
RANGE

the short story collection featuring George and Ernie

NIGHTMARE RANGE

The mama-san didn't know how long the body had been out there. "Three, maybe four days," she said. Her girls had just conducted their business a few yards farther away from it each day.

"Where is it now?" I asked.

"Policeman take go." She waved her cigarette, and smoke filtered through the darkened gaps between her teeth.

The morgue was in Chorwon-ni, ten miles to the south. Ten miles south of Nightmare Range, and fifteen miles from the Demilitarized Zone that slashes like a surgeon's knife through the heart of the Korean Peninsula.

The war had been over for twenty years but it still lingered: a big dumb ghost that refused to go away. No peace treaty had been signed—just a cease-fire. So the fourth and fifth largest armies in the world, armed to their squinting eyeballs, faced each other across the line, fingers on trigger housings, knuckles white, dancing to the sound of no breathing.

Our police escort, Lieutenant Pak, stood back, arms crossed, glaring at the squatting woman. He was a tall man for a Korean, slim but muscular. His khakis were starched and fit as if he had been born in them. I didn't ask him why it had taken so long to dispose of the body. The non-person status of a "business girl" follows her into death.

One by one the doors to the hooches slid open and groggy young women, their faces still puffed with sleep, gaped at us curiously. Some squatted in long underwear, their arms crossed over their knees, while others lay on the floor, beneath the wrinkled patchworks that were their blankets. All of the girls were ugly in some way: ravaged complexions, tufted hair, splotches of discolored skin. It seemed more like a ward for the incurably ill than a whorehouse.

Maybe it was both.

Lieutenant Pak asked a series of questions of the old woman and I managed, struggling, to keep up with most of it. There had been a number of American units in the field that day and just before nightfall the old woman had stationed a few of her girls near each encampment. As darkness approached, the girls called to the young GIs from just outside the concertina wire.

I'd seen the game before. Sometimes the GI would wade out into the tall grass and lie on the blanket, both he and the deformed girl protected by the enshrouding night. Sometimes the bolder fellows would bring the girls into their tents, risking the wrath of the Sergeant of the Guard and sneaking in and out of the camp with the stealth of a North Korean infiltrator.

I pulled out a map, showed it to the mama-san, and pointed to the area around Nightmare Range and the village of Mantong-ni. The old woman looked at it carefully and consulted with some of the girls. A few of them were up and dressed now. They chattered for a while and then came to a conclusion. With my pen, I marked the area beneath the old woman's gnarled fingernail.

I asked what type of unit it was. Big guns, they decided.

Lieutenant Pak wiped his hands on the sides of his khaki trousers and took a step toward the gate.

"Mama-san," I said. "This girl. What was her name?"

"Miss Chon," the old woman said. "Chon Ki-suk."

I wrote it down. "Do you have a picture of her?"

The mama-san barked an order and one of the girls handed me a tattered piece of cardboard folded in half like a small book. A VD card. Chon Ki-suk peered out at me from a small black-and-white photograph. She had a round face with full cheeks that sagged like a bloated chipmunk. All visible flesh had been pocked by the craters of skin disease. She differed little from her sisters now breathing heavily around me, a timid little girl awaiting death.

Lieutenant Pak stomped into the mud.

I stood up and walked with him to the gate. As he stooped to get through the small opening, I looked back at the rows of blemished faces sullenly watching our every move. None of them smiled. None of them said goodbye.

My partner, Ernie Bascom, was in the jeep curled up with a brown-paper-wrapped magazine from somewhere in Scandinavia. He unfolded his six-foot frame as we approached and started up the jeep. Some people said he looked like the perfect soldier: blue eyes behind round-lensed glasses, short-cropped sandy-blond hair, the aquiline nose of the European races. What had blown it for him was Vietnam. Pure horse sold by dirty-faced kids through the wire, women taken on the dusty paths between rice paddies, the terror rocket attacks during innocent hours. His placid exterior hid a soul that had written off the world as a madhouse. Looks were deceiving. Especially in Ernie's case.

We dropped Lieutenant Pak off in Mantong-ni. A dozen straw-thatched farmhouses huddled around the brick-walled police station as if longing for an extinguishing warmth.

Ernie popped the clutch, our tires spun, and we lurched forward into the misted distance.

The roads were still slick, but all that was left of the early morning rain were ponderous gray clouds rolling like slow-motion whales through the hills surrounding the long valley. We plunged into a damp tunnel, and when we came out, the valley widened before us. Dark clouds in the distance glowered at us like fat dragons lowering on their haunches for a nap.

"Nightmare Range," Ernie said. "Where generals meet to see how much their boys can take." He pumped lightly on the brakes and slid around a sharp curve. The water-filled rice paddies on either side of the road strained impatiently toward our spinning tires. This valley had been the scene of some of the most horrific battles of the Korean War. Americans, Chinese, Koreans, had all died here, and the bones of some probably still embraced each other deep beneath the piled mud. I had looked it up in the military section in the library, how many had died here. All I remember is that there was a number followed by a lot of zeros.

The austere cement-block building of the Firing Range Headquarters was painted in three alternating shades of green. Inside, a brightly colored relief map of Nightmare Range covered a huge plywood table.

An ROK Army sergeant with short, spiky black hair and a crisply pressed khaki uniform thumbed through a handwritten log of the units that had been using the training facility. He came to the correct date and the correct position and pointed to the entry: Charlie Battery, 2nd of the 71st Artillery. They had returned to their base at Camp Pelham.

"Our next stop, Camp Pelham," Ernie said.

We returned to the jeep.

"Tough duty, pal." Ernie leaned back in a patio chair at the snack stand just inside the front gate of Camp Pelham, sipping a cold can of PBR. We were dressed the same way: blue jeans, sneakers, and black nylon jackets with brilliantly hand-embroidered dragons on the back. Standard issue for GIs running the ville.

The outfit usually got us over. We were the right age, both in our early twenties, and we both had the clean, fresh-faced look of American GIs. If we played with the girls enough, laughed, horsed around, toked a few joints, no one would suspect that we were conducting a criminal investigation.

Ernie looked like the typical GI from the heartland of America. I looked like his ethnic sidekick, taller than him by about three inches, broader at the shoulders, with the short jet-black hair of my Mexican ancestors. My face often threw people. The nose was pointed enough, and the skin light enough to make them think that maybe I was just one of them. But I'd grown up on the streets of east LA and I'd heard the racial slurs before. When some GI started in on "wetbacks" somebody usually elbowed him, whispered something in his ear, and looked nervously in my direction. They didn't have to worry though. That's part of America, after all. I wouldn't deny them their fun.

The afternoon was glorious but cold. The crisp, clear blue sky of the DMZ, far away from the ravages of industrialism, seemed to welcome even the likes of us.

Camp Pelham is in the Western Corridor, about twenty miles from the Division Headquarters at Camp Casey and forty miles from Nightmare Range. The Western Corridor was the route the North Korean tanks had taken on their way to Seoul in the spring of 1950. It was expected to be the route they would take again.

The camp was small—you could walk around it in ten minutes—but it still managed to house the battalion's three batteries of six guns each. The big howitzers of Alpha and Bravo Batteries pointed to the sky, their barrels snugly sheathed in plastic behind protective bunkers. Charlie Battery was out in the field again but scheduled to return that afternoon.

We heard distant thunder and ran to the chain-link fence. Across the narrow river, rows of dilapidated wooden shacks sat jumbled behind a main street lined with nightclubs and tailor shops.

Charlie Battery rumbled down the two hundred yard strip. A small jeep maintained the lead while six big two-and-a-half ton trucks barreled after it as if trying to run it down. A half dozen 105-millimeter howitzers bounced behind the big trucks like baby elephants trotting behind their mothers.

The men of Charlie Battery stood in the beds of the trucks, shouting, their winter headgear flapping wildly in the wind.

An M-60 machine gun crowned the cab of each truck, partially hidden behind bundles of neatly tied camouflage netting. Rolls of razor-sharp concertina wire, draped over stanchions on either side of the truck bed, swayed lazily with the rattling of the trucks like huge and sinister gypsy earrings.

Some of the villagers of Sonyu-ri waved happily at the unstoppable convoy. Others scurried to get themselves and their children out of the way.

When the Camp Pelham gate guards swung open the big chain-link fence, the men yelled and laughed, and the drivers gunned the truck engines. Diesel fumes billowed into the air.

The jeep sped by and headed for the Battery Orderly Room. The truck turned in the other direction to get hosed down at the wash point and topped of with diesel at the fuel point.

We finished our beers and walked down the road. In front of the Orderly Room a disheveled-looking little man rummaged through the back of the jeep trying to locate his gear. I spotted his name tag. Sergeant Pickering, the Chief of the Firing Battery.

"Chief of Smoke," I said.

He looked up and squinted, a crooked-toothed weasel who hadn't shaved in a couple of days. "Who are you?"

I showed him my identification. "George Sueño, Criminal Investigation Division. This is my partner, Ernie Bascom."

He looked at the badge and turned back to his gear. "Why ain't you wearing a coat and tie?" he asked. "I thought you guys always wore a coat and tie."

"Not undercover," Ernie said.

The Chief of Smoke ignored us and continued to rummage through his things, sticking his hand way down into the depths of his dirty green canvas pack.

"Here's the son of a bitch," he said. "Kim! Kim! I found it."

His Korean Army driver came running out of the Orderly Room as the Chief of Smoke wrenched his hand free from the enveloping material. He held up a dirty, unwrapped white bread sandwich, and they both beamed. He tore it and handed half to the Korean. They munched contentedly and the driver, smiling, returned to the Orderly Room.

"Kimchi and bologna," the Chief of Smoke said. "Made it myself." His mouth was open. The odor of the hot pickled cabbage flushed the diesel fumes from my sinuses. He didn't offer us any.

"The last field problem you were on," I said, "you were at Nightmare Range."

The Chief looked at me, still chewing with his mouth open, but didn't say anything.

"There was a problem," I said. "Somebody from your unit went a little too far with one of the girls outside the wire."

He closed one eye completely. "What do you mean, 'too far'?"

"He killed her."

The Chief of Smoke chomped viciously on his sandwich. Cabbage crunched. "Probably deserved it." He continued to chew, turning his head to squint at the brilliantly outlined hills in the blue-sky distance. "I know my first wife did."

"Did you notice anything unusual that trip? Anything that might have . . ."

"Had to be Bogard. Only one mean enough to do it. And he was always messing with those girls out in the field. Didn't pay 'em, I don't think. Never had enough money anyway what with all the trouble he's been in."

"Trouble?"

"Yeah. Article Fifteens for not making formations, over-purchasing on his ration card, shit like that."

"Where's he at now?"

"Don't know."

"He's not in your unit anymore?"

"Well, we're still carrying him on the books. They say he's down in the ville." The Chief of Smoke swallowed the last of his rancid sandwich, turned away from the hills, and looked at me. Bread and bologna still stuck to his teeth. "He's been AWOL ever since we came back from Nightmare Range."

She propped her half-naked breasts atop my belt and rubbed her nipples against my stomach. She wore only shorts and a halter top, and her straight black hair swung back as she looked up at me and smiled through a mask of makeup.

"Where you stationed?" she asked.

"Starlight Club," I said.

She pulled back and punched me in the stomach with her small fist. "You not stationed Starlight Club. I stationed Starlight Club." She turned to Ernie. "You buy me drink?"

He pulled his beer back a few inches from his mouth and looked at her as if she were out of her mind. She left.

We were leaning against the bar of the Starlight Club, and this was the fifth joint we'd been in. The place was packed with GIs, mostly playing pool, and Korean girls, scantily dressed in outfits designed to inflame the male hormonal system. Some of them gyrated their bodies on the small dance floor, moving to the beat of the overpowering rock music. Various colored lights flashed on and off around the club, stabilized by the steady glare of the fluorescent bulbs above the pool tables.

"Tits and ass," Ernie said.

"Yeah. It's not easy being a hunter."

A group of GIs walked in and one girl shuffled and squealed across the room, throwing herself into the arms of a young man with a wispy mustache and blond hair parted in the middle of his head.

The tallest member of the group stood aside and surveyed the club from the doorway. He was exceedingly thin but energy seemed to emanate from his body. Even though he stood still, some part of his anatomy seemed always to be quivering and about to explode into movement.

His name was Duckworth. The Chief of Smoke had pointed him out to us as he sped by in his deuce-and-a-half, the first driver to finish his chores at the wash point and make it to the motor pool. "They're all into whacko weed. He'll know where Bogard is."

Duckworth and his buddies entered the club, mingled with some of the pool players, and soon he was leaning against the jukebox, sparring and flirting with one of the girls. His buddy was still enveloped by a feminine bear hug and had to hold his elbows high to tilt back his beer. The group was in constant motion, all with seemingly little adult motive, like children frolicking on a nursery room floor.

Ernie took a sip of his beer. "Shouldn't we roust him out back?"

"I don't think there's any need. As ornery as the Chief of Smoke said Bogard is, these guys probably will be glad to be rid of him."

We ordered two more beers. One of the girls walked up, and this time Ernie grabbed her. We weren't in any hurry.

Duckworth and his buddies around the jukebox yelled into one another's ears. The wall of music between us stopped any sound from getting through. They took some of the girls with them and walked past the men's latrine and out the back door.

We gulped down our beers, not even giving the suds time to settle in our stomachs. Ernie let go of his sweet and rotund young girl and followed me out the back door.

The group stood in the mud in the dark and narrow alley. They didn't move when the light from the club followed us outside, just stared at us with hugely dilated cat's eyes. A joint came toward me and I reached out my hand. The GI hesitated and looked at Duckworth. When he nodded, the small, burning ember was passed to me.

I took a hit and handed it to Ernie. I held the smoke in my lungs while I spoke. "I'm look for Bogard."

Everybody laughed.

"Usually," Duckworth said, "people are trying to get away from him."

"Why?"

Duckworth shrugged. "He's mean, he's broke, and he doesn't take no for an answer—on anything."

The GIs and the girls sniffled and snorted in their efforts not to lose any of the precious herbal fumes.

"Where can I find him?"

"If you got money, he'll find you."

I waited.

Duckworth broke the silence. "Find the River Rat, and you'll find Bogard."

"The River Rat?"

"Yeah. He lives with her. Sort of."

"Sort of?"

"She catches a lot of GIs," Duckworth said, "but usually just before curfew, when he needs a bunk, Bogard goes over to her hooch. If there's somebody there, he's just shit out of luck. Bogard tosses him out into the street."

The GIs giggled and snorted some more.

"How do I find the River Rat?"

"She lives by the river," someone said. The rush of air through nostrils increased.

"She walks the streets," Duckworth said. "And since there's only one street in the village, you can't miss her."

She blocked the way.

A GI stopped and listened to her for a moment and then shook his head. He stepped around her, but she grabbed him by the arm and seemed to be pleading with him. Keeping his hands in his pockets, he roughly pulled his elbow from her grip and continued past.

She smiled and waved her hand a little, as if saying goodbye to an old friend.

It was getting colder. Scattered flakes of snow hit the oil-splattered blacktop and vanished as if they'd never existed. GIs and half-dressed Korean girls scurried from club to club, running away from the small, blustering snow clouds that chased them like restless apparitions.

As she walked toward us, I turned to Ernie. "She's got to be the River Rat."

Her small breasts only slightly pushed out the thick, gray material of her baggy sweatshirt. She wore a pair of bedroom slippers and loose-fitting, dirty-yellow pants that were short enough to reveal her tall brown socks. Her face was plain but pleasant and seemed removed from the mundane consideration of life by the half smile that controlled it. Her unwashed black hair dripped to her shoulders.

She talked quietly to herself and looked around, not at other people but at objects on the ground and on the walls and in the windows of the small shops that lined the street. She seemed delighted by her conversation and occasionally nodded or waved with an easy twist of the wrist. A fine lady gently accentuating some important point.

She appeared happier than the people trying to avoid her. If she'd actually had a companion, looked at some of the people staring at her, or made some effort to clean herself and make herself presentable, I might not have thought she was mad.

When she got close, I spoke. "*Anyonghaseiyo.*"

She seemed surprised by the interruption. But the small smile quickly regained control of her face and she turned and pointed with her thumb back down the street. "You go?"

I gestured with my head toward Ernie. "We go."

She looked at both of us and smiled. "No sweat," she said. We followed her down the street.

About fifty yards past the Starlight Club, she turned off the main road and wound through some mud-floored alleys that got progressively narrower and darker. The stench from the river got harder to take as we went downhill. Finally, she stopped and crouched through a gate in a fence made of rotted wood. The shore of the river lapped listlessly up to within a few feet of the entranceway.

We followed her in. She kicked off her slippers, stepped up on the wooden porch, and slid back the panel leading to her room. She motioned for us to follow.

"Just a minute," I said. "We wait."

I sat down on the porch facing the entranceway. Ernie found a wooden stool and pulled it over behind the gate so anyone entering wouldn't be able to see him. He reached into the pocket of his jacket, pulled out two cans of Falstaff, and tossed one across the courtyard to me. I caught it with two hands, popped the cap, and sucked on the frothing hops.

The River Rat didn't question us but squatted on her haunches and waited. Just like I'd told her to do.

Ernie settled down on the stool, sipped on his beer, and checked under his jacket. His face calmed as he touched the shoulder holster that held the .45.

The wind gained strength and elbowed its way noisily through the cracks in the old wooden fence. The snow came down with more purpose now and began to stick on the mud, making for a slippery and clammy quagmire.

Just before midnight, I spotted a shadow lumbering along the edge of the river. At the gate, the shadow bent over and filled the entranceway completely for a moment and then popped into the compound.

At first I wasn't sure if he was human. He looked more like a moving mountain of green canvas. A small fatigue baseball cap balanced atop his big, round head, and two flaming eyes shone out from within glistening folds of black skin. His shoulders were huge and broad enough to be used as workbenches. The arms tapered slightly, like drainage pipes, and as he walked, they worked their way methodically around the gargantuan girth of his torso. The two large sections that were his legs moved alternately toward me.

My throat was suddenly dry. I held my breath and didn't move. When he got up close, he hovered for a moment, like a storm blotting out the sky, and turned and sat down next to me on the small wooden porch. It shuddered, groaned, and then held. He tilted his red eyes heavenward and took a drink from a small, crystalline bottle that seemed lost in his huge black mitt of a hand. He swallowed, grimaced, and then grinned, first at me and then at Ernie. His teeth were square blocks of yellow chalk, evenly spaced along purple gums.

He growled from deep in his throat. Laughter. And he was quivering with it. "Been waiting for you guys."

He leaned forward and reached out the bottle to me. *Soju.* I took it, rubbed the lip with the flat palm of my hand, and drank.

I got up and handed it to Ernie. Ernie drank tentatively at first, and then tilted the bottle up quickly and took an audible gulp. He returned the bottle to Bogard, and walked back and leaned against the fence.

The River Rat bounced back and forth to the kitchen, running around as if she were going to prepare some snacks to go with our rice liquor. She mumbled to herself and flitted about, touching Bogard lightly on his back.

He reached out with one huge paw, grabbed her by the shoulder, and sat her down on the porch next to him. She got quiet and stared serenely at us like a schoolgirl waiting for the presentation to begin.

Bogard's eyes were viciously bloodshot.

"Tell us about Nightmare Range," I said.

Bogard grunted a half laugh and looked at the ground.

"It was a mistake," he said. "She shouldn't have struggled like that." He looked up at me. "They always want to check you out, you know? Check to see if you got any shit. But by the time she got me checked out, there was no turning back."

"The clap?"

"No. Chancroid." It was one of the more popular venereal diseases. "They wouldn't let me come out of the field to take care of it. Just a little hole in my pecker, nothing serious. She shouldn't have looked. Then we wouldn't have this problem."

"*We* don't have a problem," Ernie said.

Bogard looked up and grinned. "You will."

I spoke too quickly, trying to pretend that I didn't understand the threat implied in his answer. "So what happened? You held her down?"

"I hit her first. But the little bitch kept struggling." He pouted and looked at his fleshy underarm. "She bit me. So I held her."

"By the throat?"

"Yeah. And when I finished, she wasn't moving anymore. There was nothing I could do for her."

The River Rat got up and started to flutter around in little circles, like a wounded bird with one good leg. She mumbled some more and made squeaking noises.

Bogard spoke to her tenderly. "Shut the fuck up."

She shut up.

"Finish your *soju*," I said. "Then you're coming with us."

Bogard let out a chortling laugh that seemed to cause his shoulders to bounce. He raised the half-empty *soju* bottle to his mouth and took huge, breathless gulps. The level of the clear, fiery liquid fell straight down into his gullet.

He burped and handed the empty bottle to the River Rat. She took it as if it were a great gift and carried it with two hands to deposit it in a safe place.

"I ain't going," Bogard said.

Ernie stood away from the fence and jammed his hands further into the pockets of his jacket.

"Think for a minute, Bogard," I said. "You've got no place to go. You can't leave the country. You have no income, except for dealing a little drugs or whatever. You can't stay here and you can't get away." He just looked at me, amused. "The last GI convicted of murder here in Korea got four years." I waited for that to sink in. "After he finished the time they sent him back to the States. No sense making it harder on yourself. Come with me, and we'll get this shit over with."

The River Rat came back into the courtyard, stopped, and stood stock still for a moment. She started flitting back and forth again, humming and talking to herself, walking amongst us on imaginary errands, a gracious hostess serving her guests.

Bogard bared his block-like teeth. "I ain't going," he said. "And it's going to take more than you two guys to bring me in."

Ernie took his hands out of his pockets and stepped away from the wall. I reached behind my back and pulled out my handcuffs. Bogard stood up, his feet shoulder-width apart, still smiling, and put his drainage pipe arms out slightly as if he were ready to embrace us.

I took a step toward him. He crouched, and I stopped. He

would pulverize me. And once I got in close, Ernie would be unable to use the .45.

Ernie pulled the big pistol out of his shoulder holster, slid back the charging handle, and shot Bogard in the leg. The River Rat screamed. Bogard doubled over, grabbed his leg, and bellowed like a wounded bear. I moved forward and snapped one of the cuffs around his huge wrist. When he realized what I was doing, he let go of his leg and swung an enormous paw at me. I went down. The River Rat jumped on Ernie; screaming and clawing at his face like a wildcat tearing the bark off a tree.

Bogard hopped on his good leg toward Ernie, his enormous girth rising and falling thunderously with each hop. I jumped up, ran at him, and rammed my shoulder into the green expanse of his side.

The foot of his wounded leg hit the ground, he screamed, and we all slammed to the ground in a huge pile. Things crunched. I rolled to my side, groped for the cuffs, and managed to get both of Bogard's hands shackled before he could recover from the pain.

Ernie hopped up and held the gun on him. Bogard rolled on the ground, his big, square teeth clenched in pain. The River Rat didn't move.

I checked her out. Her breathing was shallow. I left Ernie in the hooch and walked carefully along the lace covering of newly fallen snow to the main road. I trotted a few clubs down to an MP jeep and had them radio for an ambulance. They followed me to the mouth of the alley so they could guide the medics to the hooch.

When I returned, a few of the neighbors stood around outside talking amongst themselves. Ernie sat on the porch, hunched over, holding the .45 loosely in his hands. Bogard was still on the ground but sitting up now, slowly trying to shake the fresh snowflakes off his massive head. He clutched the upper part of his thigh, but a puddle of blood continued to grow beneath him. The River Rat hadn't moved.

The medics brought a stretcher. Cursing and howling, Bogard

managed to roll up onto it. It took four of us to carry him out of the hooch, down the alley, and then hoist him up into the ambulance. One medic stayed in the back with him, the other was about to climb into the cab.

"What about the girl?" I asked.

"Can't do nothing for her," he said. "You know that."

"You can treat civilians when it's an emergency."

"Only on the compound." He closed the door and started up the engine. Ernie climbed into the back of the MP jeep. I told him to wait, and I trotted back down the alley to the hooch.

The River Rat still lay on the ground, unmoving, and a few of the neighbors had wandered inside. I checked her pulse. Faint. She was becoming pale.

I talked to one of the old women. She told me that the hooch's owner had been notified and was on her way. In Korea, going to a hospital requires front money, in cash, and I didn't have much. The MP jeep honked its horn. I ran back down the alley, got in the jeep, and we spun our tires all the way back to Camp Pelham.

Bogard was all right. The bone had been broken, but not shattered, and the chopper came and took him to the army hospital in Seoul.

Ernie and I spent some extra time on the paperwork. The shooting meant that if it wasn't done right, it would be our ass.

The MPs at Camp Pelham treated us like heroes, slapping us on the back and congratulating us. They were glad to have Bogard out of their village.

It was well past curfew, but I managed to convince the Desk Sergeant to give me a jeep. At the main gate the guard came out in the snow and rolled back the fence for me, just wide enough for the vehicle to squeeze through.

The village of Sonyu-ri was completely dark. Not even the glimmer of stray light from behind shuttered windows was visible to mar the beauty of the moon-cast glow on the white shrouded street. The road was slippery, and I drove slowly.

I parked the jeep, locked the security chain around the steering wheel, and felt my way down the pitch black alley. The stench from the river seemed lessened now, and the murky waters lapped peacefully against the glistening mud of the shore.

The gate was open. Inside, the moonlight shone down on the unsullied snow, and the River Rat lay on the ground where I had left her. I brushed the frozen lace from her hair and pressed my fingers into the base of her neck.

I waited a long time. When I got up, I brushed the snow from my knees and walked away from the unblinking eyes that followed me.

If you enjoyed this short story, look for *Nightmare Range*, Martin Limón's complete collection of nineteen short stories featuring George Sueño and Ernie Bascom.

OTHER TITLES IN THE SOHO CRIME SERIES